All rights reserved.
Copyright ©2008 Changeling Press LLC

ISBN: 978-1-59596-820-3

Publisher:
Changeling Press LLC
PO Box 1046
Martinsburg WV 25402-1046
www.ChangelingPress.com

Printed in the U.S.A.
Lightning Source, Inc.
1246 Heil Quaker Blvd
La Vergne TN 37086
www.lightningsource.com

Anthology Editors: Chrissie Henderson, Margaret Riley, Crystal Esau, Sheri Ross Fogarty, Connie Alberts
Cover Layout and Design: Bryan Keller

The individual stories in this anthology have been previously released in E-Book format.

No part of this publication may be reproduced or shared by any electronic or mechanical means, including but not limited to reprinting, photocopying, or digital reproduction, without prior written permission from Changeling Press LLC.

This book contains sexually explicit scenes and adult language which some may find offensive and which is not appropriate for a young audience. Changeling Press books are for sale to adults, only, as defined by the laws of the country in which you made your purchase.

# Paranormal Mates Society: Insomnia

Kira Stone

# What reviewers are saying about the stories in Paranormal Mates Society Vol. III

## Paranormal Mates Society: Insomnia — Kira Stone

"Kira Stone used a wicked sense of word play paired with whimsical characters to create a laugh-out-loud tale... As to the heat, all I can say is oh-la-la!"

—*Belle Rouge, Romance Junkies*

## Paranormal Mates Society: O Positive — Ann Jacobs

"The erotic passion that can be found in and out of the bedroom is hot, hot, hot and tantalizing. My fingertips are still smoking from reading this story."

—*Jessica, Fallen Angel Reviews*

## Paranormal Mates Society: Loving Fury — Amelia Elias

"Reading about them falling in love was like waiting for World War 3 to break loose... A must read for its sexy escapades and the hysterical laughter that abounds."

—*Sheryl, Ecataromance Reviews*

## Paranormal Mates Society: Playing with Matches — Cat Marsters

"Cat Marsters has created a tale where redemption and passion go hand in hand, and also where love knows no bounds, not even time itself."

—*Sheryl, Ecataromance Reviews*

## Paranormal Mates Society: The Midnight Hour — Isabella Jordan

"A great treat for anyone to pick up and enjoy."

—*Lainey, Coffeetime Romance Reviews*

www.ChangelingPress.com

Paranormal Mates Society Vol. III

Kira Stone
Ann Jacobs
Amelia Elias
Cat Marsters
Isabella Jordan

# Chapter One
# Rising to the Bottom

Sanders L. Mann toyed with his favorite dildo as he waited for the DVD to load on his office computer. Inspiration to accompany his evening's entertainment. The highlight of the night was definitely to come.

The most exciting bout of hot passion he'd had in *years* had been courtesy of one of the best bottoms in the business, Sean Storm, a porn star turned bareback video producer. No one else could make him feel the way Sean did.

On video, that is. He'd never gotten the chance to meet the talented man in person. Sean would be in Snoozeville as soon as Sandy introduced himself, should that glorious event ever happen. No, on-screen action would have to suffice. Luckily, Sean's company, Cre8tive Juices, had a new release for him to enjoy.

Tonight he'd get his first taste of *Hole Milk*. Sandy was really looking forward to it. He could use a happy ending to a boring, plain vanilla day as manager of the Inn of Quiet Repose. A dearth of absorbing details had given him far too much time to dwell on old memories. Thirty-seven years to the night since his last boyfriend had left him, and he still felt the empty ache each anniversary.

"It's not you, it's me." Sandy mimicked the parting words Vincent had uttered to him. "I'm just not able to keep up with you." So they'd had one last goodbye fuck that the old vamp somehow managed *not* to sleep through—who'd ever heard of a narcoleptic vampire?—and parted ways.

For a few months, it had been a relief not to bear the strain of keeping their sexual relationship afloat. Then depression set in as Sandy discovered the vampire wasn't the only creature who suddenly dropped into a deep slumber whenever he was around.

These days Sandy was resigned to spending the remainder of his supernatural existence with Mr. Hand and a Ph.D. in self-gratification for companionship. At least then he could be sure his partner wouldn't drift off to sleep mid-coitus.

Finally, the video popped up on the monitor, the logo for Cre8tive Juices and Sean's pretty hole begging for attention. "It's just you and me tonight, stud. Show me how you do it."

The warning info faded to black, then Sean appeared on screen in all his butt-naked glory. The bareback porn star had a fuck-me-hard body, short dark hair and warm brown eyes that invited the viewer to join in on the fun. Sandy planned to do exactly that.

As the opening images flickered by, Sandy unbuckled his belt and shimmied his hips to send his trousers to the floor. He kicked them off, along with his shoes and blue bikini briefs. The shirt would stay on, for now.

Already blood was flowing into his cock. It didn't take much to get him going. That was another reason he used the quiet nights at the inn to watch porn and jerk off. Kept him from walking among the guests with a stiffie all day.

"But now it's playtime," Sandy told the gorgeous, naked men on the monitor as the main attraction began.

A dream sequence, perfect. Sean was getting rimmed by a man who looked like he was enjoying the job. Sandy wet his finger with his tongue and gave himself similar treatment. Little teasing forays into his puckered hole. So good.

Sandy dropped into the leather executive chair and hooked his knees over the armrests. It wasn't as sexy as the position Sean had adopted on a couch, his ass in the air where his lover had easy access, but it achieved the same result. Sandy was spread open, ready to be fucked.

As the guy on top pushed his cock into Sean's hole, Sandy lubed up his dildo. The plastic beast was thick and long, the shade of dark brown sugar. Ridges in all the right places, down to the vein traversing its length. He gasped as he inserted it with a little less care than usual. Hard to concentrate when Sean was getting royally fucked right in front of him.

"Work it, baby. That's right," he told the top on the screen.

Responding to his own order, Sandy slid the rubber shaft in and out of his anus in sync with the action unfolding in front of him. His muscles clenched around the flexible yet solid dildo, trying to suck it in deeper.

"Like that? You bet your ass you do," Sandy murmured.

The action heated up as the man on top thrust faster. Sean wriggled and writhed in pure lusty enjoyment, egging the man on. Both came in the way a good wet dream should end. Sandy didn't mind the quick close. For him, it was just the beginning.

The next scene... wow. It had been so long since Sandy had intimately embraced a real dick that his ass no longer knew the difference between flesh and synthetic. Sean, however, had lots of experience with prime cock. The fact that he'd chosen a blue glow stick over a penis hand-crafted by Mother Nature caused Sandy to wonder about the porn star's mental state. But what Sean was doing with the stick was... incredible. It illuminated his hole from the inside out.

Sandy tried to imagine what fucking a glow stick would feel like. "Is it hot? Does it burn? Tell me how much you love it."

Sean groaned appreciatively in response. Sandy made a mental note to add the luminary device to his next supply order. If it felt half as good as Sean made it sound, he was game to give it a try.

Mesmerized, Sandy watched the man love his job until a persistent ringing pulled him out of the scene. He paused the player and jabbed the button to activate the speaker phone on his desk. "Yes?"

"Mr. Moore wishes to see you, sir," Zachary, the zombie manning the Reception Desk, informed him.

"Mr. Moore?" Sandy ran through the current guest list in his head, but found no match. Not amongst his staff or vendors either. Must be a salesman, but who the hell made a cold call after midnight? No one Sandy wanted to talk to, that's for sure. "Tell him to make an appointment."

"Very good, sir."

Sandy resumed play, both on-screen and off. His balls rolled between the fingers of one hand while he lightly caressed his pulsing shaft with the other. His cock ached for release. He refused to give in so soon. Sean wasn't done entertaining him…

Again, the phone rang. Zachary rarely ran into a situation he couldn't handle on his own. If he was calling, Sandy had to answer. *Damn it*!

"What is it now?" Sandy bit his lip to keep from tacking on a groan to the end of that sentence. It had nothing to do with the annoying interruption, and everything to do with the delicious scene playing out before him. He'd hit the mute instead of the pause by mistake, and now Sean and his buddies were doing some incredibly kinky things with a funnel. A blue funnel. In Sean's ass. By the gods, the man was hot!

"Mr. Moore, sir. He insists he has made an appointment and wishes to see you."

Sandy glared down at his hard cock, then gazed at the screen where white streams of semen were being funneled into Sean's hungry hole. "I coulda been a contender," he said in his best—which, admittedly, was lousy—Godfather imitation.

"Sir?"

Zombies made great employees, but Sandy had yet to encounter one with a sense of humor. "Skip it, Zachary. About this Moore guy. What's his beef?"

"A matter he will only discuss with you. Privately." There was a pause, and Sandy imagined that Zachary had turned away from his present company for a bit of privacy. "I believe, sir, it would be in your best interests to speak with him. Now."

Okaaay. Zombies didn't venture an opinion very often. Something had spooked the front desk clerk out of his usual complacency. That alone compelled Sandy to investigate. Well, he would as soon as he took care of a much more immediate, personal piece of business.

"Send him up in ten," Sandy instructed.

"Very good, sir." Zachary sounded faintly relieved.

A click of the mouse released Sean from his silence. Cum dripped from his ass, an erotic sight. Sandy wanted to be filled that way. Stuffed with man-love. Or rather with the love of one man. A man capable of dealing with the side effects of Sandy's job. He could think of only one who fit the description, his boss. And his boss didn't bat for the home team.

His erection began to soften, and Sandy decided it was time to move on to the next stage, given that he had only minutes left before Mr. Moore would arrive.

The large plastic penis slurped as he removed it from his ass. After putting it in the bar sink for washing later, he extracted another toy from the bottom drawer of his desk, a dildo with a suction cup at the base. The cup grabbed the leather seat of his executive chair and held on tight. With practiced ease, Sandy lowered himself upon it.

The action on the screen had advanced to a new scenario where Sean had impaled himself upon a stranger's cock thrust through a hole in a public bathroom wall. *Oh, yeah.*

"Harder. Faster. Fuck me," Sandy chanted over the men's conversation.

While riding the inanimate shaft, Sandy stroked his cock. Pre-cum oozed from the tip. His balls tightened, preparing for release. Greased fingers squeezed his cock in an urgent rhythm. Sandy closed his eyes and tried hard to imagine that they were not his own.

Somewhere in the back of his mind, Sandy registered the sound of a door opening and closing, but didn't draw any of the logical conclusions. His body sang with the rush of hormones. The effect stole his breath, his nerves tingled, making his head empty of thought.

"Oh, yeah. Oh, fuck. Do me, big boy. Make me scream."

The vision of being the one grabbing his ankles, receiving the cum of a well-hung stud like Austin Shadow, hurled Sandy over the climactic edge. His body bowed, his glutes clenched.

Orgasm seized his cock as he grunted to announce his release along with Sean's co-star.

Sandy feverishly pumped his cock as droplets burst from the slit. Muscles shook with each contraction as he squeezed out more cum, showering his chest, arms and god-only-knows-what-else with it. One last shudder, a final spurt, and then it was over.

Sandy let his limbs go limp as he gasped for oxygen. Sean had done it to him again. Given him one heck of an anniversary present.

"Are you finished?" a male voice drawled with exaggerated patience.

Horror replaced the ecstasy of release when Sandy opened his eyes to find his boss standing beside him. Wearing a pearlescent necklace of seminal fluid. "Ohmygod."

"Thanks for the tithe," Morpheus said dryly, staring at the wet stain spreading across his black satin shirt. "But I'd prefer it if you saved your offerings for those better able to appreciate them."

Mortified, Sandy tore a few tissues out of the box on his desk with his free hand, then nudged the container toward his boss. "I thought, after last time, we agreed your visits would be scheduled in advance."

"We did."

"Then why show up unannounced?"

"I didn't."

"No, you—" Sandy suddenly realized what it was about the late night visitor that had made Zachary so nervous. "Mr. Moore, I presume."

Morpheus made his soiled shirt vanish with a magical snap of his fingers, revealing the body of a god. Sculpted muscle, gorgeous skin with a slight dusting of black hair swirling around his nipples. Despite his recent release, the erotic sight caused a fresh coil of heat to unfurl in Sandy's belly.

Damn the immortal! Morpheus was exuding sex appeal on purpose to get back at Sandy for the mess. "More than five minutes notice would be good."

The god of dreams glared at him. "*Lasting* more than five minutes would be good. Not everything needs to be done in a New York minute, you know."

Sandy grabbed his trousers from the floor next to his chair and stood up. In his haste, the dildo came with him and there was no way to extract it without further embarrassment.

*To hell with dignity* Sandy decided as he removed the toy and set it in the sink alongside the other. His ego was shredded anyway. "Did you come here for a purpose other than to rake my ego over the coals?"

"SAND delivery."

Sleep Aid for Nocturnal Dreaming, the primary reason his guests continually ranked the Inn of Quiet Repose number one in quality slumber. Sandy glanced at the meter on the wall outside the storage chamber. Sixty-two percent. Hardly a shortage crisis requiring an emergency visit.

Yet Morpheus was here, and now that Sandy took the time to look, he wasn't alone. A pair of Night Mares stood by the office door, acting all twitchy and nervous. Their moonlight drenched, diaphanous gowns floated around their hips in defiance of gravity. Sandy was reminded of bashful children doing the pee-pee dance.

"Go for it," he told Morpheus.

The dream god shot him a quicksilver grin, the kind of sexy invitation that spawned wet dreams. He led his Mares toward the heavily fortified SAND retention unit, guiding them with one hand on each well-rounded ass. The dreamy god jumped through the security hoops, both technical and divine, then ushered his fillies into the area beyond.

Sandy expected to hear the magnetic seal engage with a soft click. Instead, Morpheus returned to Sandy's side, alone. "You know what you need, Sandman?"

The lust bubbling in Sandy's veins cooled in a heartbeat as one of the girls giggled. Why couldn't his boss have the good taste to prefer male consorts? "A gay boss with a better sense of timing?"

Again, the quicksilver grin flashed across his face. "Not quite. You need to relax, get laid."

"Is that an offer? I'll take you up on it." Sandy pressed his body against the god, his re-awakening cock pulsing against Morpheus' hip. "Just you. And me. What do you say?"

Unmoved and uninterested, Morpheus replied, "In your dreams."

"In my office," Sandy countered. "Right here, right now."

He leaned in, expecting a harsh rebuff. Instead, his lips met... nothing. Startled, he opened his eyes. Morpheus stood before him, pale and opaque. The bastard had shaded on him, becoming no more substantial than a memory.

Feeling foolish, Sandy dropped into his chair and started punching computer keys at random. "The Mares will panic if you leave them alone too long. You'd better get going."

Agreeably, maddeningly, the dream god lingered. "I'm not the best employer on Olympus, but I try to solve more problems than I create. Let's see what we can do about yours."

"Morpheus, please. Leave it alone. I've been embarrassed enough for one day."

"Your problem isn't unique, you know."

"Yeah, I'm sure thousands of guys *unload* on their boss every day."

"Wouldn't know about that. Daydreams aren't my thing." Morpheus sat on the corner of the desk. "I have known a couple of Sandies though."

"Someone cue the violin music."

Sandy knew his current attitude sucked. He was just so tired of looking at prime eye candy and not being able to touch. If Morpheus hadn't interrupted, rubbing his face in the fact that he didn't have a hope in hell of getting well and truly fucked, Sandy might have made it through another day without hosting a self-pity fest. But Morpheus had, and now both of them had to deal with the consequences.

The dream god reached around his employee and punched a few keys on the keyboard.

"Paranormal Mates Society," Sandy read as the web page loaded. "What's this?"

"A dating service that caters to a clientele with… special needs."

A very handsome vampire popped up on the screen. Cuffsnfloggers was the screen name listed below his picture. He had brown hair, commanding brown eyes and a white shirt open to the waist. Not only did his confident posture announce that he was a top, but Sandy was willing to bet he was a Master as well.

"Whoa! If he's on the menu, I'm buying," Sandy replied, momentarily forgetting that vampires were allergic to him.

"Down, boy. This is the het section. You need to look over here." Morpheus clicked through the menus, bringing up "Men Seeking Men." "See anything worth taking for a test drive?"

It was like being a contestant on a game show. Pick a face, win a prize. Sandy skimmed the profiles. All sorts of non-human creatures were represented, including some Sandy had never seen or heard of before. Ones with pincers even. He could handle a little pain for pleasure, but that seemed extreme. "I'm not sure lobster boy is my type."

The dream god shrugged. "So pick someone else."

A few faces caught his attention. Some because they were brown bag ugly. Others because they had a sweet smile or a sexy pout. Only one made him stop and stare.

The man looked human, almost plainly so after viewing goblins and vampires and hellspawn of the darkest variety. Long white hair fell past his shoulders, several strands of which flirted with a white feather earring in his left lobe. His molasses-colored skin, hairless chest and prominent cheekbones marked him as a Native American. Sandy couldn't begin to guess from which tribe. The only indication he was something more than the human norm, albeit perfect ten, were two tattoos—a snowflake topped by a crescent moon—which glowed with a blue fire.

"IceEchoes," he read from the bottom of the picture.

Morpheus frowned. "Yeah? Why him?"

"Just look at him. He's so... cool." Sandy meant that in every definition of the word. He could name a dozen men with equally impressive bodies. His porn vids were crammed full of them. However, none radiated this man's combination of quiet power, wisdom and sex appeal. Sandy *wanted* this man. Or whatever he was.

"That's as good a reason as any, I suppose," Morpheus acknowledged.

"So now what?"

"Sign up so you can send him a vibe. Let him know you're interested." Morpheus stood and stretched, the outline of his hard cock straining the fabric below his waist as he arched his spine. "Time to make the SAND, and all that."

Alone again in his office, Sandy studied IceEchoes' face. So much character packed into a few pixels. Gray eyes, the palest shade of a winter day, gazed back at him with a wisdom mere mortals couldn't possess. So Ice was a god, or at the very least related to one. Not one of the Greeks though. Morpheus surely would have commented had Ice been one of his cousins.

Would a deity from another pantheon be immune to Sandy's slumberous aura? Or would the same problem exist, giving them no time for even a quick fuck before Ice dropped into a deep sleep? Deciding the one way to find out was by asking, Sandy completed the application for trial membership, created a profile for himself—he thought PillarsofSand gave the right impression—and sent Ice a message of introduction.

Now all he could do was wait and see what IceEchoes had to say in return. Good thing he had Sean Storm and his fuck buddies to help him pass the time. Sandy sat back in his chair and pressed the play button, letting the images take him to places he could only imagine...

## Chapter Two
## A Place to Be

Pe-Ben prowled the mouth of his cave, glaring at the snow-capped peaks surrounding his mountain home in the lands of the Abenaki people. Though the Maine landscape appeared to be in deep hibernation, he could sense the first tendrils of spring creeping in. It was... depressing.

He turned his back on the view and headed deep into his subterranean lair. If the Maiden of Spring was moving in, it was time for him to be moving out.

But where to go? Although the question came up every year, he put off making a decision as long as possible. No other place on earth appealed to him more than the ancestral seat of his people. Unfortunately, there were some universal pacts even a deity couldn't break. Timesharing dominion over the seasons was one of them.

Even if he were able to withstand the onslaught of spring, a far greater problem was the Maiden who shepherded the Abenaki tribe through the planting season. She'd been chasing after him for eons, always right on his heels. The young deity thought he'd make a good husband, opposites attract and all that. What Pe-Ben couldn't get through her stubborn head was that she wasn't his type. His type came with a penis.

The Maiden had as much divine power as he. She could assume any physical aspect she wanted. However, her personality—a far more difficult characteristic to alter—was about as masculine as a daisy. Even if she had the right equipment, Pe-Ben could never think of her as a man. So until he came up with a better tactic, he vacated his mountain home every spring to avoid the endless, fruitless debate about their romantic suitability.

And it looked like that time was rapidly approaching.

Pe-Ben ducked into his study where stalactites dripped mineral-laden water. This was one of his favorite rooms, but the high moisture content made it difficult to use electronic equipment. Instead, he'd turned a wall of ice into a big screen monitor and drew on his own power to connect to the Internet.

Within seconds, he was browsing information on vacation properties. Rental properties. Gay friendly resorts. Nothing grabbed his interest. He might as well throw a dart at a map to pick his destination. It mattered little where he went. Even if he were lucky enough to find a place suited to his tastes, he had no lover to keep him company. Nor did he have bright prospects for acquiring one.

Although his powers decreased the further he went from tribal lands, one of the more persistent characteristics was his ability to put those around him into a sleepy trance after a few minutes of conversation. It worked well for soothing agitated tribesmen, but it created one heck of a problem in the romance department.

"Wanna fuck?" That was the extent of his seductive repertoire. Any additional discussion, and he risked putting a human partner to sleep. Therefore, most of his sexual encounters with mortals took place in highway rest stops or dim back rooms of dance clubs, the kind of atmosphere where presence implied consent and lengthy discussions were discouraged.

The only men he'd found to have any immunity against his magical charms were other supernatural beings. Although it sounded good on the surface—who would be more sympathetic about the limitations of godhood than another god?—that path had inherent problems too.

Deities, by and large, were a moody, demanding, egocentric bunch. Pe-Ben liked to think he ranked low on the ego scale, but he'd met too many from the other end to seriously consider shacking up with one.

With a grimace, he recalled the one time he spent a wild month in Valhalla. Those Viking boys knew how to treat him right, but the constant boasting, blood letting and inebriation had gotten on his nerves. He couldn't out-drink them, and they weren't terribly interested in tales of winters he had known. That left nothing but sex for entertainment. Not a bad way to spend a few weeks, but far from his ideal eternity-ever-after situation.

His was not the only hard luck romance story Pe-Ben knew well. He'd spent one long season with a rather unique man named Danny, who recounted an ill-fated romance story about circumstances even death, courage and love failed to overcome. Which is why Pe-Ben had joined the Paranormal Mates Society. To get expert advice on finding a suitable mate. So far, nothing had come of his Heavenly membership but he had faith that their method of match-making would prove superior to his own. After all, how could it be worse?

Pe-Ben directed his Internet browser to load their web page. It had been a few days since he'd checked his account. He'd gotten distracted by a magnificent weather pattern which allowed him to blanket his tribal lands in snow several feet deep. It had been a deeply gratifying display of his abilities, probably the last of this winter. Spring was coming…

Since he was looking for a place to go, he might as well check in with PMS to see if he'd gotten any new offers.

There were a few barely intelligible messages from the boys in Asgard, inviting him back for another romp. Pe-Ben didn't feel so much as a twitch of interest. He sent them a polite decline. Perhaps the lack of an immortal playmate would force them to rest in between orgies. Then again, knowing the Vikings, it probably wouldn't even slow them down.

Grinning with memories—there'd been a few enjoyable moments in Viking heaven—Pe-Ben flipped through the rest of his messages. One in particular caught his eye. Of course, that could be blamed on the vibe attachment that practically knocked him over when he opened it. Whoever had sent it certainly packed a punch.

As he waited for the tingling in his body to subside, Pe-Ben pulled up the sender's profile to see what PillarsofSand was all about.

The man was, in a word, edible. Thick, dark hair capped a ruggedly handsome face. Green eyes drew in the light surrounding him and held it captive. A shadow of a beard helped to define his jaw and cheek while adding to his overall sex appeal. Who was this gorgeous creature? And what was he doing on a dating website when there were any number of eligible gays who'd love to love him?

Pe-Ben scanned the rest of the man's profile. The manager of a Canadian seaside resort. Out of his territory… but not too far up the coast. A native New Yorker who had relocated north of the border. That could mean a lot of things. Still, nothing on the form told him what paranormal aspect made him eligible for PMS's unique services. What if they weren't magically compatible?

PMS was supposed to rate their suitability as a couple, but Pillars had a temporary membership. The fact that his message had been put through meant someone at PMS didn't see an issue, but that was far from the iron-clad guarantee his level of membership was supposed to supply.

Pe-Ben needed to find someone resistant to his winter aura. He'd prefer to use his energy to seduce a partner rather than to keep them awake. Without evidence that PillarsofSand could withstand his supernatural presence, Pe-Ben refused to lock himself into spending his summer with the man. No matter how cute he was.

He bookmarked the hotel manager's profile and moved on to the remaining messages. More offers from old friends, former fucks, but none that excited him half as much as Pillars. Was it the challenge of getting to know someone fresh and new? Had he been drawn in by the almost palpable energy that radiated from the screen whenever his visage appeared?

Pe-Ben was immune to most forms of manipulation. No one could dominate his mind without his permission. Except this man. PillarsofSand. He felt, just by looking at him, that their lives were somehow intertwined…

Nonsense! He had no life. He *existed*, sustained by the love of his people. They understood him. They needed him. To be with anyone else was just… temporary.

But temporary also meant empty. It was extremely difficult to form a lasting bond with someone he saw only part of the year. PMS promised they'd find him an understanding mate. A compatible mate. Apparently, someone behind the scenes thought PillarsofSand fit the order.

Well, he'd make up his own mind about that.

Pe-Ben shut down the magic feed to the Internet and climbed into his glacier-sized bed. Over the centuries, the stalactites had produced a puddle around his bed, like a moat. The mattress was dry though. Down-filled quilts and plush pillows covered its surface. A love nest, if he'd ever seen one.

He dove into the middle of it. As a god, he had no need for sleep, but there were times it was nice to have a comfortable place to stretch out and think. That's what he did now, taking a split second to banish his formal robes as he fell onto the fluffy surface.

The contrast between his golden skin and the white fabric pleased him. He could change his appearance at will, but preferred the features that identified him as a member of his people's tribe. His tats were enough to mark him as a god.

Now his cock, that was another matter. He couldn't settle for average. Even above average didn't suit him. Though it had taken a few centuries to get the right look, he'd finally crafted an uncut rod that was long and thick, with a pair of heavy balls that dangled low. His lovers had expressed appreciation for his sexual tackle in the past. But what would Pillars think of it?

All right, so he was a bit vain. About that much at least. Pe-Ben wouldn't waste the words to ask, but would the hotel manager be enthralled by it? Beg to be speared by it?

The profile didn't claim a preference for top over bottom. Good thing, because Pe-Ben didn't bend over for anyone. He did, however, know how to please a lover when given the chance. Hearing his name bellowed out during climax was a thrill, one hard to come by outside his godly duties. Sure, his people praised him for the deep snow that would create rivers of fresh water under the Maiden's warm touch. He derived satisfaction from that. Still, it wasn't the same as personal, direct gratitude for a job well done.

He closed his eyes, sliding one hand from chest to abs, and down to the base of his shaft. He toyed with it, stroked it, his mind adrift in search of the man who fascinated him. *Pillars, where are you?*

Because the hotel manager was not of his tribe, he was much harder to find amidst the sea of humanity residing on the planet. However, another thing Pe-Ben was adept at was locating friends half a world away. Using the PMS vibe as a kind of beacon, he homed in on his target.

Making a psychic connection to the man set off a buzz in his body, a brand new experience. Like gripping a live wire. It shot straight to his loins, making his cock sit up and take notice. Despite its arousing qualities, he wasn't sure he liked it.

Once he'd adjusted to the sensation, he was able to absorb other impressions. Though Pe-Ben had no more substance than a shadow, he could feel the heat emanating from the human's body. Pillars was as naked as he. In an office, presumably his own. But what was he doing?

Pe-Ben watched him for a bit as the man bobbed up and down. It took a few seconds of observation to figure out he must be riding a dildo. That triggered a jolt of pure lust to surge through Pe-Ben's hard cock. He could easily imagine himself walking into the room, plucking Pillars out of the chair and substituting his own erection for the fake one. Seating himself inside Pillars' tight ass. Deeply. Completely.

If he decided to go.

Despite the seemingly mutual attraction, Pe-Ben still wasn't convinced that was the right decision. If only he knew what other talents the man possessed. Hence this seek and find mission. Did it tell him what he needed to know?

Given his gorgeous olive skin, he could rule out Pillars as being one of the undead. No shed fur or scales in sight, so he wasn't a were. Another deity would have sensed Pe-Ben's presence by now, so he could scratch that as a possibility. But there had to be something special about him, aside from his gorgeous looks. The hot jolt from a simple shadowing connection implied Pillars wasn't human.

There'd been some glitches in the PMS computer system when it first went on-line. Pe-Ben was inclined to believe this match was the result of one error that hadn't been purged. Except for that damn spark.

Deep in thought, Pe-Ben stroked his cock the way another being might stroke their chin. Pillars did the same, using frantic jerky movements. For him, the journey was almost over rather than just beginning.

Several seconds later, Pe-Ben's prediction came true. The hotel manager balled up as cum spurted from his cock in a shower of white droplets. They hit the surface of his desk, barely missing the keyboard. As the orgasm ended, he remained slumped over for so long Pe-Ben thought he might never regain enough strength to move.

But move he did, slowly swiveling the chair to look at the place where Pe-Ben hovered. Pillars' eyes probed the space. He reached out a tentative hand. Pe-Ben couldn't help himself. He thrust his hard cock into the man's open palm. If it registered at all, the other man should only feel a cool brush of air.

To his great surprise, Pe-Ben watched Pillars react as if he'd been shocked, snatching back his hand so quickly that the leather chair rolled back a few inches. Apparently his prospective mate could sense their connection too. Interesting. Interesting enough to spend a few weeks at the Inn of Quiet Repose to find out what this man was all about.

With half a thought, Pe-Ben established a link to PMS's server and typed out a response to PillarsofSand. *I'll come before spring. Reserve a room. IceEchoes.*

Somehow, the thought of the Maiden arriving a bit early no longer seemed quite so bad.

# Chapter Three
# Coming Together

Before spring. What the hell did that mean? Sandy had been puzzling over that ever since he'd gotten the message a month ago. Keeping a room empty, out of circulation, had been difficult. After a week, Sandy gave up. They could always shuffle guests around later if Ice actually showed.

Sandy was starting to have serious doubts about that. The long silence, combined with his own misgivings about how well the pairing would work, strengthened his belief that anticipating a meeting between them was just plain foolish. A god, or even a half-god, certainly had better things to do than come to his sleepy corner of the globe.

At least, Morpheus often did.

Yet, Sandy couldn't entirely discount the idea either. There'd been one night, right after he sent the vibe message, when he could have sworn another presence watched him as he pleasured himself. The voyeur aspect had heightened his enjoyment of the moment, but that was the only time it had happened. Had Ice lost interest?

Really, the only man a guy could depend on was himself.

Sandy patted the flat screen monitor. "Looks like it's going to be just you and me again."

He was half in, half out of his pants when his phone rang. He jabbed the speaker button with his finger. "Zachary, you really need to work on your timing."

"My most humble apologies, sir."

He waited a beat for the zombie to continue. When he didn't, Sandy prodded him. "Well, what is it?"

"A Mr. Benjamin is here to see you, sir. He believes you are expecting him."

Mr. Benjamin. Sandy couldn't translate that into any subtle form of Morpheus, nor did he recall an appointment with anyone by that name. Unless… "Please ask the gentleman if his arrival is related to IceEchoes."

A few moments of mumbled conversation passed, then Zachary returned. "Yes, sir. I believe so."

"I'll be right there!"

He took one step toward the door before he tripped. Swearing at himself, Sandy yanked his pants on, tucked in the burgundy collarless shirt which marked him as an employee of the inn and fastened his belt. Again he started for the door, but then abruptly stopped.

"Better make sure I haven't forgotten anything else."

"Sir?"

Damn, he'd left the line open too. "Nothing, Zach. I'll be down in a minute." He severed the connection, then ducked into the executive washroom.

The mirror reflected a grinning face. His green eyes danced with excitement. Not quite the cool, sexy air he wanted to project. But try as he might, he couldn't replace his expression with anything approaching sobriety.

He finger-combed his dark curls into a sultry disarray. The effect was… chaotic. Now he looked like a very happy yet not entirely sane person. A bit of water smoothed it back into place. Shaving would definitely take too long. Ice—Mr. Benjamin—would have to take him as is.

The lobby was empty, making it easy to spot his visitor. Not that he'd have trouble finding the man if they'd been on opposite sides of Times Square as the ball fell on New Year's Eve. His special guest had a presence that was hard to miss.

Mr. Benjamin looked even better up close than in the photo on the PMS website. His long white hair—not the yellowish color of the elderly, but pure snow white—had been captured in a single braid that hung down his back. A brown suede jacket, more like a sports coat than something a motorcycle gang would wear, hung from his broad shoulders. Fine linen covered his chest, the whiteness of it matching his hair. Black jeans hid the tops of a pair of fashionable black boots. Sandy followed the long legs to his crotch, and almost fainted with delight when he spotted a very promising package.

*Well, hello, Mr. Benjamin!*

Sandy's cheek muscles ached from sustaining a happy expression for so long, but he kept it in place as he crossed the plush carpet to greet his special guest. "I'm Sanders L. Mann. Sandy. Welcome to the Inn of Quiet Repose."

"Pete Benjamin," the man said, clasping his hand in a firm grip.

Palm brushing palm generated a static shock. Blue energy arced up, making Zachary, who was safely ensconced on the other side of the reception desk, draw back in alarm. Sandy glanced at his hand, half afraid of what he'd see. Thankfully, it appeared to be intact, if a little tingly from the contact.

"Wow, that was some greeting."

Pete slowly slipped his hands into his jeans pockets, his face blank, his only response a terse nod.

Sandy turned to Zachary. "Is Mr. Benjamin checked in?"

Looking more animated than he ever had before, the desk clerk gave a jerky shake of his head. "No, sir."

"Why not?"

He leaned in and lowered his voice. Sandy had to strain to hear him. "No reservation."

Of course not. Sandy hadn't made one. No name to put it under, no ETA. And they were booked up solid for the next three nights. Shit! "Give him mine."

"209?"

"Mine," Sandy repeated. He never used it anyway. Well, not often. He could live out of his office for a few days, until something opened up. He turned his attention back to his guest. "So how was your trip in?"

"Fine."

"Travel is usually pretty good this time of year. No holidays traffic to slow people down."

Pete nodded absently. His eyes roamed the décor. Nothing in his face advertised his impressions though.

Sandy got a sinking feeling in his stomach. This wasn't going the way he'd hoped it would at all. "Can I get you something to drink? Are you hungry?"

Those winter-gray eyes blinked languorously. Again, a slight twist of his head indicated the negative.

Zachary placed an access card on the counter along with the standard registration form for Pete to sign. Sandy made a mental note to adjust the room rate to zero dollars per night. He wasn't going to have Pete paying for the privilege of sleeping in his bed. That was too much like... well, he just wasn't going to have it.

"I'll take you to your room now. I'm sure you're tired, being so late at night and all." Sandy forced himself to yawn. He was pretty convincing, having practiced in front of the guests for the last forty years.

Pete frowned, but picked up the key from where Zachary had left it.

"Do you have any bags?"

"No."

Must not plan on staying long. To hide his disappointment, Sandy headed for the corridor that would take them through the public areas. He tossed off casual facts—how long the hotel had been in existence, when and where meals were served, the indoor pool and view of the beach—until his throat ran dry, and still he got very little from Pete in response.

Sandy wished he knew more about the man. The profile had been brief, mostly talking about the beauty of Maine winters and the Native Americans living in the area. Surely there was more to his life than that. But Pete offered no clues.

Perhaps the man just wasn't interested. Too bad, because Sandy had plenty of interest. Pete Benjamin moved with a panther's grace. He had gorgeous, smooth skin. And enough raw sexual energy to keep the inn running for days. Maybe tomorrow he'd feel more like talking. Sandy decided to cut the tour short and get him settled in.

His suite served as a buffer between the administrative offices of the hotel and the guest rooms beyond. As far as he could recall, there was nothing embarrassing lying around. He kept his toys and videos in his office next door, where they were close at hand.

As they stopped before his door, Pete rested against the wall. Close enough for Sandy to get a whiff of his personal scent. No cologne to dilute the crisp, clean scent of the man. Like a cold breeze off a snow-capped mountain. Sandy managed to swallow a needy whimper, but he fumbled a bit working the lock with his own card.

"This is it," Sandy announced as he gave the door a gentle push.

He gestured for the other man to precede him. Sandy followed, switching on the lights and closing the door. *Nice ass. By Morpheus's nose, I hope he changes his mind about me.*

Sandy rushed around, sticking his head into each room. He announced their purpose as he went. "Bedroom here... Bathroom through this one... Small kitchenette. If you don't like what's stocked—"

He'd run into an obstacle. A very large, solid obstacle.

"Sandy?" Pete's voice was soft as his hands settled on Sandy's hips, and another frission of static arced through his body.

"Yes?" *Ohmygod, did my voice just crack?*

"Shut up."

The directive was said gently, but the way Pete captured his lips in a searing kiss was not. Though the tingling from the initial shock was absent, there was no shortage of energy bouncing between them.

Pete opened his mouth and Sandy eagerly swept his tongue inside. Minty cool, as if he'd just brushed his teeth. The taste sent a shiver down Sandy's spine. He rested his hands on Pete's chest. Receiving no protest, he explored the masculine planes as they kissed. Hard muscle flexed under his hands as Pete shifted, widening his stance and encouraging Sandy to come closer. The rigid column of Pete's cock pressed against Sandy's groin.

It felt divine to be in the arms of someone real. Sandy had been waiting so long for something like this to happen. It was almost a miracle. The way the man moved, how he seemed to instinctively know what Sandy wanted without having to be told. As if their pairing had been choreographed by the gods.

*So why isn't my dick responding?*

Sandy froze and reviewed that last thought. It was shamefully true. Though his body tingled with desire, his cock lay quiescent against his thigh. Hell of a time for it to get shy!

"Trouble?" Pete asked.

The man's eyes twinkled with the blue found deep inside glaciers. Oxygen rich. Life giving. Sandy wrapped his arms around Pete's waist and drank him in. "No. None at all."

Pete's lips curved in a half smile. "Good."

The man's next kiss stole Sandy's breath and replaced it with pure desire. Sandy allowed himself to be marched in reverse until his back met a wall. Pete's fingers remained locked on Sandy's hips, his thumbs stroking the area over and over.

"Wanna fuck you," Pete murmured, though their lips were still touching.

"I want that too." Assuming, of course, he could get hard. His cock still refused to rise to the occasion. Sandy didn't understand why his physical response had gone AWOL, but it was starting to seriously scare him. He couldn't hide such a critical detail from Pete much longer.

*What the hell am I going to do?*

# Chapter Four
# An Ounce of Cure

Pe-Ben knew something was wrong. Sandy's reactions were a touch slow, a barely perceptible hesitation. Despite his words, he wasn't ready. And Pe-Ben didn't know if he should press on or back off. "You sure?"

"Yes." There was a "but" tacked on to the end of that sentence, and Pe-Ben waited for Sandy to fish it out. "But maybe right now isn't such a good time."

Pe-Ben got a good look at Sandy's molars as he yawned. Damn it! Those idiots at PMS had been wrong. Though he'd been very careful to keep conversation to a minimum, he was putting Sandy to sleep. All that waiting and wanting, and for nothing! They were no more compatible than Danny and his Siren.

Pe-Ben slammed the flat of his hand against the wall. Must have been too near Sandy's head, for the man jumped. He ducked out of the way and Pe-Ben let him go. He was making such a mess of this. "Sorry."

"*I'm* sorry," Sandy apologized. "I don't know what's wrong. Too much excitement perhaps." Embarrassment crept over his face. "Could we try again tomorrow?"

"Yeah." Pe-Ben stuffed his hands into his pockets to keep from reaching for Sandy. He didn't want to be alone tonight, not after waiting so long to see him. However, if the guy was too tired for sex, well, there was no one to blame but himself. He'd just have to do a better job of keeping his mouth shut tomorrow.

Sandy approached until less than a foot separated them. "I really am glad you're here."

Pe-Ben might be a god, but even he had his limits. He could no more hold himself back from touching Sandy than he could stop the moon from orbiting the earth. He cupped Sandy's jaw and traced his lips with the pad of his thumb. "Me too."

"You're not mad?"

"Disappointed." In himself for believing that he had a chance. In PMS for failing to live up to its advertising. Still, he'd take what he could get. He had a lot of empty days ahead until he could return to his ice cavern. He might as well spend them here. Maybe over time, Sandy would build up more of a resistance to his slumberous speech.

By the stars that hung in the heavens, Pe-Ben prayed it would be so.

"Anything I can do to make you more comfortable?" Sandy asked.

He pressed a kiss to the shorter man's lips. "Tomorrow."

Sandy groaned softly and swayed into him. "You sure?" Almost immediately, he stepped back, shaking his head. "No, no. Forget I said that. You're right. Tomorrow is better." He backpedaled toward the door, fumbled for it behind his back and finally opened it. "Good night, Pete."

"Night." He added a small wave.

And then Sandy was gone.

Pe-Ben let out the deep sigh he'd been holding back. Nothing to do now but count the seconds as they ticked by. Modern entertainment held little appeal for him. He could surf the net, check in on friends. Instead, he banished his clothes with a thought and lay down on the king-size bed.

Sandy. The man's natural scent was all around him. Though it didn't bring to mind any one thing in particular, he was nonetheless reminded of a day at the beach. Hot sun on warm sand. A swallow from a cold beverage that left an icy trail all the way down one's throat. Salty night breezes and relentless tides. It was all there in the essence of Sanders L. Mann.

If Sandy really was paranormal—and there was nothing normal about the shock they got whenever they connected—then the Internet wasn't likely to have much information on him. However, he did have other resources to tap. By far, the simplest thing to do would be to have a peek inside Sandy's mind.

Unfortunately, Sandy didn't have a trace of Abenaki in him. Without it, Pe-Ben couldn't do more than shadow him.

The Paranormal Mates Society didn't give out personal details on their matches, nothing the member didn't make public themselves. Violation of privacy. Besides, you were supposed to trust PMS not to fuck up.

But what was he supposed to do when they did? He needed information, damn it.

"Hi."

Pe-Ben sat up abruptly to find a man standing at the foot of Sandy's bed. Tall, dark and handsome. Too perfect. And immortal, but not one Pe-Ben had crossed paths with before. "Who the hell are you?"

"Sandy's boss. He around?"

Since Mr. Perfect didn't appear to be fazed in the least by his lack of dress, or interested by it, Pe-Ben crossed his legs Indian style and replied, "Yeah. He's around."

"Here?"

Pe-Ben shook his head.

"Look, can you give him a message for me?"

"Can't you do it yourself?" Not that he wanted to be uncharitable, but Pe-Ben didn't think Sandy was ready to see him again. Quite honestly, neither was he. Not until he had a better handle on what had gone wrong.

"Yeah, if I want to spend all night chasing after him. That boy can move faster than a comet." The god ran a hand through his hair, ruffling the dark curls. It was sexy, if you were into that sort of thing. It failed to move Pe-Ben beyond a gay man's appreciation for the male form. "Tell him to adjust the SAND mixture. The guests aren't dreaming the way they should."

"I will. Tomorrow."

The god's face darkened. "Look, my friend, you may be exchanging bodily fluids with my Sandman, but he still has work to do. Important work."

"Sandman?"

"SAND-man," the god emphasized. "You know, the guy who escorts people to Dreamland each night?"

"I don't dream."

"Your choice, but I have to tell you you're missing out on some really great stuff. Thanks for playing messenger. Shouldn't take Sandy long. Then you can get back to… whatever you were doing and I can finish my business."

Before Pe-Ben could protest, or ask another question, the strange god was gone. With typical divine arrogance, he hadn't introduced himself or acknowledged that Pe-Ben was hardly an ignorant mortal to be ordered around. His initial response was to refuse to carry out the request. However, that would only create more problems for Sandy, and it certainly wouldn't solve any issues between the two of them.

Pe-Ben slid off the bed. On his way to the door, the same clothes he'd been wearing earlier coalesced around his body. Half his mind was occupied with the task of creating the shadowing connection which would tell him where to find Sandy. The other half of his considerable brain power grappled with how to explain why he was getting involved in hotel business in the first place.

At first, Sandy seemed to be in three places at once. And they all looked the same. Entering a guest room where he'd apologize to the occupants, make some adjustment to a vent, then leave. The pattern repeated itself over and over, with only the extras changing. By the time Sandy got to a landmark Pe-Ben could recognize, he realized his target was heading right back toward him.

"Problem?" Pe-Ben asked as Sandy paused outside another door further down the hall.

"No, not really."

Pe-Ben walked toward him, that magnetic pull in his gut once more on galactic strength. "Your boss thinks otherwise."

"Morpheus? You talked to him?"

Confusion and hurt mingled in his voice. Pe-Ben reached out to soothe, but Sandy was already moving away, inside the door he'd just opened.

"Morpheus," Pe-Ben repeated as he followed the other man into what appeared to be Sandy's office. "Your boss?"

"Yeah. Morpheus. God of dreams. Did he have the Mares with him?"

"No, no horses."

Sandy stretched, arching back. It pulled his burgundy shirt over his sculpted chest. Just looking at him made Pe-Ben's mouth water. Even if it didn't lead to anything—and Pe-Ben vowed one day soon it would, even if it meant magically sealing his own mouth for the duration—he wanted to be closer to the man. He crossed the carpet and leaned against the edge of the desk as Sandy dropped into the black leather chair.

"Then he wasn't here to make a SAND delivery. Not that we need it. The vault is still pretty full." He glanced over his shoulder at a meter on the wall. It read eighty-eight percent from what Pe-Ben could see. "I wonder what he wanted."

"More SAND. The guests are restless."

"Tell me about it." Sandy rubbed his hands over his face, seemingly exhausted. "I don't think I've ever had a night with so many complaints. Heater doesn't work. Water is too cold. Neighbors having sex, keeping them awake. Zachary called in Zelma to help him answer the phones. It's just wild."

"Seems quiet now."

"Yes, it does, thank the gods." He took a sip from a cup on his desk, then spat it back out. "Yuck! Cold coffee. Let me go dump this out. Would you like a cup?"

"No."

Sandy carried the mug to the small bar and rinsed out the dark liquid. When he didn't immediately return, Pe-Ben called over to him. "Need help?"

"Ah, no. Thanks. I've got this."

Nervous. Must be. But what could there be about doing dishes to make him sound so fearful?

Curiosity drew Pe-Ben to Sandy's side once more. The man had filled the sink with bubbles and was stirring up more by the second, soaking the sleeves of his shirt, and quite a bit of the rest of him as well, in the process.

Pe-Ben reached around from behind, his chest pressed against Sandy's back. He ran his hands down Sandy's arms, and into the water.

Sandy bowed his head. "Please don't."

"Why?" Pe-Ben placed a kiss on the bare nape of Sandy's neck.

"Because I've already disappointed you once tonight."

Realization hit Pe-Ben with whiplash intensity. Whatever their other problems were, he'd compounded them with his terse speech. In absence of a full explanation for his disappointment, Sandy had assumed the blame. *Hellfire!*

He spun Sandy around. Water sprayed out in an arc, catching them both. Sandy hooked his arms over Pe-Ben's shoulders to keep from falling. Pe-Ben didn't mind a bit. The closer they got, the happier he was.

"You did not disappoint me," he said slowly.

Pe-Ben feared those five words might send Sandy into a deep sleep. He only hoped the Sandman would remember them when he woke.

But instead of sagging into his ready arms, Sandy's green eyes sparkled with relief. "I thought... You said..."

Pe-Ben kissed him. "I failed. PMS failed. Not you."

"You? PMS? How?"

Hearing the clipped language from someone else brought a chuckle to Pe-Ben's lips. Did he really sound like a verbal machine gun when he spoke? "PMS ensured a compatible match. We aren't compatible. Not completely."

The happy light in his green eyes dimmed. "What makes you say that?"

Pe-Ben stole a quick kiss before answering. "I make you sleepy."

"Huh?"

Bafflement wasn't the response Pe-Ben had expected. "You yawned."

"I faked it. In case you were tired. I didn't want you to think you had to stay up for me."

That didn't make one bit of sense to Pe-Ben, but it didn't need to. Sandy, for his own reasons, had faked being tired. There was hope for them after all. "The sound of my voice doesn't make you sleepy?"

"Sexy, not sleepy." He nibbled at the sensitive skin under Pe-Ben's ear.

"Thought you wanted to wait," Pe-Ben said, even though his eager fingers were already prying the shirt tails out of Sandy's waistband.

"I changed my mind."

# Chapter Five
# Fully Engaged

*What the hell am I doing?* That thought collided with the haze of lust clouding Sandy's brain. He wanted Pete, craved his touch. Thinking beyond that proved too difficult a task for him to master. He wiggled against the larger man, pulled him closer… and smacked the back of Pete's head with a plastic schlong.

*Morpheus, if you have any mercy in you, now would be a good time to whisk me away.* But apparently his boss wasn't listening, or didn't care to get involved. Sandy could only wait as Pete absorbed what had just happened.

Pete pulled Sandy's arm down to get a better look at the object Sandy could no longer hide. "Nice toy."

"Thanks."

"Yours?"

"Yeah." Sandy brought the object in his other hand around for inspection too. "So is this one."

Pete glanced over Sandy's shoulder, presumably at the sink which was still full of suds. "Got more in there?"

"More, yes. There, no."

Pete's eyes roamed as much of Sandy's body as he could, given their proximity. "No disappointment at all."

Sandy chucked the dildos over his shoulder, not minding when water splashed out of the sink and soaked through the back of his shirt. "Prove it."

A heartbeat sped by, and then another. And a third. Then, with a sudden smile, Pete lifted Sandy by the waist and set him down on the edge of the counter next to the sink. He leaned in, teasing Sandy with little flicks of his tongue. On his lips. His nose. His ear. Wherever Sandy was least expecting it.

With a growl of frustration, Sandy gripped Pete's head with both hands to hold him still, then kissed him deeply. His tongue berated that of the other man with several playful slaps. Desire hummed through his veins, this time giving his cock more than a lick and a promise toward assuming full stature.

Pete unbuttoned Sandy's shirt. The fabric made an audible, wet sound when it peeled away from his skin. Even though he was slightly chilled from the water, Pete's fingers felt cold. Stiff.

Sandy raised Pete's hand to his mouth and drew one finger in between his lips. He sucked it, nibbled on the tip. Swirled his tongue over it. In his mind, he imagined the way Pete's cock would taste when he subjected it to the same treatment.

Pete trailed his hand along Sandy's ribcage, then around to tweak his pebbled nipple. "Top or bottom?"

He let go of Pete's finger with a pop. "Bottom. Definitely."

"Excellent."

Time to do a little unveiling of his own. Sandy tugged at the belt buckle, releasing the long length of leather. It gave him so many ideas…

"Wait. Watch." Pete took a step back. Half a blink later, the man was completely naked. And impressively aroused.

Sandy took in the long, rigid length of Pete's uncut cock. The white hair at its base matched the thick strands now freely floating around his wide shoulders. A pair of twin globes nestled in between his thighs. His smooth, hairless chest was marked by the blue tattoos Sandy recalled from the PMS photo. Without a doubt, the man was a god.

"Not impressed?"

Sandy twitched, startled out of his musings. He'd been silent too long. This was not a good time for him to be tongue-tied. "Very impressed. Which heaven do you belong to?"

"Huh?"

"Which heaven? Which god are you?"

"Pe-Ben. God of Winter to the Abenaki people. Does it matter?"

Of course. Pe-Ben. Pete Benjamin. Made sense. "Not to me."

Pe-Ben spread his arms. "Well then?"

Morpheus wasn't high maintenance, for a god. It didn't seem like Pe-Ben was either. However, it appeared that both had a tendency to expect their needs to be addressed first and foremost. That might become a problem later on, when work interfered with play, but for now it was an arrangement Sandy could live with. He really wanted his mouth around that divine cock.

Sandy kicked off his shoes and hopped off the counter. When he reached Pe-Ben, he dropped to his knees.

"Not what I meant," the winter god said on a gasp as Sandy took one testicle in his mouth.

Sandy looked up at him. "Want me to stop?"

Pe-Ben's eyes were brighter than sunlight reflecting off a fresh layer of snow. "No."

"Good," Sandy replied, although his response was muffled as he resumed his oral caress of Pe-Ben's balls. First one and then the other, inhaling deeply the intimate scent of the man.

Fingers replaced tongue as he licked the arrow-straight shaft, along the vein throbbing under the sensitive skin. By the time he reached the tip, a pearl of moisture had formed. Sandy sucked it off, letting the fluid linger on his tongue to fully absorb Pe-Ben's unique flavor. He stroked the god's shaft with his hand, drawing out more liquid for him to sample. Ambrosia. Nectar of the gods. Is this where it came from?

"Good?"

So good that the crotch of Sandy's pants was fixed to burst, struggling to contain his erection. "Uh-huh."

Pe-Ben spread his legs apart, giving Sandy more room to play. His cock was so big Sandy knew he couldn't swallow all of it. Instead, he did the reverse, allowing his lips to surround little more than the tip. His fingers sought out the inch-long strip of skin behind his balls and tickled it. Pe-Ben thrust his cock deeply into Sandy's mouth.

"Oh, fuck."

*Indeed.* Sandy freed his erection from his pants. He pumped it with one hand while he caressed Pe-Ben's cock with the other. Their moans blended together. Pe-Ben increased Sandy's slow rhythm by flexing his hips. He fucked Sandy's mouth with rigid control. Sandy wanted to snap it, drive the god beyond restraint. Someday, when they learned each other better...

"Wanna come inside your ass," Pe-Ben announced through gritted teeth.

"Uh-uh." Next time, maybe, but Sandy wanted to swallow Pe-Ben's cum. To take him inside where no one could separate them. "Next time."

Sandy felt the brush of Pe-Ben's hand against his hair. "Next time. Good."

Sandy palmed Pe-Ben's ass with both hands. His own cock rubbed against the winter god's calf, no doubt leaving pecker tracks. There was nothing he could do about that, probably wouldn't even if he could. It felt too good. Skin just cool enough to comfort the burning hot flesh that was full and heavy with blood.

Strong masculine hands gave Sandy's shoulder a squeeze before he felt the weight lift. When he looked up, he saw Pe-Ben had his head thrown back, the cords on his neck standing out. Could Sandy be everywhere at once? Could he be sucking dick, tongue-fucking ass, fusing mouths and nibbling neck all at the same time? No, but he could enjoy the hell out of watching the rapturous expressions cross the god's face as each adjustment Sandy made brought him closer to climax.

"Coming," Pe-Ben announced.

No doubt. Sandy could feel the god's shaft quivering with the first tremors of release. He burrowed his fingers into the cleft of Pe-Ben's ass, finding the hyper-sensitive ring of tissue. Even an exclusive top liked to be rimmed. Fingering wasn't quite as good, but this time it would have to do.

As Sandy pressed his index finger against that small rosette, Pe-Ben erupted into his ready mouth. The load was so large that Sandy had trouble swallowing it all. The second load came, adding to the first deposit. Using his tongue, he parked Pe-Ben's cock against the roof of his mouth. This also blocked his esophagus. It was better to wait a few seconds and enjoy it rather than risk choking or — may the gods save him from such a fate — throwing up on Pe-Ben's feet if he gagged.

Utterly spent, Pe-Ben pulled away from Sandy's grasp. "Have any left over?"

Sandy nodded. He liked the unique flavor of the god's cum so much that he hadn't been willing to swallow all of it in one greedy gulp.

"Come here."

Pe-Ben helped him to his feet, then dove into his mouth for a tongue-tangling kiss. Semen and saliva mixed in a new, erotic way of sharing. *Snowballing. I never thought I'd find a lover who'd do this with me.*

But Pe-Ben wasn't just any man. He was a god, a very generous one.

"Thank you," Sandy said when their kiss finally ended.

The winter god gathered Sandy to his chest, surrounding him with a cool, secure embrace. "My pleasure."

"Mine too." Under his cheek, he could feel Pe-Ben's heart hammer with excitement.

A chill cocoon enveloped Sandy's cock. "What about this?" Pe-Ben asked. "Does this bring you pleasure?"

A new voice intruded, shattering the mood. "It'll have to wait. I think you've taken up enough of my Sandman's time for one night."

Sandy turned around, aware of Pe-Ben behind him, still naked. His own rapidly deflating dick hung out of his pants. Shit. "Hello, Morpheus. Did we have an appointment?"

"I think you can forgive my unexpected intrusion *when all hell is breaking loose!*"

Pe-Ben's arm slid around Sandy's waist and pulled him close until they touched, chest to back. Whether it was out of modesty or a need to feel close, Sandy appreciated the extra support. "I already took care of it."

"Then why is the switchboard lit up like a solar flare?"

"What?" He twisted in Pe-Ben's embrace to check the communications console on his desk. It was true. Every line into the reception desk pulsed with activity. "This has to be some kind of malfunction."

"I agree. Your malfunction."

"Mine?" He hadn't done anything different than usual. There'd been a few complaints, but he'd talked to each guest personally. Smoothed it over. Gave them a personal escort to Dreamland. Why were the guests still up?

"The guests aren't sleeping. Whose fault is that?" Morpheus stormed over to the SAND chamber and started the process of clearing the security. "Say goodbye to your boy toy. You've got work to do."

Sandy mentally hurled every vile curse he could think of at his boss's retreating back as he returned his cock to his pants.

Pe-Ben whispered, "Want to quit?"

"No."

He couldn't. Working for Morpheus sustained him, prolonged his life. Without that divine benefit, he wasn't sure what would happen. Perhaps he'd turn to dust on the spot. Definitely lose whatever chance he had at a relationship with Pe-Ben. He'd be a mortal. A pure mortal. Maybe even a dead one. And mortals, whatever their condition, didn't consort with gods. Not for long, anyway.

Pe-Ben turned him so they faced each other. "Want me to leave?"

"No!" Sandy quelled the panic rising in him. No one wanted a desperate man. "I mean, not unless you want to."

"I can wait."

That was a big compromise. Gods weren't used to waiting for anyone or anything. They were the ultimate instant gratification boys. Sandy kissed Pe-Ben, trying to convey his relief and gratitude. "I need to get dressed. Morpheus won't be as patient."

Pe-Ben held out his hand. A white shirt materialized over it. "Use mine."

Gladly. If Sandy had to spend the rest of the night with a cranky immortal, at least he could do it surrounded by the fragrance of one who felt a lot more kindly toward him. "Thanks."

He shrugged into it. The material hung loose on his frame, but not so much that it would look sloppy when he went to talk to the guests. "I'm really sorry about this. It's never happened before. Most nights around here would make a graveyard look like a happening place."

"Quiet, huh?"

"Yeah." He finished getting his clothing in order, then settled his hands on Pe-Ben's naked hips. "I'd really like to make this up to you. How about dinner tomorrow?"

Pe-Ben rubbed Sandy's belly with the back of his fingers. "Sure."

"It'll be late, after my rounds, but I guarantee we won't be disturbed." After tonight, the guests who remained would get an extra dose of SAND. If exhaustion didn't make them sleep through the night, that certainly would.

"Fine."

"Five seconds, Sandy, or I'm transferring you to the stables!" Morpheus called from within the vault.

"Gotta go," Sandy said softly. He kissed the winter god's lips one last time. "Tomorrow. Dinner. 10:00 pm."

\* \* \*

If he were at home, Pe-Ben would have blanketed the inn in a slumberous wintry cocoon, resolving Sandy's professional problem in less time than it took to discuss it. Outside his power base and surrounded by so few who could nominally claim to be of his tribe, he could do little to influence the sequence of events. And Morpheus certainly didn't want him messing around with his turf.

Turf that included Sandy? Were they more than boss and employee?

Sandy's reaction to the dream god seemed to indicate otherwise. And Pe-Ben knew from personal experience that

Morpheus didn't hit on every man who came around. Maybe they'd been down that road and parted ways...

Should he do the same? Asgard wasn't nearly as peaceful as the Inn of Quiet Repose, even under the current circumstances. However, there he never had to worry about his lover being called away. Passed out drunk, maybe, but certainly not absent. Was Sandy worth the inconvenience?

One phenomenal blow job did not a relationship make. His divine instinct warned of even more potential pitfalls ahead if he chose to stay with Sandy. There was also the possibility of great reward. The Sandman seemed to have more tolerance for his company than any other normal or paranormal creature he'd met. Aside from other gods, that is. He'd already rejected the idea of mating with one of them for all eternity.

Again his vast thought processes brought him full circle, back to the original question. Should he stay or should he go? He'd told Sandy he could wait, a possibility not a promise. Sandy wouldn't see it that way though, and Pe-Ben didn't want to hurt the man needlessly. If he chose to leave, he'd be honest about it.

They'd barely scratched the surface of getting to know each other, but Pe-Ben knew there'd be a permanent hole in his being without the sexy Sandman around. He had to decide what was best not only for himself, but also for Sandy. And then he'd decide whether or not he could live with the answer.

In order to do that, he needed to get to know the man better. Sandy's office seemed like a good place to start.

The desk held a myriad of sexual toys. Sandy hadn't been kidding when he admitted to having more dildos. They almost overflowed the deep bottom drawer. Nothing too kinky, but definitely an assortment to cater to a wide variety of tastes. Apparently Sandy enjoyed variety and trying new things. That was good to know.

The next drawer up contained a stockpile of DVDs. Porn vids covering as many fetishes and genres as the toys. Pe-Ben recognized a lot of the names from his web surfing. A few of his personal favorites in the mix. Sexual compatibility wasn't going to be a problem, not from that angle.

Nothing he saw told him much about the man under the skin though. Maybe Sandy's computer would hold a few hints.

The screen saver required a password. Pe-Ben cheated by using a god command to override it. A series of warnings flashed across the screen. He read them as fast as they appeared. Apparently Sandy had a program that alerted him each time a complaint was logged. One hundred and thirty-seven in the last two days, the overwhelming majority being logged in the last twelve hours. Since he'd arrived.

Were the two events related? How could that be? It wasn't like he'd held a tribal dance or announced his arrival with a heavenly fanfare.

No, it had to be something else. Something mundane. Sandy and Morpheus would figure it out and then Pe-Ben and Sandy could have a few hours to themselves.

Leaving the red flags alone, Pe-Ben started poking around in other electronic files. The desktop photo was obscured by dozens of shortcuts. Instead of testing each one, he used a utility to show which ones got the most use. Some were business related. Others were definitely not.

The top spot belonged to the DVD drive. No doubt it saw a lot of action, given the drawer was stuffed with movies. Pe-Ben clicked on it to see what was in the drive now. A few seconds later, Sean Storm popped up on the screen.

Pe-Ben knew Sean's face well. He'd seen it many, many times. It was tough to identify the man behind the Halloween mask, but it had to be Ian Rawlings, the international porn star of mystery. No one else associated with Sean Storm was so careful not to get his face caught on film.

Pe-Ben sat back in Sandy's chair, his hands caressing the leather armrests as he watched Sean and Ian make up. How many nights had Sandy spent doing this very thing in this exact spot? Had he ever had someone to teach him the joys of being a bottom? Had all his research been put to practical application?

Probably not. Sandy was more a prisoner of his responsibilities than Pe-Ben had ever been. He could damn well do what he pleased, in most things. Sandy was governed almost entirely by his job. He couldn't miss a night of work. Couldn't visit with guests longer than it took to tuck them in at night. In other words, Sandy was as lonely as Pe-Ben himself, if not more so.

Pe-Ben would put a stop to that. As Ian climaxed for the camera and slipped his cock back into Sean's waiting hole, he started to make plans for a night both he and Sandy would remember for a long, long time.

# Chapter Six
## Chemistry Lesson

After guiding his guests into Morpheus's waiting arms, Sandy nervously paced the length of his office. Every few seconds he'd glance at the phone, counting the number of lines in use. So far so good, but he wasn't completely reassured. Things could go haywire at any minute, just like the night before.

Last night had been a nightmare. Not literally. Sandy would love to lay the blame for the chaos at the hooves of Morpheus's Mares. Unfortunately, as far as he and his boss could tell, the girls didn't have a thing to do with the rampant chaos that had swept through the Inn of Quiet Repose. None of the deities on Olympus, or their minions, had taken credit for what appeared to be a prank of cosmic proportions, although they all professed their appreciation for such a good joke.

No, as near as Sandy could tell, reality had reversed itself for about an hour. Whispered sexy words were broadcast through the hotel. Hot became cold. Peace became chaos. None of it made any sense.

He was not looking forward to a repeat. Thankfully, one didn't seem to be in the offing. His dinner with Pe-Ben could take place as planned.

Sandy was very much looking forward to it. Although Morpheus had kept him running all over the inn, soothing guests and investigating potential causes of the disturbances, every spare second of thought belonged to the winter god.

Pe-Ben, as he looked on the website, all cool and remote yet sexier than any Hollywood hero.

Pe-Ben, naked and aroused.

Pe-Ben, thrusting into him with passionate abandon as they—

Sandy shook his head. Better to do it than to dream about it. That's what he planned to do tonight. Make some of his fantasies come true.

He dialed the front desk. "Has dinner been delivered to my suite?"

"Yes, sir." Zachary's tone was flat, factual.

"Good. Any problems?"

"No, sir."

Another straight answer, no hesitation. No edge of panic to the zombie's voice. Things really were okay. "Thank you, Zachary. I'll be in my suite the rest of the night. Don't disturb me unless it's a dire emergency."

"Very good, sir."

"Not even for Mr. Moore." The last thing he needed was Morpheus barging in on them again. The god really needed to work on his timing.

"Not even for Mr. Moore," Zachary repeated. "Enjoy your evening off, sir."

Sandy felt a sudden lightness in his chest as he disconnected the call. For the first time in almost four decades, he had a date. With someone other than Mr. Hand.

He ducked into his office bathroom to freshen up. Fifteen minutes later, he knocked on the door of his own living quarters, quelling the urge to bounce on the balls of his feet with anticipation.

The lock on the door released and the door opened, seemingly of its own volition.

"Enter."

The room was dark, almost pitch black, except for a line of votive candles forming a trail between the entry and his bedroom. Though the smells in the air indicated that dinner had indeed been delivered, Sandy saw no evidence of that. Confused but pleased by the notion that Pe-Ben had taken some trouble to make their evening special, Sandy followed the course laid out for him.

As soon as he crossed the threshold into the bedroom, the air changed, became charged. Sandy didn't know what had stolen his breath... whether it was the sight of a sex swing that had been hibernating in his closet or the fact that such care had been taken to create a romantic setting, with silver dishes, candlelight and roses that hadn't come from any of the inn's stock set out on his dresser.

His heart slowly flipped over. Whatever else happened between them, this was a night Sandy was never going to forget.

"Like it?"

Pe-Ben's voice came from the shadows behind him. He turned, but couldn't see more than a dark outline of the man except for the faint blue glow outlining his tattoos. "Gods, yes."

"Which hunger shall we feed first?"

Sex or food? "You decide."

"Then I choose my hunger for you."

Sparks showered all around them as Pe-Ben placed his hands on Sandy's shoulders. They were white hot, yet arctic cold at the same time. Sandy jumped.

"You hurt?"

"No, just surprised." With spots from the brilliance of the electric spray still dancing in his eyes, he relaxed into Pe-Ben's embrace. "We've got to stop meeting like this."

The winter god's voice rumbled with laughter as he brought their bodies into contact from shoulder to thigh. "I like meeting you like *this*."

Pe-Ben was naked. Wherever Sandy's hands roamed, all he met was flesh. Beautiful, muscled, naked flesh. He groaned with desire, wanting to do much more than merely touch. "You said something about hunger?"

"Yes. Hunger for you."

Pe-Ben captured Sandy's mouth in the most erotic kiss imaginable. Their tongues tangled, their lips fused and their bodies swayed into each other as if they'd always belonged together. His perfect mate. His soul mate.

Sandy froze, waiting for the punch line. This had to be a joke. No one wanted him this much. Did they?

"Afraid?"

"Yes." Afraid it was real. Afraid it wasn't.
"Of me?" Pe-Ben asked.
"Of finding out this is just a dream." He nuzzled against the skin at Pe-Ben's throat, breathing him in.
"We don't dream, you and I. Reality is all we have." He took Sandy by the hand and led him to the swing. "Undress. I want a bigger bite of you."

Sandy complied, though his motions were slow and jerky. Performance anxiety tightened his gut. As he stripped off his underwear, he prayed his dwindling confidence wouldn't cause something else to shrink too.

The winter god gestured toward the chair. "Sit."
"Pe-Ben, I—"
"Call me Pete. Tonight I'm more man than god." He leaned in and nibbled along Sandy's ear. "I want to fuck you in every way humanly possible."

Still, doubt nagged at him. "What if I'm not *up* to your standards?" he asked, running a finger along the length of the god's stiff cock to emphasize the point he was trying to make.

"Then I wouldn't be here." He nudged Sandy backward until his thighs brushed against the leather seat. "Since I am, you can be assured you meet all my standards."

Relief, or perhaps it was the intense look in Pete's gray eyes, weakened his knees. Either way, Sandy sagged into the swing. Pete helped to arrange his limbs, putting his feet through the leather loops to support his legs up and out of the way. His hands were buckled in straps attached to the metal chains. The result was surprisingly comfortable, but left him completely open to Pete's gaze.

"Exquisite. I knew you would be."

The compliment restored his confidence. Whatever came next, Sandy was ready for it.

"Hungry yet?" Pete asked.
"Yes."

"Good." He walked over to the buffet and peeked through the dishes. He selected one and brought the serving platter to a table set slightly behind Sandy's head, out of his sight. "Try this."

Sandy sucked the offered finger in his mouth, swirling the sauce away with his tongue. Perhaps the orange beef he'd ordered. "Hmm."

"More?"

"Yes, please."

The finger slipped out of his mouth, then returned a few seconds later with a piece of beef. Slowly, he ate, licking Pete's skin clean after every bite. After a sip of plum wine to clear his palate, Pete fed him a few spicy string beans. Peppery heat burned his taste buds, but it was a good kind of pain. Like being so close to Pete without being able to touch him. To kiss him. To be fucked by him.

But without a doubt, those thoughts were in Pete's mind too. Every time their gazes locked, he telegraphed his desires. *I want you. I want to bury myself inside you so deeply that glaciers will become lakes before I could part from you. I want to feel your body wrapped around mine, living on your heat because I need nothing more to sustain me.*

Sandy groaned, squirmed, did everything he could think of to signal he wanted to be taken now, hard and fast and deep. Still Pete kept him waiting.

The next dish wasn't one Sandy knew, another spicy flavor with bits of duck. Rich and decadent, but a few bites was enough. He was full. Now his stomach burned with a deeper, darker craving. One only Pete could fill.

"My turn," the winter god said, seeming to read his mind. He turned Sandy's head to the side, toward him. The result placed his mouth inches from Pete's hard cock. "Suck me."

Sandy wrapped his lips around the velvet-soft head. Pete brushed Sandy's dark curls back from his face as Sandy worked his mouth over Pete's thick shaft. His other hand cupped Sandy's jaw. Sandy didn't have to look up to know Pete was watching him.

"So beautiful."

The hand at his jaw grazed his neck, then traveled lower. It swirled over one pec and then the other, stimulating his sensitive nipples. As if any part of Sandy needed further stimulation. His cock had reached full capacity and then some.

"You're too good at that," Pete said as he withdrew. He turned away, ferrying the dishes back to the buffet. His white mane of hair, down for the occasion, shimmered like fresh snow in the candlelight.

This time when Pete returned, he stood between Sandy's legs. He took Sandy's erection in his hand and lightly stroked it. Nothing more than a feather-light caress up and down the length. All the while, Pete's eyes were riveted on Sandy, gauging the reaction to his touch.

"More," Sandy begged. "Take me."

"Not just yet."

But Pete did lower his mouth over the tip and lick the pre-cum from the crown of Sandy's cock. He must have put something hot in his mouth. The spice burned through his sensitive skin, inflaming his blood, making him sweat. "What the hell?"

"A little surprise. You like?"

His cock burned and yet Pete's cool mouth was there to soothe the sting away. Sandy grabbed the chains near his wrists and tried to lift himself higher, thrusting deep into Pete's suction as the heated sensation reached his balls.

"It's too much."

"No, Sandy, you're wrong. It's not nearly enough."

The winter god knelt and buried his face between Sandy's legs. His tongue laved the length of his shaft, his chill breath chasing away the fire and replacing it with a tingle that went far deeper. Each time Pete reached the base, he sucked on the loose skin surrounding his balls.

Sandy's body was awash with desire. He tugged against the restraints, wanting to help. To guide. To get his hands on the man driving him wild.

"Patience," Pete cautioned.

"It's never—" Sandy stopped before he got that thought out. Of course sex had never been like this before. He'd never been with Pete until now. He tried again. "I don't—"

"I do."

Pete spread Sandy's ass cheeks apart and speared the puckered hole he'd revealed with his tongue. Sandy hissed in surprise, the sensation was so powerful. The overwhelming sensation stopped almost immediately. "Sorry, sorry. It's just—"

"I know." Pete grinned. "I like how you respond."

"Then you'll do it again?"

Pete slapped Sandy's ass, chuckling. "Yes."

This time Sandy tensed up well in advance. Pete's tongue didn't penetrate far. However, the god continued to nibble and lick, sending waves of pleasure over Sandy's body. His marble-hard cock left dots of sticky pre-cum on his stomach every time it throbbed with need.

Pete had already given him so much, but it still wasn't enough. "Fuck me," Sandy begged. "Please."

"Making demands of me?"

Chagrined that he might have gone too far, Sandy blushed. "Yeah. Sorry."

"Don't be." He got to his feet, but couldn't seem to resist touching Sandy. Pete's hands caressed Sandy's legs, his ass, his belly. Always moving, exploring. "Tell me again."

Sandy loved the way his eyes glittered like icicles in the sun. Sharp and clear. "I want your cock inside me."

"So be it."

The initial breach brought a slight sting of pain. He always felt it, no matter how well prepared he was. Fast penetration was almost better, and Pete seemed to understand this. He sheathed himself deeply in one long thrust, until his balls slapped Sandy's ass, then gave him a few seconds to adjust to the welcome intrusion.

"So good," Sandy gasped out. "You feel so damn good."

"As do you."

Pete began to move his hips in small circles, grinding in. He held Sandy by the thighs so the swing wouldn't carry him away.

"Faster. Harder," Sandy urged him.

Pete withdrew until the tip of his cock could barely be detected, then slammed it back in with a fierce growl.

Lack of blood to his brain, because so much of it now swelled his cock, was making him delirious. Surely that's why Sandy heard the sound of bells ringing. "Don't stop. Don't stop."

"Never."

Sandy struggled against the strips of leather restricting his movements. He tried to impale himself on Pete's cock with more force, deeper penetration. Pete let go of Sandy with one hand and, with each thrust, he pumped Sandy's cock in his tight fist.

The shrill bells in his head were getting louder as he got closer to orgasm. "I'm coming! I'm coming!" Sandy realized he was screaming, but it was the only way to force the words past the tightness gathering in his body.

"No!" Morpheus popped into existence beside the swing. With a wave of a muscled arm, he thrust Pe-Ben backward, sending him crashing into the bedroom wall. "Put that dick down!"

# Chapter Seven
# Love Is in the Air

Fury rolled through Pe-Ben. His fingers curled into fists, ready to rip the snowcaps off mountains. The dream god was about to take a long walk off a short cloud!

He stepped forward, wanting to use physical force as Morpheus had done, even though it wasn't necessary for what he had in mind. The Maiden pined for a playmate. Pe-Ben was going to send her one.

"Hey, Pe-Nut," Morpheus said, his hands now raised in self-defense. "It's not what you think."

"Any interest I had in your intentions is long gone," Pe-Ben growled. "As you should be."

Sandy struggled to sit up, but the restraints held him in place. "What is it now, Morpheus? I checked with Zachary before dinner, and everything was fine."

"Maybe then it was." Morpheus didn't take his eyes off Pe-Ben. "It's not now."

"Well, help me up and—"

Pe-Ben iced over the buckles on the restraints with a flick of his mind. "You're not going anywhere, Sandman. *He* is."

Mid-protest, Morpheus was flung to a remote cave on the coast of Maine. Pe-Ben didn't pay much attention to which one since he had no intention of fetching him back. The Maiden would find him sooner or later, and then the meddlesome Geek of Dreams would be someone else's problem.

"Now, where were we?" Pe-Ben leaned down to blow a wisp of cool air over Sandy's cock. "Right about here?"

"Been there, done that," Sandy reminded him with a sly grin.

Pe-Ben chuckled, sending a chilly stream of air over his lover's heated flesh. The man shivered. Pe-Ben vowed he'd make up for it soon.

"Then maybe it was here?" He licked the seam between Sandy's almost perfectly matched balls.

Sandy's breath hitched. "Done that too."

"Ahh. So I did." Pe-Ben inserted his thumb into Sandy's anus, searching for the spongy spot that would make the man jump with inner joy. "Did we do this?"

"Oh, yeah. But you can do it again if you want." Sandy wiggled, trying to help.

"Hmm. I hate repeating myself." Still, he continued to probe until he found the spot. He pressed it just enough to let Sandy know how good it would feel when his cock brushed against it, then removed the digit. He positioned his cock at the opening to Sandy's anus. "Then I guess I should—"

Once again they were interrupted by a slight popping sound. Morpheus appeared, his black shirt ripped in several places as if someone had grabbed him and he'd had to fight his way free. Petals and other kinds of forest debris were tangled in his hair. "Don't *ever* do that to me again!"

"Don't get in my way again," Pe-Ben warned in return.

"Look, I have a crisis here. I need my Sandman."

"I need Sandy too." Gods weren't supposed to have needs. Not ones that couldn't be sated with a snap of their fingers. Yet the truth was impossible to deny. Right now, Pe-Ben needed Sandy, as a lover and as a companion. How long could a relationship between them last? How long was eternity?

Sandy used the side of his foot, the only part of him that remained independently mobile, to stroke Pe-Ben's arm. "I need you too."

"Touching," Morpheus replied, clearly not meaning it. "Are you through?"

"Close, but not quite." Even if the world came to an end around them, Pe-Ben was going to make sure he and Sandy got one bright, orgasmic moment together.

"I'm not going to stand here and watch you fuck my employee!" Morpheus thundered.

"So go. Either way it's going to happen." Pe-Ben kept his eye on his lover rather than the angry deity. Sandy's smile made all the hassles worthwhile. "You ready?"

"Your sex life doesn't take precedence here. The peaceful dreams of a couple hundred mortals—"

Sandy cut him off. "What about my dreams, Morpheus?"

"You don't dream."

"Sure I do. Just because you don't deliver them to me, just because they don't come to me while I sleep, doesn't mean they're not real." He shifted his gaze back to Pe-Ben. "Please, let me have my dream."

Morpheus might have been able to resist the plea in Sandy's voice, but Pe-Ben could not. Without waiting for the dream god's consent, Pe-Ben leaned between the legs of his lover and kissed his lips. "As you wish."

"Free my arms, let me touch you."

"Not yet."

Morpheus vanished once it was clear he wasn't going to get their full attention in the near future. Pete didn't even take time to rejoice in this minor victory. His sole focus was on his lover.

He kissed his way down Sandy's body, taking time to lick his lover's nipples until they hardened. Kissed the inside of Sandy's thighs. Nibbled his ass. By the time he tongued Sandy's puckered hole, the man was writhing again, begging for his cock.

"Now, Pete. Now."

He poised his cock, already primed, at Sandy's tight opening. He thrust home with one long push.

"Yes," Sandy hissed through his teeth. "Oh, yes."

Willing a bit of frost to form on the end of his finger, he drew a cold, invisible line down the center of Sandy's erection. Sandy shivered from the touch, tightening around Pe-Ben's enshrouded shaft, hugging him intimately. Pe-Ben performed the trick a second time, enjoying his lover's reaction to the hilt.

The warmth of Sandy's expression melted far more than the ice from his finger. Pe-Ben was falling for this generous, funny, verbose bottom-boy. Falling hard and fast.

A push of his hips set the swing in motion. He let the chains do the work, sending his cock into a retreat, then burying himself in Sandy's tight ass. Though it gave him great pleasure to watch his thick erection slide in and out of his lover's body, he took greater pleasure in watching the erotic storm brewing in the man's green eyes.

"If you won't let me touch you, at least free one hand so I can jack off. I'm dying here," Sandy insisted.

Pe-Ben shook his head. Sandy was far from being in mortal peril. The pulse hammering through his veins, the rapid rise and fall of his chest, the moans that left his talented mouth… they all proved that Sandy was very, very much alive.

Pe-Ben wrapped his fist around Sandy's shaft. Again the swing supplied the bulk of the effort, rocking back and forth to provide friction, causing both men to tremble.

Tingling rose within his balls. Pe-Ben could hold out longer, but knew sooner or later Morpheus's patience would wear thin. Thinner, rather. The last thing he wanted right now was another interruption so he didn't hold himself back. He let the orgasm build inside him.

"In or out?" he asked his partner.

Sandy bit his lip, considering. "In. No, out!"

Pe-Ben leaned into the next thrust, penetrating extra deep. "In or out. Choose one."

"I can't!"

Maybe some day he'd grow another cock just to see if it doubled their pleasure, but today he had to work with the one he had. "In," Pe-Ben decided. "In so far…" He clamped onto Sandy's thighs, just above the hip. "So deep…" He drove himself into his lover's body again, his cock straining for release. "Can't separate…" Pe-Ben arched his back as a climax ripped through him, coming in one long, steamy rush. "Us!"

"Fuck. Oh. Fuck me. Yes, yes!"

Pe-Ben continued to plunge and withdraw in an orgasmic frenzy. He used magic to keep his cock pulsing and throbbing inside Sandy's ass as the man experienced his own climax. White gouts of semen arced between them, to land on Sandy's olive-tan chest. The droplets sparkled upon the dark, curly hair bisecting his torso.

"That was… divine," Sandy said, panting heavily.

It still was, as far as Pe-Ben was concerned. His softening cock remained lodged in Sandy's ass. He wasn't ready to end that intimacy just yet. "Worth the wait?"

Sandy's expression changed, becoming blank, indecipherable. "Release me."

Thinking he'd somehow hurt or upset his new love, Pe-Ben quickly undid the buckles that had kept Sandy's limbs out of the way.

As soon as he had use of them, Sandy wrapped his legs around Pe-Ben, forcing him to tumble forward. Before he could right himself, Sandy grabbed a fistful of hair and jerked his head up for a kiss. Not just any kiss, but a raw-fucking, all consuming kiss.

By the time Sandy released him, Pe-Ben was primed for another round. He rocked his hips in a gentle pace, just fast enough to keep them both interested. Sweat and semen lubricated the places where their bodies connected. Nothing in his existence had felt so perfect.

"What was that for?"

Sandy tucked Pe-Ben's white mane of hair over his shoulder and traced the outline of his pectoral tattoos. "If I had to wait a hundred years, or even a thousand, to be with you, it would have been worth the wait."

"Same goes, my Sandman."

Pe-Ben stood up and helped Sandy out of the leather seat. He wobbled a bit after, his muscles protesting movement after being in one position for so long. Sandy leaned into his support, using the position to its best advantage to explore Pe-Ben's body in a way he hadn't been able to do just a short while before.

"Silly idea," Pe-Ben murmured, nuzzling Sandy's neck.

"What was?"

"Keeping your hands off me."

Sandy chuckled and hugged him hard. "What inspired you to do it in the first place?"

"Remember the scene at the end of *Hole Milk*?"

Sandy's eyes widened in surprise. "You have a thing for Sean Storm too?"

"I do now."

"Wait a second. His hands weren't tied in that scene."

Pe-Ben guided him into the small private bathroom. "I improvised. Next time I'll know better."

"When's next time?"

Pe-Ben groaned when he felt the nudging interest of Sandy's cock against his hip. "About five seconds after your boss is through with you for the night."

"Shit! I forgot he was waiting. We'd better hurry. Morpheus's temper doesn't improve over time."

Once they'd freshened up and dressed in matching green robes Pe-Ben had conjured from out of the ether, they walked into the sitting area where Morpheus was conferring with several of his horse-faced nags.

At their entrance, he looked up, one brow raised in a sardonic arch. "Done so soon?"

"Fuck you," Sandy said without a trace of his usual good humor. "You're the one that encouraged me to get a boyfriend who wasn't made of plastic. Now that I have, you're doing everything in your power to ruin it. Why is that?"

"If I wanted to get rid of your new boyfriend," the dream god replied, stepping away from his ring of clingy sycophants, "he'd be gone. I'm not the problem here."

"You're in my living room, pissing me off. That's a problem."

As much as he enjoyed listening to Sandy rise to his defense, Pe-Ben preferred not to waste more time verbally sparring on it. He was staying in Sandy's life. No one on earth, Olympus or any other plane of existence was going to change that. "Ease up, both of you."

"Ease up? What—"

Pe-Ben kissed Sandy, giving that remarkably facile tongue something better to do than wag in the wind. There were times for talk and times for silence. The latter was called for now, at least until Morpheus had expelled whatever bug had crawled up his ass on this occasion.

As he released his lover, he gently said, "Shut up and listen."

Sandy didn't seem too thrilled with the idea, but he turned his attention to his boss. "Well?"

"No one in the inn is sleeping," Morpheus explained, running his hand over the rump of a mare brave enough—or scared enough—to approach him for comfort. "Not to dream anyway."

Pe-Ben listened but didn't hear the noise that had been all but impossible to ignore the previous night. As if they'd been long-time companions who knew each other's minds, Sandy voiced what both of them had been thinking. "Pretty damn quiet for a chaos convention."

"That's because while you were *busy*, my father tranced all the human guests."

"Hypnos is here?"

"No. He's got better things to do than to hang out here and clean up your mess."

"*My* mess? How can you say I caused this? Last night you seemed to think contaminated SAND was to blame."

"I still do."

Sandy folded his arms over his chest. "Then I suggest you find out which of your Night Mares has gone off her feed. Thank you for seeing yourself out, and good night."

Pe-Ben fought against a smile. Sandy was just too cute when he got irritated. Pe-Ben looked forward to smoothing his ruffled feathers later.

The mares gathered around their stallion, as if seeking safety in numbers. Morpheus did his best to reassure the four of them as he replied, "My fillies put down pure SAND last night. It's not clean now. Something happened to it between the time we left this morning and your rounds this evening."

"I haven't done anything but—" Uncertainty clouded the brilliance of his green eyes.

Again, Pe-Ben knew the thoughts tumbling through his lover's mind. "Be with me."

Sandy blinked and gave him a smile full of happy memories. "Yes."

"Well, there's the problem and the answer," Morpheus announced. "Looks like it's Splitsville for the two of you!"

# Chapter Eight
# A Dream Come True

"No!" Pete and Sandy shouted in unison.

"I sure as hell can't have a Sandman who keeps people up all night."

Sandy looked toward Pete, seeking reassurance that this major hitch in their relationship wasn't going to doom it.

The winter god placed his arm around Sandy's waist before answering. "I won't leave him."

The wave of relief he felt hearing Pete's response made him a bit dizzy. It also stiffened his spine. "Ditto. And if you fire me, I won't be immune from Pete's other charms. I'd like to spend more than five minutes in his arms before I fall asleep. There has to be another solution."

"What are the complaints?" Pete asked.

Morpheus started writing in thin air, his finger leaving a trail of wispy letters. "No heat. Loud, raunchy neighbors. Requests for condoms, lube and ice cubes." The nags tittered in amusement.

Pete raised an eyebrow. "Ice cubes?"

"I'm not finished," Morpheus said, displeased at having been interrupted. "Dim lights. Cold water from the hot tap. Requests for headache meds and sleeping pills. Referrals to prostitutes who deliver."

"Sounds pretty typical for any large hotel," Sandy commented.

"Not this one," Morpheus replied flatly. "Disgruntled guests are leaving in droves. The ones who are staying have been ordering oysters and the porn channel like you wouldn't believe."

"Good for them." Pete sank onto the couch and spread his arms along the back of it.

"No it's not," Morpheus barked. "And the guests aren't the only ones ready to walk out. The zombies are threatening to shuffle off their reanimated coils and go back to the graveyard if we don't get things under control soon."

Sandy was torn between jumping his lover and saving his job. It was a much tougher decision than it should have been. "Morpheus is right. Our reputation is based on providing a quiet, restful place to spend the night. If the place isn't quiet or comfortable, business will suffer."

"So change the name to the Inn of Passionate Seduction. Probably get more customers with that name anyway."

The girls snickered in their horsy way. Morpheus didn't. He didn't even crack a smile. "I'll let someone else in the family run a fuck shack. The goal here is dreams. The guests can't dream if they're too busy shagging, or shivering, in their beds!"

Pete remained unmoved. "This isn't the end of the world. You've had a couple bad nights. That's all."

"That's all?" Morpheus started mumbling under his breath. The language wasn't English though. Sandy wasn't even sure it was human.

"I'm still not convinced Pete and I did anything wrong. Surely other Sandys have had sex near the SAND. It didn't cause this kind of commotion, did it?"

"No, it didn't."

"Other than the timing, what evidence has you convinced that we're to blame?"

"We eliminated all the other possibilities, and even some wild theories last night. It's the only viable explanation left."

"Prove it," Pete demanded softly.

Sandy walked behind the couch to stand by his lover. "How? We don't have any idea what's happening, let alone how to test it."

"Sure we do. Fresh SAND goes bad when the two of you get frisky. That's the theory, right?"

"That's *your* theory," Sandy reminded his boss.

"Whatever. So I'll get the girls to pony up some fresh SAND and you guys get happy and we'll see what happens. Agreed?"

"Get happy?" Pete murmured.

Through lips strained from repressing a giggle, he replied, "Yes." Thankfully the answer covered both questions.

Morpheus led one of the Mares out of the room. The others shuffled nervously in his absence. Sandy could relate. He didn't miss the dream god, but there was no question that he was anxious to get this matter settled. "What if—"

"—if we wait to worry about problems that haven't surfaced yet," Pete finished for him. "Sit with me instead."

An offer he couldn't refuse. At Pete's urging, Sandy stretched out, his head in his lover's lap. The winter god stroked his hair with one hand and rested the other over his chest. Sandy came as close as he ever did to sleep, lying there with his lover. He felt relaxed, almost dreamy. It was a fine way to spend the time, far better than worrying about every little thing.

When Morpheus returned, Mare in tow, he looked a bit disheveled as he usually did after a SAND delivery. Sandy had asked, more than once, what the process involved, but his boss would never give the smallest hint. He didn't think he'd get an answer this time either, so he didn't waste the question.

Morpheus held up a clear vial filled with the familiar pink substance. The top was stoppered with a cork. He pulled it out and dribbled the SAND on the coffee table, making a miniature heap. "Your turn, I believe."

Pe-Ben gathered Sandy in his arms and sealed their lips together. The electrical tingle he'd come to anticipate threaded through his nervous system, a live, low level current that heightened all his senses. It brought life to him in high-definition, vibrant color. Being with Pete did that.

"All right, guys. That's enough. Open your eyes and see what you've done."

They stared at the mottled SAND. Its neon pink color had degraded into a variegated purple. The same discoloration they'd found in the SAND chamber last night.

Sandy interlaced his fingers with Pete's. "What are we going to do?"

Morpheus shrugged. "The options remain the same. Either you two break up or Sandy finds another place to work."

"What if there were another possibility? Would you consider it?" Pete asked.

"Depends on how stupid it is."

"Morpheus, please!" Sandy protested. This was getting way out of hand. The Greek deity must be under extreme pressure, not being able to deliver his nocturnal messages. However, this wrangling was giving him a migraine.

Morpheus sighed, being overly dramatic. "All right, Pe-Nut. Let's hear it."

"Trade places with me."

"*What?*"

Morpheus and Sandy's collective shout was enough to bring Zachary running into the suite from the front desk. His black skin looked unnaturally pale while his eyes scanned the room for signs of trouble. "Sir, is there a problem?"

"Stand down, Zachary," Sandy said soothingly, although his gentle tone was to prevent the Mares from starting a stampede rather than pacify his desk clerk. "False alarm."

"If you say so, sir." Zachary backed out of the room, closing the door behind him when he reached the hall.

With his heart in his throat—and, he feared, love reflected in his eyes—Sandy turned to Pete. "You want to trade me for the Night Mares?"

"No. Of course not," Pete replied instantly.

"Well, I'm certainly not about to hand you my job," Morpheus said, hands on hips and braced for war.

"I don't want that either," Pete said. His gray eyes turned smoky, a trick Sandy found signaled deep desire. "I want to stay here, with your Sandman."

"We got that, Pe-Nut. The problem is you and Sandy can't keep your hands off each other, which means you can't live near the SAND."

"That's why I suggested we switch places."

Sandy placed his hand over Pete's and squeezed it gently. "Umm, honey, perhaps you should explain what you mean by that instead of leaving us to guess."

"The way your boss keeps popping in and out of here, I figure he's got to have a place nearby where he rests. Or whatever."

"I do," Morpheus interjected. "What of it?"

"My cave—state of the art electronics, climate controlled, no public access, plenty of chambers for… guests—in exchange for your… whatever you call a home."

Sandy didn't want Pete to regret the sacrifice he was making. "What about your people? Don't you have to be near them?"

"Only when it's cold. By then we'll come up with a solution to that problem." Pete turned toward the dream god. "So, is it a deal?"

"I fail to see how it would solve your problem. You'd be closer to Sandy, not farther away."

"But the SAND wouldn't."

Sandy caught on to what Pete had in mind and put it in terms Morpheus would understand. "Pete or the SAND, one of them has to go. Pete doesn't want to leave." Sandy got butterflies in his stomach every time he thought about that. "So we'll move the SAND instead."

"Into my quarters," Morpheus said, clearly displeased by the notion.

"Into *my* quarters," Pete reminded him. "If Sandy can find a bed for me here, that is."

Not only did he have one available, he knew exactly what he wanted to do with Pete once they were in it. "That's doable."

"That's great, guys, but what happens when it comes to Dream Time? That requires SAND, you know."

"I know." Hope and love swirled in Sandy's heart, making it pound. He gave in to the desire to rub his head against Pete's shoulder where the robe no longer concealed his tan skin. "It's only fresh SAND that's vulnerable to our sexual chemistry." He nibbled the cord of muscle along his neck that Pete made available to him.

"So during delivery, I'll stay out of the way," Pete added so Sandy didn't have to stop what he was doing.

Sandy rose to his hands and knees, knowing that he offered Pete a look inside the robe where his cock throbbed with fresh blood, coming to life. He stayed in place, stretching out the sexual tension with his eyes locked on his lover as he finished the explanation. "No appointments. No interruptions. Just leave a bucket with Zachary when it's time for my rounds."

"And in the meantime I'm supposed to live in a freezer?"

This petulant behavior was out of character for Morpheus, even at his godliest. It was almost as if… "You're jealous!" Sandy shouted in surprise.

The dream god scoffed. "Of Pe-Nut? Don't be absurd."

Sandy shot Pete a look of apology, then cut his boss out of the herd of Mares to address him privately. "You're jealous, Morpheus. Admit it."

He smiled, but the sexual heat that usually swam in its depths was missing. "What do I have to be jealous about? I'm not gay."

"No, you're not. But you *are* my friend. And you're used to having my full attention whenever you want it. Now you have to share. That's not a concept that sits well with you."

Morpheus rubbed his jaw as if he'd been socked a good one. "There could be a hint of truth in that, I suppose."

"Could you try being happy for your friend rather than angry at your employee?"

He nodded, slowly. "This is the one you've been waiting for, huh?"

"Yeah. I think I love him." It scared the crap out of him that he could feel so much so quickly, but sometimes love was like that.

"Then may all your romantic dreams come true." Morpheus leaned over and kissed him. Not a peck on the cheek, but a gut-tightening, tongue-down-the-throat kiss. Stunned by the suddenness of it, Sandy could do little but hold on to the brawny shoulders of the man devouring him.

A deep rumble started in the background, the sound of an avalanche in its infancy. Definitely not a human sound. It grew in intensity as the kiss went on until the floor vibrated with the power of it.

Just as Sandy was about to protest, sensing real danger headed their way, Morpheus released him. "Tell your boyfriend to leave directions to his place with the zombie at the desk."

Morpheus and the Night Mares winked out of sight. Sandy turned to find Pete sitting on the couch, right where he'd left him. A thin layer of frost covered him, and his breath formed white puffs of vapor. "I thought that bastard had no claims on you."

"He doesn't." Sandy loosened the belt at his waist and let the robe slip from his shoulders. It pooled on the floor at his feet.

"Then what was that all about?"

Sandy puzzled over it as he unwrapped Pete's muscular body. He slid his hands over the smooth skin, warming him. But when the answer came, he started to chuckle.

"Something amuses you?"

"Morpheus." Sandy cuddled against Pete's side, regardless of the stiff welcome he received. "Once, before I met you, I got desperate enough to throw myself at him. He replied, 'Only in your dreams.' Tonight, I told him I thought you were everything I'd ever dreamed of in a boyfriend. The kiss was his way of telling me he'd do his part to make my dreams come true. My dreams with you."

The world spun away in a cosmic twist. When it came back in living color, Sandy found they'd been transported to his bedroom. The robes hadn't come along for the ride.

Pete covered him with his own body. The tattoo on his chest cast a blue glow on his face. He'd never looked more powerful, more god-like. "Tired?"

Sandy hugged Pe-Ben—for he was now dealing with the god rather than the human soul inside—around his waist, embracing him with his legs. He lifted his hips off the bed and clung to the winter god, bringing their solid erections into contact. "I think I've come down with a permanent case of insomnia."

"That's good, because I plan on keeping you awake for a long, long time."

## Kira Stone

Kira Stone lives in a warm, many-chambered cave tucked away in the Scottish Highlands. A small band of ever-changing heroes keeps her company. As they relax in front of a roaring fire, devils dance and angels sing her bawdy songs. Faerie folk often stop in for a cup of mulled wine and to listen to her spin a yarn or two. And when daylight turns to dusk, together they somehow find a way to keep the cold, uncaring world at bay for another night…

Okay, maybe not. LOL. When Kira isn't living in a fantasy world, she's writing about one from her ordinary house in Ohio with a few feline companions (who don't sing nearly as well as the angels do). Is it any wonder she prefers the cave?

You can check out Kira's website at www.kirastonebooks.com, or join her Yahoo! group at http://groups.yahoo.//.

# Paranormal Mates Society: O Positive

# Ann Jacobs

# Chapter One

It sucked, literally.

Erica Stone rubbed at the bruise she'd gotten on her ass not from the flogging she'd wanted the masked Master to give her, but from having been booted out of yet another Atlanta dungeon.

All because she'd scared another big, strong Master with her fucking fangs.

Pretty soon she'd be reduced to self-flagellation whenever she wanted satisfaction. Unless she could remember to keep her lips sealed, and that was mighty hard to do and still perform the cock sucking every Dom she'd ever run into seemed to want as proof of her submissiveness.

She looked in the mirror and grimaced. There was no hiding the long, pointed incisors she'd grown overnight six months ago after dying at the bottom of a north Georgia ravine. At the time she'd been grateful to the good Samaritan who'd climbed out of the back of a chauffeured limo on top of the hill and brought her around. After all, what twenty-something woman in her right mind wanted to be dead?

She hadn't even minded much when she learned she'd traded maybe fifty-sixty years of mortal living for more or less eternal life as a vampire like her aristocratic savior. *Admit it, Erica. You sort of liked the idea of drinking blood instead of chowing down on chocolates. Good for keeping the hips under control.*

Being a vamp wouldn't have been tough to take at all, if only it weren't for the *fangs*. How was she to survive if she couldn't find a Dom who was man enough to master a sub with fangs?

Erica sat in front of the computer where she wrote her best-selling erotic romances and stared at a blank screen, but words wouldn't come. How the fuck was she to write about sex when she hadn't had any for more than six months now? Disgusted, she clicked on Internet Explorer and started to surf. Had to find inspiration somehow. Some way. Inspiration or a mate willing to take on a novice vampire with strong submissive tendencies.

Google. Couldn't hurt to try. Running her tongue over a fang—it felt strange but vaguely erotic to stroke the hollow tip— Erica gave a few minutes' thought to the search. *Vampire Lonely Hearts Club.* That had to be it. *Wanted Single Male Vampire.*

Nothing. Nothing but a sidebar on the last search she'd tried. It linked to a site called ParanormalMatesSociety.com. Might as well give that a shot. Vamps definitely fit the description of paranormal—though not as much as some of the site's former clients who beamed from the home page with their testimonials of having found love eternal through the Society's computer matching.

Her vampire heart beating less slowly than usual, Erica got out her credit card and started to fill in the registration form for the Heavenly Plan. In less than fifteen minutes, the Society had taken her money for a three-month subscription, massaged the information she'd entered, and come up with the ad it assured her would attract just the sort of mate she wanted:

SWF vamp seeks SM, vampires only need apply.

Five feet six, well-nourished blonde with blue eyes and vamp-pale complexion seeks another of her kind for long-term relationship, possibly marriage and family. The right guy must like taking his nourishment from cups, not throats, and he'll prefer high-rises in big American cities to dreary castles in Transylvania. Oh, yes, he'll also choose a bed for sleeping—and other things—not a musty old coffin. Interested? E-Mail lonelyheartvamp☐@Paranormal.com

Satisfied with the ad, Erica clicked "OK," signed off the site, and sat back, hopeful that soon she'd find a Master who wasn't intimidated by the fangs.

Maybe now she could get in the mood to get some writing done. If she didn't, she'd soon be drinking her blood from living mortal victims instead of buying her supply from the local blood bank.

* * *

"Mr. Wilder, your mother's on line two. She's most insistent that she talk with you now."

Anthony Wilder looked up from the report he'd been studying about a struggling dungeon he was thinking of buying and shook his head at his longsuffering personal assistant. "I'll talk to her, Barb. It's okay. You've put her off longer than I thought was possible." Longer than any of Tony's previous assistants had ever managed to shield him from Magdalene Wilder over the past two hundred years. Maybe he ought to marry Barbara.

No. While he had no trouble imagining the plump redhead being his right hand woman in the office for forty years or more, he couldn't picture her being as submissive in bed. Come to think of it, he couldn't imagine her in his bed at all. No chemistry. That was a good thing, because he couldn't imagine her with vampire fangs framing the prominent front teeth that should have attracted the attention of an orthodontist during her childhood.

He pressed the button on the speakerphone as soon as Barb walked out. "Good afternoon, Mother."

"Anthony, darling. When are you going to find a nice girl and make me a grandmother? Just today Myra called. Your cousin Harold is marrying Libby Grant next month. A vampire wedding! The first one in our circles in nearly a hundred years."

Tony gave up trying to study the financials. His mother had been on his back to "find a good woman and settle down" for more than half his life it seemed, at least since he'd hit a hundred and fifty, about the time Sherman burned Atlanta and wiped out most of its native vampire population. Mother obviously wasn't going to lay off him until he took the matrimonial plunge. "Who do you suggest I marry, Mother? Suitable female vampires don't grow on every tree." On top of which, none of the eminently suitable daughters of his mother's friends was a sexual submissive, and the Dom in him demanded he take a slave as his mate.

Magdalene reeled off some names—the same ones she'd been putting forth since women had paraded around in bustles and parasols instead of miniskirts and string bikinis. At least she'd deleted the names of those who'd found mates or moved away in the century or so since she'd begun her matrimonial hunt. "Really, darling, you must marry. It's unseemly for a man your age..." Her words trailed off, and for a long time she kept quiet. "You're not *gay*, are you?"

"No, Mother. I'm not gay." He considered spilling the news on her that he was a Dom, into the sorts of BDSM sex play that would make gay sex seem tame—and that the Cotton Factor, which kept her in vintage blood and diamonds, was an exclusive members-only BDSM sex club, not the cotton brokerage that once occupied this redbrick building a carpet-bagging Yankee had built back in 1876.

Tony leaned back and laced his fingers together behind his head as he stared at the St. Andrew's cross along the opposite wall. While Magdalene rattled on about potential mates for him, he imagined a naked sub restrained there, awaiting the bite of his flogger. It was damn hard, having a mother whose mind, at least part of it, stayed firmly rooted in the antebellum South. Her sole purpose in life was to see that he marry well, provide her with a daughter-in-law to diss and a couple of vampire babies to spoil.

"I have a meeting, Mother. I have to go, but I'll try to drop by to see you this weekend." He ended the connection before she could protest and beeped for Barb.

"The next time she calls back, tell her I've gone for the day and forgot to pick up my cell phone," he said to his longsuffering assistant.

"Sixteen," Barb said two hours later—two hours before her quitting time, but from the fact that she had her plain brown cloth coat on and her handbag slung over her shoulder, Tony deduced she planned to leave. "She's called sixteen times since you spoke with her, each time more demanding that you be found. I've had it."

So Magdalene had gone one better than her previous record of fifteen calls in less than two hours' time. And Tony had lost yet another personal assistant. "I couldn't persuade you to stay?"

"God couldn't talk me into staying. Your mother..."

Obviously Barb couldn't think of anything she could say about Magdalene that was both accurate and diplomatic. Neither could he. Still, he figured he ought to try because the eternally annoying vampire was his mom. His mind came up blank, so he shot Barb a toothy grin. "I understand. I'll add two weeks to your last check. Consider it combat pay."

Tony needed a drink. No, he didn't. What he needed was a nice long session with the sub of his dreams—a session he didn't dare indulge himself with because he was afraid he'd lose control and turn his mortal partner. Or kill her. He'd almost done it last month, with a club sub his mother would *not* have wanted him to take as his vampire slave for life. Much less his wife.

His balls ached, from disuse he imagined, as he strode into the main salon of the dungeon and watched a masked, leather-clad Domme standing over a naked sub, grinding her pelvis into his face while he tongue-fucked her dripping cunt. Felicia. The only female vampire member of the Cotton Factor, and she had to be a dyed-in-the-wool Dominant. She'd never in a thousand years submit to any Master. Even him.

But Felicia had a way of stirring his hormones into action. Come to think of it, she wasn't the only one. Beneath his conservative pleated slacks his cock swelled. Uncomfortably hot, he unbuttoned the top button of his white dress shirt, laying it open at the collar. Damn it, he had to do something not only to get his mother off his back, but to get himself a ready supply of submissive vampire pussy before his balls rotted off from disuse. Stalking back into his office, he sat at the computer and began his search.

*ParanormalMatesSociety.com*. Not a bad place to start, Tony guessed, even though the featured couple on the home page—a pair of gay gargoyles from the look of them—gave him a moment's pause. Slowly, painstakingly, he keyed in his credit card number and completed the registration he hoped would bring him the relief he sought:

> Looking for a walk on the wild side? Then I'm your man.
>
> SWM vampire seeks SF playmate for D/s fun and games, possible long-term relationship. Black hair, blue eyes, six foot four of solid muscle just waiting to please the right woman. I'm even filthy rich and most of my lovers consider me mildly civilized. My ideal mate must like O-Negative sipped from fine crystal stemware, impromptu travel, and the BDSM lifestyle I've enjoyed for centuries now. If she pleases me, I'll make her my beloved slave. Interested? E-Mail cuffsnfloggers@paranormal.com

# Chapter Two

From the beginning, Tony had suspected the mating service was too good to be true. Here he'd shelled out good money for what these charlatans called The Heavenly Package, and the idiots from Paranormal Mates Society had tried to match him up with a Fury.

Not that Thera wasn't attractive enough—as Furies went. And *not*, Tony told himself, that he was afraid of her. But imagining her razorlike teeth digging into his cock had done a real number on his libido. Besides, he'd clearly specified he was only interested in another vampire, and he didn't take well to being screwed unless it involved getting hot and sweaty and *off* with one or more subs of the opposite sex.

Tony's day had started off early and bad, and chances were it would only get worse. In addition to his disturbing—he wouldn't admit to frightening—online encounter with Thera the Fury, Magdalene was back in town. He imagined she'd spent large sums of his money in Paris, which was okay because it had kept her out of his hair for three days. But it was only a matter of time before she'd rise and start bombarding the Cotton Factor staff again. So far he hadn't been able to wheedle any of the women the employment agency had sent into taking on the job of personal assistant to the boss of a BDSM dungeon, however upscale it might be, so he was reduced, for the most part, to answering the phone himself.

*Ringgggggggggg.*

Scowling, Tony strode to the phone. It had damn well better be the manager of that crooked dating service returning his call. After all, he'd wakened early for the sole purpose of taking the boss at Paranormal Mates Society to task. "Anthony Wilder here," he snapped, not caring at the moment if it was Mother or that if it was, she'd ream him a new asshole for his lack of courtesy.

It wasn't. Tony listened to the apologies from Ms. Defoe, apparently the General Manager of Paranormal Mates Society. He gauged the soft-spoken woman's apologies as being too abject and profuse to be sincere. "What do you intend to do about it?" he asked, cutting her off before she could prostrate herself on the floor or start sucking his cock right through the phone.

"Normally we don't steer our clients, Mr. Wilder, but since you were the victim of this *inexcusable* computer glitch, I'm going to break my own rule. Are you in front of your computer now?"

"Yes. I am." What the fuck was she up to? Trying to talk him out of demanding his money back? "I still want a refund."

"Well, if you want one after you see the client I'm going to show you, I'll have it processed right away. Indulge me though. Go to the site, then key in this URL." She gave him a series of slashes and dashes that would take him, if he read the URL correctly, to a private section of the website. The page that opened on the screen said, "Bite Me—To Be Processed." It contained only two profiles, both of them for females. The first had been crossed through with a big "X". It was the second photo that caught Tony's eye.

She was a blonde, with the sort of ladylike long pageboy hairdo Magdalene would love and big blue eyes. What attracted Tony, though, was the look of the red leather bustier she had on. Still, he couldn't help imagining her in a classy dress like the ones society women wore to tea parties at the club. Mother would love her if she could carry that off. What Tony liked, beyond her full breasts with pert, ringed nipples that overflowed the bustier and a generous mouth made for sucking cock, was her fangs. Small, dainty fangs that made it clear she was a vampire. She might as well have worn a sign around her neck.

He also liked the diffident way she'd worded the ad below her picture. If she weren't a sub now, she should be easy enough to mold into his lifestyle. "I'll try the one on the bottom. Erica." He liked the way her name rolled off his tongue. "But mind you, if she doesn't work out, I'm going to want my money back." Tony couldn't help staring at the screen, imagining the woman on her knees, cupping his balls while she sucked him off, those cute little fangs gently scraping his rock-hard flesh. He could practically feel her silky hair sliding between his fingers as he pushed her head lower, made her swallow his cock and clamp those blood-red lips down hard at its root, sucking out his come.

Except for occasionally dressing her up for dinner with Magdalene, he'd keep her naked after dark, wearing nothing but the wide collar that would mark her as his slave. And maybe a bauble or two—a jeweled chain to join those nipple rings, maybe—for when he brought her to the dungeon, if only to show the other Doms how much he cherished her.

"I'll have her contact you if your profile interests her," Ms. Defoe promised as she did something that wiped the screen and left only a blinking message that said BITE ME. "I'm certain this will be a match made in heaven. Again, I can't tell you how sorry I am that our computers sent you a potential mate not to your liking."

Yeah, she'd better be sorry. Tony had lawyers—a couple of the meanest mortals he'd ever seen when they were doing their thing in court. They got their rocks off several nights a week at Cotton Factor by submitting to the sexual whims of any available Dom, male or female. In the early hours of morning they'd crawl out of the dungeon shaved baby-smooth from head to toe, their backs bloody from the cats and floggers they always begged their tormentors to use on them. Their cocks were always locked securely into chastity devices, their reddened assholes stretched with butt plugs so they'd be ready for more reamings from Dominants' cocks or dildos.

If Tony hadn't seen them in action in their professional capacity before one of the other members had recommended them for Cotton Factor membership, he'd never have guessed they'd be the formidable legal fighters they were. He'd also never have imagined their three-piece suits hid irrefutable proof they were sexual submissives.

Now when he glanced through the one-way glass that separated his office from the main dungeon, he saw them—Peter and Paul, last names never uttered in the dungeon—crawling in naked, their heads and bodies freshly shaved. They were obviously looking for action from the messages sent by cock leashes they'd attached to their Prince Alberts and draped over their already paddle-marked asses.

Hopefully Tony wouldn't need to engage their services, legal or otherwise. "I will wait for her call," he told Ms. Defoe, keeping his tone noncommittal.

"Good. I can't help but believe Erica will be the woman of your dreams."

Tony hoped she was right, but he'd been convinced for years that such a woman didn't exist. A sub to please him, a society girl to please Mother… and a vampire to boot, all rolled into one arousing package? Well, if he had to, he could always turn a mortal who met the first two requirements into the third—bad as he hated the thought of doing it. "I hope so. For your sake as much as mine."

When he hung up the phone, Tony stared at the blank screen for a few minutes, wishing Ms. Defoe had left the picture up. Then he crossed to the big sofa where he sometimes stole a catnap, stretched out, and closed his eyes. Three in the afternoon was too early for him to have been stirring, especially after last night's encounter with the Fury. He drifted off, imagining the blonde vampire strapped onto the St. Andrew's Cross along the other wall, awaiting his pleasure.

\* \* \*

A vampire Dom. Erica's dream come true. She could barely stop herself from drooling when she looked at his picture on the screen. His smile… fangs *not* showing, she noticed, self-conscious because she hadn't learned how to keep hers retracted when not in use… and omigod, those full, sensual lips. She imagined they'd feel soft as velvet when he clamped them shut over her clit, her nipples. Her sex-starved pussy grew wet just thinking about what those lips could do.

And she could drown in his eyes. Dark, dangerous eyes that could compel a woman to do anything. Anything to make those eyes light up with lust for her. Though the photo was a head shot, she could guess from seeing his thick neck and broad shoulders that he'd be powerful—able to make her submit to anything and like it.

Her fingers shook as she lifted the print-out of Ms. Defoe's email and read through it again. It was very unusual to get a "bite" so soon, before her information had even gone live, but the match had been perfect, the woman said. Well, almost. Her dream Dom's requirements were for a high-society mate and, as the CEO had pointed out in her email, Erica was strictly middle-class. Could she fake it?

She didn't know, and she wasn't sure she'd ever learn to keep her fangs retracted so as not to do injury to his undoubtedly huge, beautiful cock. But every instinct told her to try. This guy had to be the vamp of her wildest fantasies...

She hit "Reply" and started typing.

> Yes, I want to meet this vampire. I think he may be the man of my dreams. As to handling the needs of a sexual dominant? Not a problem. And yes, I'm sure I can manage to choose the right blood type to go with a fish entrée.

Oh, no. That would never do. As far as she knew, not even high-society vampires ate mortal food. They drank blood, same as she'd been doing since having been turned. She had no clue about vintages—she just ordered her weekly quart from the local blood bank, sucked down a pint at the time, right out of the bag it came in, and curled up in her lonely bed to sleep off its effects.

Erica deleted that last sentence, rapidly replaced it with another.

> Given enough time and money, I can figure out how to dress and hobnob with the best of them.

Thinking about her wardrobe—mostly jeans and shorts and ratty T-shirts that were her writing wardrobe, plus the few dress-up outfits she wore to book signings and the occasional conference—she decided she'd better spend her next royalty check on a new wardrobe if she wanted to impress this obviously upscale vamp.

"And to think I was going to buy a new car." She blinked at the late afternoon sunlight when she looked through the window at a six year old Honda she'd gotten with the insurance settlement after she and her previous wheels had bitten the dust at the bottom of that ravine. "Guess you'll have to do for a while. Looks like I'll be shelling out the bucks on clothes instead of your replacement," she said, turning back to the monitor and hitting Send.

\* \* \*

Erica scrambled through the perennial stack of papers on her desk, knowing she'd eventually unearth her cell phone.

When she did, she called number in the email she'd just received to set up a meeting for tonight—at the Cotton Factor, the most exclusive BDSM dungeon in Atlanta from what she'd heard. Her slowly-beating heart sped up at the thought of submitting to the hot-looking vampire Dom... of putting herself into his able hands and fulfilling his every demand.

He sent another email after they'd talked on the phone. She'd practically climaxed when she'd read it.

> I want your entire body slippery-smooth as a baby's ass, and those pretty blonde curls pulled up in a pony tail on top of your head. Wear six-inch stilettos, that red bustier you had on in the picture, a matching harness holding an eight-inch dildo in your cunt and the biggest butt plug you can take up your tight little asshole. Do not play with yourself, and don't even think about coming until I give you permission.

After tweezing her brows into thin, arched lines and putting on what she thought of as her "I'm gonna get fucked" makeup, Erica slid her hands along her arms and legs. She stopped as she inspected her pussy to tweak the ring that dangled from her clit. Complying with his first command would be no problem. No razor or wax—the mere idea made her cringe—needed, for when she'd awakened to find herself with fangs, she'd noticed to her delight that the only hair she had was on her head.

Not for long, maybe, she thought with a shudder as she dragged the mass of curls that hit her midway down her back atop her head and secured it with a red elastic band. She hoped he'd let her keep it intact. If not, hair was a small thing to give up for a Master who didn't mind her fangs. She laced herself into the bustier as tightly as she could manage by herself, wondering—hoping—he'd pull the strings even tighter. Another good thing about being a vampire, the lack of a need to breathe in lots of air.

Other than that and the blessed lack of body hair, it sucked. She missed snarfing down a pizza at three AM when she was finishing up edits on a book, and tasting cotton candy at the church festival down the street. Not that she'd have dared go there now, anyhow, in case the rumors about crosses immolating vamps were true. Damn it, Erica even missed those inconvenient bodily functions she no longer had to worry about.

She reminded herself there was a certain benefit in not having to give herself an enema in preparation for a night at the dungeon.

She stepped into the red leather harness that matched her bustier, wincing as she worked the well-lubricated butt plug up her ass. The eight inch dildo slid easily into her dripping cunt. Would her vampire Dom share her with a friend? Moisture gushed over her fingers when she visualized a ménage. Erica barely resisted the urge to fuck herself with the toys, but reminded herself of her potential Master's order not to play and strapped the harness into place.

The six-inch stilettos went on next, followed by a beige raincoat so she wouldn't get dragged off to jail on the way to meeting her potential Master. Eager to become Anthony Wilder's sex slave, Erica teetered on the "fuck-me" footwear, the toys stimulating her into a sexual frenzy as she made her way outside and slid behind the wheel of her car.

## Chapter Three

As eager as a kid anticipating his first fuck, Tony stood in the doorway of the Cotton Factor, watching his new PMS match wobbling on stiletto heels as she got out of a middle-aged Honda. The car stood out like a sore thumb in the sea of Porsches, Mercedes and Humvees, giving him a sinking feeling the woman herself might make a similarly less than glowing impression on his snooty mother. But that didn't matter for the moment. Erica looked delectable, as he'd known she would after seeing her picture—but also stolidly middle-class wearing that wrinkled trench coat that had obviously seen more than a season's use.

His cock twitched against the silver-studded leather jock that matched his chaps and vest when he visualized what she had on under that coat. Or rather, what she'd be wearing *if* she'd followed his orders. If she was the obedient little sub of his wildest fantasies. From the way she swung her hips when she walked, he guessed she'd stuffed her cunt and ass the way he'd told her to—that and the look of sexual excitement on her face, the slackness of those full lips she'd painted a brilliant red.

She paused at the entrance, her pale skin reflecting the green neon of the discreet sign that identified the club. Tony liked the way she'd pulled her hair up into a blonde cascade that fell from the crown of her head—just as he'd instructed her. He moved out of the shadows, took her hands and drew her inside. "Welcome to the Cotton Factor, Erica."

"Tony?" Her eyes widened when she got a look at him—as had been his intention when he'd donned a Master's dungeon attire instead of the slacks and sports jacket he might have worn to meet a woman at his mother's country club. "Omigod, you're a real, live Master!" She threw off the ugly coat and went down on her knees, kissing the pointed toes of his black cowboy boots.

Oh, yeah. This one had all the signs of being a keeper, and he sure as fuck couldn't fault her for disobedience. Tony reached down and laced his fingers through the silky strands of her ponytail, tugged her to her feet. "Stand still and let me look at you."

His mouth watered at the sight of her tits spilling over that tightly laced bustier—the same one she'd had on in the picture Ms. Defoe had shown him. But it was her pale, incredibly soft vampire skin more than the taut pink nipples dangling modest gold hoops that had his cock at full attention, his balls aching for action. "I wonder if I can reach all the way around your tiny waist."

"If you can't, you can always tighten the laces, Master."

"Yes, I can. But I don't think I'll have to." He liked the way she grinned before looking sheepish and clamping her lips shut to hide the fangs. "Come here."

Even wearing the stilettos as he'd commanded, she gave the impression of delicacy. The top of her respectfully inclined head came to eye level when she complied with his order and moved closer. He could smell not only her perfume, but the musk of arousal that said louder than words that she wanted to be fucked as much as he wanted to fuck her.

As he'd guessed it would when he looked at her picture, her hair looked and felt as silky smooth as spun gold. And his fingertips collided when he spanned her corseted waist with both his hands. "Welcome to my dungeon," he said, lifting her and turning her toward the main salon where the two naked lawyers groveled at the feet of a vampire Domme and her two submissive helpers who were wielding cats o' nine.

"Oh, my." Her tongue darted out when she took in the milieu.

"You like the kiss of the whip then?"

When she shivered, the rings in her nipples swayed. "Whatever brings my Master pleasure," she said so softly he could barely hear her.

Oh, yeah. She was a sub, all right. An experienced one who'd probably felt the sting of the lash, who he sensed would enjoy taking part in a ménage. "It pleases me to bring pleasure to my slave." He slipped a hand between her legs, felt the moisture there when he tweaked her hardened clit and caught the tiny ring on the tip of his little finger.

From the pocket of his chaps he pulled a slim chain leash and attached it to the clit ring. "On your knees, now, and crawl over to that fucking swing. I can tell you're ready to join in the fun." As he gave a tug on the leash, he motioned for the lawyer subs to join them. He'd fuck her first, then see if she could pass muster with Mom. But he wouldn't claim her yet as his vampire mate, because he was sure that if he did he'd never be able to let her go.

\* \* \*

She thought he'd never ask. Head bent, Erica crawled on all fours across the plush carpeted floor, careful to keep her head lower than her ass. A dozen pairs of eyes seared her cool vampire flesh as they followed her progress, their focus seemingly on the leash her soon-to-be master held in his hand. With every movement it tugged her clit, making her inner muscles clench around the dildo and butt plug held firmly in place by the harness. Her nipples hardened with anticipation when she glanced forward at the elaborate swing.

She felt something warm, strong at her corseted waist... felt herself being lifted onto the swing as though she weighed no more than a child. "Suck my cock while my two friends ready your ass and cunt for my pleasure," he said once he'd secured the straps that held her at the waist, thighs, and upper arms. "Mind you, do not draw blood."

As he stepped up, released the leather jock he'd worn, and fed her his long thick cock, he snapped a collar around her throat, attaching it to the swing to ensure she stayed at the proper angle to deep-throat him. "Suck, my beautiful slave."

## Chapter Four

Oh, God. What seemed like a dozen hands skimmed over her body, some stroking, others sharply prodding and poking at her while she feasted on her Master's cock. Impatient tugs at the harness buckles and the rings in her nipples and clit contrasted sensually with the soft dampness of mortal breath on her ass cheeks, her swollen cunt.

Talk about sensual overload! Erica gasped as waves of pent-up pleasure sluiced over her. Mindless with the pleasure of it all, she clamped down on her Master's cock.

And felt the bite of a flogger on her naked ass. "I told you not to bite," he said, stepping back far enough that she could see the puncture marks near the base of his long, thick shaft.

"I am sorry, Master. Punish me. Please."

*Thwackkkkkkkk.* The sting of the flogger had her ass cheeks burning, her cunt muscles contracting wildly against the dildo someone was working in and out with maddening slowness.

"Looks like I'll have to teach you how to retract those pretty fangs," her Master said as he stuffed a ball gag into her mouth and buckled it in place. "Hell, they could be considered lethal weapons."

"Mmmff."

He didn't answer her as he strode around her left side. Was he angry? Was he planning to leave her to the mercies of the matched pair of men he'd summoned while he led her here? If she'd been mortal, she'd have started hyperventilating, because the two burly subs looked as though they might be fierce—dangerously so, if a Master ordered them. Since she was no longer mortal, she simply worried.

She needn't have. She'd have known her Master's touch anywhere, and she recognized it when he shooed one of the subs aside and stepped between her legs. His touch was strong, sure—

yet surprisingly gentle for one so large. He let out a groan when he found her cunt wet and swollen.

"Seems Peter's fond of vampire pussy. Good job. Now you may busy yourself tasting my lady's plump vampire nipples. Paul, you may nibble on her clit." Tony drew in a deep breath, expelling it hard against the stretched, sensitive tissue around her anus. "I think I'll fuck you here first."

Erica wanted to move, to put her ass and pussy in closer proximity to Tony's sensual lips, but the insubstantial looking swing held her firmly in place. Trapped, helpless to whatever erotic tortures her Master might have in mind for her.

She loved it. Loved the shiver of fear that wove its way from her sex-starved brain to her belly, the element that added exponentially to the pleasure of sexual stimulation. Tension built inside her as her Master popped out the butt plug bump by bump until it emerged with a pop. Even that pop sounded sexy, probably because it reminded her he intended to replace it with his own huge tool. Her muscles clenched in anticipation of the pleasure-pain she'd missed these last few months.

But it didn't come. Instead she felt the cool, wet sensation of another dildo being worked into her cunt... and the buzzing warmth when the toy began to vibrate, gently at first, then harder and faster. When her master slipped two fingers up her ass and probed her there, she started to pant.

"I'm giving you my cock now," he said, his breath warm against her upper back as she felt herself stretching... expanding... her flesh molding around his massive cock. "Relax. You can take it all. Oh, yeah. Clamp down on me, hard. Tell me you want me to fuck your pretty ass."

"Mmmffffffffft." God, yes, she wanted him to fuck her ass. Her cunt. Her mouth too, although she figured that was out unless she could learn how to make the goddamn fangs retract and stay that way. She welcomed the heat of mortal mouths on her, suckling like large twin babies, but it was her Master's touch that had her ready to explode. *Face it, Erica, you want him to possess you. Not just tonight, but always.*

He took her slow and easy, mindful that a tool the size of his could hurt her. Then, frustrated at the self-instituted restraint, he pulled out, took out the vibrator from her cunt, and plunged his cock inside. "So tight. So wet. So *mine*," he mumbled as he pounded into her, his strokes long, deep, hard enough to set the swing to vibrating.

Grasping his slave's constricted waist, he slammed into her harder, faster. His balls tightened, slammed into her clit with every stroke. Her ecstatic moans fueled his own lust, driving him over the edge.

Barely conscious that he was doing what he'd sworn he wouldn't, Tony bent over her delectable body to remove the gag from her mouth... and bit her neck, tasting her blood and mingling it with his own as he came, spurting his seed deep into her womb.

"My slave," he said when he rested his head against her shoulder.

"My Master. Remember, Master dearest, I drew your blood first." She laughed, a happy sound. A sound that made Tony think of antebellum mansions, iced O-Negative on columned porches, and the patter of little vampire feet.

Now all he had to do was persuade his mother Erica was the woman of his dreams.

No big deal.

*Right. Tell that to anybody who's ever met Magdalene.*

# Chapter Five

So what if his Mother didn't approve of the woman he wanted to warm his bed?

Tony knew it was his cock talking, but he couldn't still the voice inside him that kept the memory of how sweetly Erica submitted to his every whim, how eagerly she obeyed his most complex order. As he headed to her place the following Saturday to pick her up for The Meeting with Magdalene, he hoped like hell he'd managed to convey his wishes that his slave come across like the perfect Southern lady.

He pulled his Maserati up to the curb on a street filled with neat but modest homes and bounded up the rock walkway with its border of low-growing shrubs. When he rang the doorbell, he heard a low rumbling sound much like the growl of a large, vicious dog. It was like Erica, he thought, recalling her sense of humor he'd discovered when they'd relaxed at his favorite vampire bar over iced O-Positive the night before last, after enjoying an intense four days of sexual excesses.

"Coming," she yelled from somewhere in the back of the small bungalow.

Coming? His cock twitched at the prospect, although there certainly wasn't time for *that* now. Not when Magdalene was expecting them for cocktails at the family mansion in less than half an hour.

Sure, they could fly, but his mother would find it unseemly if they showed up on her doorstep with dust of the city smearing their cheeks. Impatient, he pushed the bell again, shaking his head at the novelty sound it made.

The door swung open and there was Erica. Stark naked except for the ruby and diamond collar he'd locked around her pretty neck before sending her home three days earlier so he could interview a few potential personal assistants. "What the fuck?"

She went to her knees, her head respectfully inclined. "I didn't know what would be best to wear, Master, so I thought I'd let you choose. If you don't mind, that is."

Mind? Tony would have liked nothing better than to take her to her bedroom, order her to lie down and spread her pretty legs, and fuck her until they both were spent. But they didn't have time. "Get up," he ordered gruffly. "You have two minutes to put on some clothes. My mother will be insulted if we don't arrive on time."

She took his hand. "I put two outfits out for you to pick from. Come with me, please."

Come. He'd never wanted more to come than he did right now, looking at his slave's clit ring dangling merrily between her legs, the hoops in her nipples swaying with her every move. His fangs elongated, and his mouth watered at the idea of feasting not on Magdalene's finest vintage blood types, but on the ivory column of his slave's slender throat. "I'm right behind you," he said, desperate not to utter the word that had his balls aching and his cock tenting the front of his beige linen slacks.

Her bed looked soft, inviting, its girly-looking ruffled coverlet a soothing shade of baby blue that showcased the two dresses she'd mentioned — a black one and a floaty pale-pink one. He wanted Erica on that bed, the clothes off. "Put them up if you don't want them wrinkled," he growled, reaching in his pocket for his phone. "Mother can wait. I can't."

"Yes, Master," Erica said sweetly as Tony dialed his mother's number and waited for her to answer.

"No, Mother, we won't make it today. Something's come up." His cock, mainly, but he wasn't about to tell Magdalene that. "I'll call you later." Much later, he thought as he shut off the cell phone and laid it on the antique table by Erica's bed.

"We're not going?"

"Not until I come. You need to be punished for getting me all hot when I was supposed to be taking you to meet my mother." He whipped off his belt and gave her a playful swat on the ass. "Now get these clothes off me. I can't wait to get inside your tight little cunt."

Her fingers brushed his near-to-bursting cock as she loosened his pants and slid them down, kneeling as she did and very gently taking his cock head in her mouth. "Careful, baby." Sometime soon he had to find time to teach her how to keep those fangs retracted in moments like this. When he'd get enough of her that he could forego fucking her for long enough to give her lessons in vampire etiquette, he had no idea. "You wouldn't want me to have to spank you."

"Mmmmfffff." She just sucked him harder, nailing his cock with the sharp edge of a fang.

"I forgot. You like being spanked." Tony shrugged out of his shirt and laced his fingers through Erica's hair, caressing her scalp before lifting her off his cock. "On the bed. On your knees," he ordered as he toed off his loafers and stepped out of his slacks and underwear.

She had the prettiest ass, all pale and plump and practically begging for the flat of his hand. But he didn't want to turn that inviting flesh red, no matter how much she provoked him. Instead of smacking her, he bent and nipped her left ass cheek with his teeth, extending his own fangs and letting them sink in and draw a drop of her blood.

"Ouch, Master."

"Ouch is right. Imagine how it feels when you do it to me. I imagine my cock's a lot more sensitive than your delicious little buttocks. If I ever find a personal assistant again, maybe I'll have time to teach you how to keep those lethal weapons put away, but right now I've got to fuck you."

She smelled of sweet cologne and female in heat. When he slid a finger along her slit, he found her wet and swollen, the small butt plug he'd ordered her to wear firmly embedded in her rear passage. "Good slave," he said, giving the plug a jiggle as he moved in behind her and slid his cock into her tight, wet cunt. "Squeeze me."

"Like this?" When she tightened her pussy muscles around him, it felt like a thousand tiny fingers playing along his shaft, milking him.

"Oh, yeah. Keep it up and it'll be all over too soon." He reached around and caught the rings in her nipples between his fingers, tugging them and eliciting a moan of pleasure from her as he pumped into her slow and deep. His balls tightened as they bounced into her rigid little clit.

"Oh, yessss, Master. I'm… coming." The last word came out loud, almost a scream as her cunt began to spasm around his cock. Her breath came hard, fast. Tony couldn't wait. He thrust into her, hard and deep, bending over and burying his fangs in the silken column of her throat. Fed by her climax, he came. Hard, staccato bursts into her spasming cunt that seemed to go on forever.

\* \* \*

"I don't intend to have you out of my sight from now on," Tony said, his tone gruff as he toyed with Erica's hair while they lay together on her bed. "You may write your books at the Cotton Factor, but you've just become my personal assistant."

"Because no one else will take the job, Master?" Erica didn't mind. The idea of spending her days and nights naked, gagged, blindfolded, and bound to the elaborate St. Andrew's Cross in Tony's office wasn't at all unpleasant. Especially when she considered the anticipation… awaiting the pleasure-pain of his flogger, the delicious touch of his tongue and teeth—fangs—the heat of his cock invading her cunt or ass when she least expected it. She'd deal with his mother's frequent calls—maybe even bite her if she came to see what her precious son was up to. "Tell me about it."

"You'll be naked except for these—" He tweaked the rings in her nipples and clit "—and the chains I've ordered to connect them all. You'll answer my private phone and see to all my personal needs. And you'll spend a few hours every day on the cross so you won't forget you're my slave. Perhaps I'll bring in a fucking swing," he said, a thoughtful look on his handsome face.

Hmm. That meant no gag, at least while he wanted her to answer the phone. "Aren't you afraid I'll scare away your guests with my fangs?"

"We'll have to work on that. Not that I care if you scare the members, but I want to use your mouth the way I use your cunt and ass, and I don't like my cock being fed on, not even by my precious slave." He slapped her smartly, then slipped the vibrator from her pussy. "Climb on my cock, and I'll think about what your duties will be."

Erica straddled him, her gaze on his as she impaled herself inch by inch on his erection. "Good slave. Now, move slowly. Let me see how your little cunt glistens while I play with your beautiful breasts."

He loved the silky smoothness of the round, firm globes, the contrast of pale pink nipples ringed with gold against her ivory skin. Her cunt caressed him, the feel similar to the sensation of having his cock in her asshole, yet different. Both were arousing. Raising his head, he caught a nipple in his mouth and sucked hard. At her ecstatic moan, he bit the turgid flesh, catching the ring on a fang and tugging at it briefly while she clenched his cock harder.

Fuck if he wasn't about to come again. Lifting her at the waist, he pushed her to her back and straddled her face. "Take me in your mouth. If you bite, I'll have to punish you."

She opened wide, concentrated. Mustn't scrape his magnificent cock with her lousy fangs. Not if she wanted to taste his come, and she did. With her tongue she traced the vein that ran the length of his shaft, then circled his cock head and tongue-fucked the slit at its tip.

"Swallow it. Now." When he tugged at her clit ring, she opened her mouth and took him in. Relaxed. Let his cock slide down her throat. Felt the pulsing of his flesh with every convulsive swallowing motion she made. So good. So right. So delicious, his smooth flesh, the salty pre-come she tasted with every swipe of her tongue.

She needed... her cunt clenched as she took him deeper, as he played with her clit. He bent over, forcing his cock farther down her throat, and tongue-fucked her cunt. Demanding... forcing a climax when she'd thought she could come no more.

As she came, he let go, spurting hot bursts of semen she gulped down greedily as though it were his blood. Her sustenance. She moaned in pleasure as his fangs punctured the entrance to her cunt. Her fangs sank into his cock.

Oh, shit. "I'm sorry, Master. I didn't mean..."

"On the way to the dungeon, I'll be thinking of appropriate ways to punish you. Vampire payback," he said with a grin when he turned around and took her in his arms.

## Chapter Six

Anticipation. The most delicious form of punishment. Erica sat in Tony's sleek sports car, the wind whipping at her hair. Her cunt still twitched, and she felt the sting from four small holes Tony had left on her cunt with his fangs—fangs she had yet to actually *see*.

Would he take her to his private office? Or would her punishment involve others like the two hairless mortal subs who'd joined them for their first encounter? Tony apparently liked them. Erica shivered as she fantasized that he'd take her hair and brand her ass the way the two mortals who'd joined her and Tony in the ménage had been branded. Maybe Tony would have a flogger made from her blonde locks, like a Dom had done to one of her friends in a less upscale dungeon she'd frequented as a mortal.

Her pussy clenched at the thought of him binding her to that cross, her mouth and ass and pussy all open to him and the other Doms and Dommes she'd seen in the Cotton Factor. Of being fucked in every way she could imagine and then some, of feeling the touch of callused hands and smooth ones, of silken floggers and a metal-tipped cat o'nine.

"I think I'll keep you to myself for the time being, my beautiful slave, even though I enjoy listening in on your kinky fantasies."

"Listening? Master, I didn't say a word."

"Didn't you know? Most experienced vampires can get into the heads of younger, weaker vamps almost as easily as they can read a mortal's mind." Tony pulled into the Cotton Factor's parking lot and stopped in the space painted with his name. Not waiting for her, he slid out of the car. "Come on. I find I'm not anxious to show you off this way to any club members who might be lurking out here."

Erica opened the door, glanced around, saw no one. Still, she hesitated to get out, for Tony had insisted she go as she was — stark naked but for his collar, a pair of stiletto heels, and the black silk scarf he'd found and threaded through her clit and nipple rings. He hadn't even let her grab her raincoat. Shivering, she followed his order, hoping no one would suddenly materialize before they could get inside the dungeon.

\* \* \*

There were Peter and Paul, in stocks, their stretched assholes being reamed by the club's two fucking machines that seemed to have been set at maximum speed and force. Felicia looked on, her red lips curled in a cruel smile. Their cocks looked painfully hard, and Tony wondered how they'd managed to keep from coming — Felicia's orders not to do so notwithstanding — until he noticed the lassos constricting them. "Take it easy, Felicia. We don't want any incidents." Tony made a mental note to have the maintenance man put governors on the machines — he'd hesitated to add them to the dungeon's bag of tricks but given he'd finally in to a chorus of begging from the Dommes.

"Do you need help with your slave?" the vampire Domme asked, shooting a lascivious look Erica's way.

Tony found he didn't much like anybody even thinking of poaching on his property. "Unplug the lawyers and let them come. I need them to ready my slave." He didn't, but at least that way he wouldn't worry that Peter and Paul would wise up and slap a lawsuit on the club. Obviously Felicia had been doling out some vicious punishment, and this time Tony thought she might have been going a little too far in the name of giving pleasure through pain.

She let them go, and the two lawyers crawled to Tony's side with unseemly haste. Tony was damn glad he didn't have to face either of them in court next week — Felicia's session had to have worked them up into full fighting shape. "Come with us. I want you to guard my office door."

"Yes, Master," they said in unison.

"Don't let anyone past you."

One of them—Peter, he thought—shivered. "Not even your mother, Master?"

"Especially not my mother." It irked Tony that Magdalene had earned a certain amount of notoriety with the members at Cotton Factor, even though she'd never set foot in the place. If the gods were looking out for him, they'd make sure she never did.

\* \* \*

Erica followed Tony into his office. Before she could do more than visualize herself bound to his St. Andrew's Cross, he had her secured to it, her legs spread. A pair of buzzing vibrators stimulated her cunt and ass, sent swirls of sensation through her that ebbed and flowed and drove her crazy with arousal she was helpless to satisfy.

"Enjoy, sweetheart, while I check my messages. If you're good, we'll play once I'm done here," he told her as he turned on the speakerphone, accessed his voice mail, and leaned back in the massive black leather chair behind his desk.

"Anthony, I need to speak with you right away." His mother, Erica surmised. She'd never heard anybody else call Tony that. The voice sounded genteel, Southern. It reminded her of towering magnolias and live oaks dripping Spanish moss.

A few business calls followed, nothing that could distract Erica from her growing arousal—her growing need to give in to the need to come, with or without her Master's say-so. She watched him, taking in his sure way of taking over conversations, the ease with which he seemed to take care of whatever problems he was called on to solve.

For a few minutes she enjoyed the silence while Tony scribbled some notes on a pad. From his expression she surmised he liked what the last caller had said. But then the phone rang again, its tone strident amidst the peaceful quietness.

"No, Mother. I do not have time to drop everything now and come reassure you that I haven't met some heinous end. Yes, I will bring Erica to meet you just as soon as I can." A frown creased his brow as he held the phone away from his ear and shook his head.

"Anthony Wilder, I will not be put off. I am going to see you, one way or another." The voice didn't sound so soft and genteel now. Tension crackled through the phone line, reflected on Tony's face—and in Erica's body, where the sound of Mrs. Wilder's voice warred with arousing vibrations, leaving her with a funny, not altogether pleasant set of sensations.

"Yes, Mother." Tony sounded half resigned, half pissed off when he depressed the "Off" button. "I need a break."

Erica's usually slow heartbeat raced when Tony stalked across the room, his gaze glued to her exposed crotch, his expression purposeful. "I'm here for you, Master," she said, laughing at herself when she realized how silly that sounded since there was no way she could *not* have been there considering how efficiently he'd bound her to the cross.

"Be glad I'm not into taking out my frustrations on my slave," he growled, going to his knees and sliding the vibrators aside. "If I were, I'd bring welts up on your pretty skin. But I won't. I'm going to eat your pussy."

He bent his head to her, nipped gently at her clit before bathing the length of her slit with his agile tongue. She couldn't help moaning with the pure sensual pleasure of his touch, the warmth of his breath against her most sensitive flesh. "Oh, yes, Master, please don't stop."

He didn't. She was writhing against her bonds, wanting to give him more—to feel not just his tongue but his huge, hard cock in her. Fucking her cunt and ass until…

\* \* \*

"No. You can't go in there. Paul, stop her."

"Degenerates! What are you doing outside my son's office door, stark naked? Get your hands off me. When my son hears how you're manhandling me, he'll…"

"What the fuck?" Tony pulled away at the sound of the commotion outside the door. He should have known Magdalene wouldn't have taken no for an answer. "I think you're about to meet Mother," he said, hurriedly releasing Erica's legs and arms and lifting her off the St. Andrew's Cross. "Quick, put this on." He peeled off his shirt and tossed it her way.

It seemed as though his hard-on should have gone as fast as Erica's flush of arousal chilled, but when she looked, she saw it still tented the front of his pants. At least he had on pants, which was more than she could say. *What a hell of a way to meet the prospective mother-in-law, wearing nothing but your Master's shirt and a pair of red stiletto heels!*

Rubbing at her wrists and hoping the rope burns wouldn't be too noticeable, Erica allowed herself a wistful wish for one of the two new dresses now draped over a chair in her bedroom. Meanwhile the conversation outside the door grew louder, more intense.

"Let me go, I said! Young man, my son will deal with you."

"Ma'am, I only wish I could."

A dull thud was followed immediately by a loud scream. Peter? Or Paul? Erica imagined whichever unfortunate twin was holding on to Mama for dear life had to be clutching at his crotch because that scream sounded like ones she'd heard in dungeons when a Dom or Domme was practicing some hard-core cock and ball torture.

"Master, don't you think you should let your mother in?" Erica asked, clutching the tails of Tony's shirt so they wouldn't gape open and show her pussy.

He shot her a dubious look. "Baby, I love you. I want you to know that before—"

The door burst open, filled with a tiny white-haired dynamo flanked by the two naked lawyers. "Anthony, what do you mean, having these—these creatures—guarding your door? And why are you not wearing a shirt?"

Erica knew immediately when Tony's mom noticed her from the horrified gasp that came out of her mouth.

*Say something, Tony. Say anything. Just get your mother's scandalized gaze off me. Please.* She might have been brought up in a household firmly ensconced in the middle class, but she knew enough to realize one didn't make much of an impression on a *grande dame* by standing in the shadow of a sex dungeon toy, wearing nothing but her lover's shirt and a sheepish grin.

"I take it this is the young woman you wanted me to meet," Magdalene said to Tony.

He had the balls to shoot Erica a brilliant smile. "Yes. Mother, this is Erica. Sweetheart, I'd like you to meet my mother, Magdalene Wilder."

What a time to fall back on the manners he had to have learned at this woman's knee! Erica tried to smile, dared to let go the tail of her shirt so she could extend her hand. "I'm happy to meet you, Mrs. Wilder."

"And I'm—pleased—to meet you too, my dear." Magdalene sounded anything but happy, much like Erica herself felt at the moment. "What a unique dress you're wearing."

Unique indeed. Not half as unique as this meeting, with Tony brazening out the scene, acting as though there was nothing unusual about having two hairless, naked men guarding his office door, nothing remarkable about him being topless and his slave bottomless while carrying on a more or less conventional conversation with his mother.

"I wasn't expecting—"

Magdalene smiled at that. "Obviously my son wasn't expecting me either. Tony, I've known for years you're into this strange lifestyle. I've despaired for centuries that you'd ever find a woman to join you in it, but apparently I was wrong. Welcome to the family, my dear. I do hope I can coax you into something more conventional for your engagement party."

"But we're not engaged." The words poured out before Erica could call them back, just as Tony took her hand.

"A formality. My darling slave, will you marry me?"

She didn't know what to say, but then she didn't have to because Magdalene was on her, hugging her, bestowing a vampire kiss on her throat. Peter and Paul both gaped at the scene.

It was out of her hands. In her Master's. As Erica relaxed later in Tony's arms, she thought it wasn't too bad after all, this being a vampire…

# Epilogue

Dear ParanormalMatesSociety.com,

You're the best! Our sincere thanks to Ms. Defoe for realizing our match was one made in heaven. Tony and I hope you'll join us at the Wilder Plantation on Saturday, June 10th, for what his mother assures us will be Atlanta's wedding not of the year, but of the century. You're welcome to post this email so others will know what a great job you do of matching up lovers for a lifetime!

Sincerely, Erica Stone
Tony's faithful slave and soon-to-be-bride…

# Ann Jacobs

Ann Jacobs has lost track of how many books she's published. At least thirty at last count. That count includes several awards, including Eppies, Golden Quill awards, More Than Magic awards, and two Lories. Ann has multiple personalities—she also writes as Sara Jarrod, Ann Josephson, and Shana Nichols.

Ann loves to hear from readers. You may contact her through her website, www.annjacobs.us.

Paranormal Mates Society: Loving Fury

Amelia Elias

Dedication:

To the ladies of the Bat Cave, for snark above and beyond the call of duty.

# Prologue

Fingers flew over the keyboard, each keystroke a digital chisel that chipped away at the final firewall separating him from the inner sanctum.

Ceyx grinned as the firewall gave in to the pressure, finally showing a weakness he could exploit. Slipping through, he typed a few careful commands. Passwords were no problem for him. He'd been doing this since computers had been created.

Ahh. Success.

Logged in as Administrator, Ceyx took a moment to scroll through the client list. Quite a variety, he mused, glancing at the profiles. Angels, demons, nymphs, werefolk—with photos of both their forms—and vampires, complete with artist sketches to compensate for the impossibility of photographs. Every type of mythological creature seemed to have a representative here.

Including a certain satyr who should really have known better than to get wasted and accept a dare.

Well, easy enough to fix it now. He scrolled through until he found his photo and "ad." Just reading it was enough to make him wince. Luckily, the hit counter at the bottom of the page registered 0001—only one person had viewed his profile, probably the agency's true administrator.

Breathing a silent sigh of relief, Ceyx selected the file and hit delete.

**Error**
**Error**
**Unauthorized Command**
**Access Denied**
**Network Administrator Contacted**

The screen went black. Ceyx swore aloud and backed out of the program, thinking fast. What possible detail had he overlooked? He'd never been caught hacking before, and he damn sure wasn't planning to ruin his perfect record tonight.

He paused, drumming his fingers on the table. Damn it! Failure just wasn't an option. Well, where one way into a program existed, there were usually more, and he knew how to find them. It didn't take long before he was back in the system.

All right, so he couldn't delete files. That left only one alternative.

He accessed the compatibility database, the system that matched couples according to shared interests, goals, and, in the case of weres and vampires, clan or species. Pulling up the algorithm took no time at all. He'd just tweak the system a bit so his name never came up.

Quickly scanning the options, he shook his head. This was so simple — why on earth did anyone need a computer for this? Did it really take an algorithm to determine that vampires and river sprites were incompatible? That shared interests increased the probability of a successful date? That angels and trolls were unlikely to see eye-to-eye on major political issues — or anything else?

For Loki's sake, he could do this kind of matchmaking in his sleep! The profiles were ridiculous too. Even his drunken attempt at a profile read better than these.

Holy shit — was that a real *god* on here? He scanned the profile and shook his head in disbelief. Oh, how the mighty had fallen if a god needed help to get laid!

And with that thought, the familiar mischievous urge tickled his mind. His hands hovered over the keys, hesitating only a moment before beginning to type again.

It wasn't so bad, really — he was just helping these poor, misguided fools to see how silly it was to leave such an important process in the hands of a stranger. Besides, if he was ever — Loki forbid — sent out on a date, he could quite honestly say that they had nothing in common. He'd be well within his rights to withdraw his profile and get a refund after such a disaster.

But first… the opportunity to mess with a few heads was just too tempting to pass up.

**Save changes to profile?**
**Save.**
**Reset to default settings?**
**Accept.**
**New match alignment protocols?**

Ceyx smiled as he keyed in the new parameters. Really, this was barely troublemaking at all. He was simply giving ParanormalMatesSociety.com a little help with their overly-simplistic matching system and helping a certain god realize the error of his ways.

Opposites attract, after all.

# Chapter One

**You've got a vibe!**

I stared at the blinking message on my screen for a full minute, waiting for it to disappear or reveal itself as a figment of my imagination. Neither would surprise me.

The real thing, now… that would shock the hell out of me at this point.

It kept right on blinking.

**Vibe! Vibe! Vibe!**

It was almost enough to make a girl start singing the Beach Boys out loud.

Still, you can't blame me for my disbelief. It had been almost a month since I'd joined www.ParanormalMatesSociety.com—at the most expensive level, no less—and in all that time, I hadn't gotten a single iota of interest. No matter how many profiles I perused, how many vibes I sent out or e-mails I typed, one cold, hard fact kept slapping me right in the face.

No sane male wanted to date a Fury, and even the insane ones were wary.

Much as I hated it, I supposed I couldn't blame them. I am the Alekto, the Force of Natural Destruction—the most obvious one of the three Erinyes, or in the modern translation, the Furies. My sisters and I don't exactly have a warm and friendly reputation. I've lost count of the eruptions, earthquakes, and floods I've engineered, and I've wrecked so many cities that it's not even special anymore.

Does that mean I'm doomed to never get laid throughout the rest of eternity?

The www.ParanormalMatesSociety.com thing was my last and best hope. The slogan grabbed my interest and pulled me in the first time I read it:

### Paranormal Mates Society III — Stone, Jacobs, Elias, Marsters, Jordan

Welcome to Paranormal Mates Society, where finding the love of your life is supernatural, super easy.

Tired of squeamish humans passing you over because blood is your beverage of choice? Do you long to indulge in intimate moonlit jaunts with a potential Pet Smart Companion? Are your fins fed up with the goldfish bowl of dating? Did the devil make you give up on ever finding your soul mate? Long to soar to the heavens with the match of your dreams?

Fill out our in-depth entry form. Browse thousands of profiles from paranormals just like you! Make new friends — find the immortal man or woman of your dreams with just one easy click.

Talk about exactly what I needed — a service that could find a male who wouldn't run screaming the first time my hair hissed at him or dump me if I accidentally knocked his house down.

But after spending hours agonizing over my profile, begging one of my sisters to take a flattering picture of me and searching hundreds of profiles, I hadn't gotten a single response.

Until now.

That **Vibe! Vibe!** blinked at me and I couldn't stop myself from grinning. Someone, somewhere, was finally brave enough to talk to me! I clicked the button and pulled up the profile, biting my lip to keep from giggling with excitement.

"Aaron S.," I read aloud, savoring the name. He was a wind sprite — I wasn't quite sure what that was, but it sounded good to me. I mean, I'm the Fury in charge of natural disasters. I can do all kinds of weather stuff — some of it even on purpose — so there's something we'd have in common.

My excitement built as I read more. No age listed, which I couldn't fault him for since I hadn't listed mine either. Let's face it, there comes a point when the numbers become somewhat meaningless and you're either old, damn old, or *way* damn old.

In the hobbies section he'd listed walks on the beach and surfing. Great! Big waves are something of a specialty of mine, so we could certainly have fun doing that.

But it was his self-description that really sucked me in.

Sensitive, gentle immortal seeking a strong female to share my eternity with; a lady with a taste for the finer things, who loves to snuggle and won't mind if I cry at romantic movies.

*Perfect.*

Aaron sounded exactly like the mate I'd been hoping to find.

After thousands of years of mindless destruction at the whims of the multitude of petty, vengeful deities, I was just about sick of the macho-god type. Hurling lightning and dodging the angry curses of my victims had gotten old a very long time ago. A little sensitivity would go a long way in my book. I mean, yeah, I can kick ass and crumble mountains with the best of 'em, but what I really, truly want more than anything else has nothing to do with power or divinity.

Fun. A little "me" time and a chance to unwind.

A few dozen stellar orgasms wouldn't go amiss either. And Aaron sounded like just the one to give them to me.

I clicked the "e-mail me" button as another alert popped up on my screen.

Oh my heavens. No freaking *way* was I this lucky!

I held my breath and clicked the alert, and yet again, I wasn't imagining it. Aaron had not only sent me a vibe, he'd e-mailed me! I grinned from ear-to-ear and indulged in a little chair-dance of elation as I opened the e-mail. He really did want to flirt with me!

Maybe my joy was a bit more than the situation called for, but this had never happened to me before. Could he really not be put off by my rather… unique… skill set?

Dearest Thera,

I do hope this isn't too forward of me, but I find myself fascinated by your profile and your beautiful photograph. I'd love to take you out to dinner, if some other lucky male hasn't already snapped you up. I beg your indulgence for rushing things. Would you meet me for dinner tonight? I'll wait for you on the balcony of the Plaza Hotel's rooftop restaurant—I'll bring a night-blooming orchid, so that you may know it is me. I hope to see you soon, lovely Fury!

Yours, Aaron S.

*Tonight?*
He wanted to take me out to dinner *tonight?* Talk about a change of fortunes! Three and a half weeks of an utter drought that would put the Sahara to shame, and now this great guy was falling all over himself to meet me.

This kind of news had to be shared. I ran out of the office, dying to find my sisters and gloat.

Our office was modern, but our home certainly was not. The Great Temple of the Erinyes has always been the home of the Furies, and it was designed with intimidation in mind. All creamy marble with bright shining patches of gilding, high-ceilinged and filled with statues twice and three times taller than the largest man, it was a monument to our power and ruthlessness. The great open spaces only made the supplicant feel small. The brutal images meticulously rendered in the mosaic tile reminded any who entered of just what the three of us could do, should they displease us.

Home, sweet home.

I sailed through the great central courtyard and ducked between two of the enormous marble columns that created our Temple's outer border. As I'd expected, my older sister was lounging beside the enormous bathing pool, relaxing on velvet cushions and wearing a gauzy *peplos* made of cloth of gold. Three acolytes attended her, one feeding bits of delicacies to her black snake-tipped tresses, one carefully painting her toenails jet black, and the last massaging her hands in preparation for a manicure.

Maura, our Megaira—the Force of Greed, Jealousy, Betrayal and Revenge—did greatly love to be pampered.

"Maura, you won't believe what just happened!"

She didn't even open her eyes. One of the black snakes snapped playfully at the acolyte, demanding another treat. "Let me guess," she said dryly. "You've come to your senses and decided to stop throwing money away on that stupid dating site."

"We're richer than Midas," I said, repeating the old argument. "What does it matter if I throw away a few bucks? You spend more than that on chocolate every *week*."

"It's the principle of it," she replied, as she always did. "And besides, it's not working, so why bother?"

Since her eyes were closed, she didn't see the face I made at her before replying. "I beg to differ," I said smugly. "I have a *date* tonight."

She still didn't open her eyes. "With who—or should I say, with what?"

"A wind sprite named Aaron."

"And what is a wind sprite?"

"I'm not exactly sure," I had to admit. "But you know that I'm in tune with the weather, so I thought we'd have that in—"

"Listen to yourself!" Maura sat up to shoot me a disdainful glare. "You're a Fury, not the Weather Channel! Listen, Thera, why won't you just go grab one of Apollo's priests and do what comes naturally? Don't let a wind sprite screw you—he sounds like a wimp anyway. You'll probably break him in half."

She reclined again, eyes closing, and I made an uglier face at her—this time adding a pair of one-fingered salutes. The acolyte at her feet bit her lip to keep from laughing. I love my sister, I truly do, but she can spoil a good mood faster than anyone I've ever met.

Then again, considering her specialty of undermining governments and dynasties, I suppose it comes naturally to her.

"Ignore the sour-puss," a sweeter voice said behind me. "You just let me know if he doesn't treat you right. I'll fix his ass up good."

I turned to smile at my other sister, the Tisiphone—she commanded the Force of Plagues. If I am brute force and Maura is intrigue, Odessa is a combination of the two. Untraceable, quiet, easy to overlook... until the outbreak is out of control, utterly devastating everything and everyone in its path. Of all of us, she looks most delicate with her white hair falling in soft waves to the dainty snake-heads and her petite figure, but of the three Furies, she is the most feared.

"Planning to give him a good dose of the clap if he stands me up?" I teased her.

She didn't smile. "I'll start with the flesh-eating virus on his balls," she said with utter seriousness. "And then I'll move on to something really uncomfortable."

I hugged her, touched by her concern. "That's sweet, sis, but I'll be fine. What I really need is some help with my hair." Maura groaned and I looked back at her. "Please? No one can charm my hair like you can. You've got a gift for dealing with the snakes, and I've never mastered it."

When dealing with Maura, flattery will usually get you everywhere.

She sighed and opened her eyes again. "I shouldn't," she said. "This is a bad idea, you mark my words."

*Shouldn't* wasn't the same as *won't*, and I knew I had her. "Consider them marked," I said, grinning again. "And you'll do it because you love me."

"No, I'll do it because then you'll go away and take this obnoxious sunshine with you. I hate it when you're happy, Thera. It hurts my eyes."

# Chapter Two

Two hours later, I flashed down into the mortal world, aiming for a stall in the lobby area ladies' room of the Plaza Hotel. When no one screamed, I sighed in relief. I'm not as good at the flashing thing as either of my sisters—let's face it, subtlety and I are only passing acquaintances—and I hated it when I miscalculate and surprise some poor human woman in the middle of what should really be a private moment.

After listening to make sure the restroom was empty, I left the stall and paused in front of the full-length mirror. Sometimes the snakes got fidgety when I teleported, and I wanted to admire myself one more time anyway.

My red waves were still tucked into a neat twist, just the way Maura had charmed them. She really did have a gift with them—not only had she persuaded them to knot themselves into this tight style, she'd arranged them so that not a single scale of their heads showed. They were all neatly tucked away, holding the style in place with strategic bites.

"Terrific job, ladies," I murmured. "Don't move a bit. You look lovely." They gave a soft hiss of pleasure when I patted them.

Then I straightened the hem of my short red dress—fire-engine red, just like my hair. Odessa had advised me to wear something understated, to try and downplay my obviously inhuman characteristics, but Aaron shouldn't mind seeing me as I truly was. After all, he wasn't human either. The dress was cut high on my thighs, low at my cleavage, and clung lovingly to everything in between. My heels were little more than a few straps and a spike, and they showed my red toenails and the small snake tattoo on my left foot to perfection.

My eyes were the only thing that didn't match the color scheme, and that was a good thing for everyone. Right now I was excited and happy, so they were the clear blue of a spring sky. I dabbed on a little more lipstick, smiled to make sure I didn't have any on my teeth, and went to meet my date.

As soon as I stepped out of the elevator and into the restaurant on the top floor, I knew I'd made the right decision to come. The dining area was absolutely lovely, a romantic dream come true — crystal chandeliers, soft music from a tuxedoed string quartet in the corner, flowers and candles on every table. Clearly, Aaron had exquisite taste.

I hadn't even seen his picture yet and I was already half in love.

"Welcome, madam. May I seat you?"

I turned to smile at the maitre d', then froze when I caught sight of his face. Gorgeous was the only word for him, with shaggy dark hair and the hint of a five o'clock shadow. His dark eyes sparkled with humor. He looked like no maitre d' I'd ever seen, even without the short horns protruding from his forehead.

"You're a satyr," I whispered, stunned. "What are you doing down here?"

He raised an eyebrow and gave me another of his devastating smiles. "Always a pleasure to serve the gods, my Lady," he replied with a smooth little bow. Everything about this satyr was smooth, despite his rough-around-the-edges appearance. His voice dripped sexual promise. "I believe I know who you're here to meet. Will you follow me, please?"

Too surprised to do anything but comply, I followed him with my mind spinning. Only now did I think to scan the diners around me for other supernatural beings — there was no way a room full of mortals wouldn't have noticed that their maitre d' came equipped with a set of horns — but everyone else in the restaurant was human.

Except for one being on the balcony.

The energy I felt from him was overwhelming, a bright ball of power and aggression. Whatever the hell a "wind sprite" was, I didn't think it would have an energy signature like that, and I stiffened with unease. "That's not Aaron," I said, stopping halfway across the dining room. "Explain, satyr."

He turned to me, still smiling. "Forgive me, my Lady," he said, bowing again. "I am but a servant to the gods and not privy to their secrets. Will you follow me and have your explanation from your date?"

I narrowed my eyes at him and had the satisfaction of seeing that smooth smile waver a fraction. Yeah, the hell he was just a servant. I stared at him a moment longer than necessary, until his gaze flickered and dropped, then adjusted the strap of my purse over my shoulder. "Lead, satyr," I said coldly. "And have a care before you play the fool with me again. You don't want to piss me off."

"No, Lady," he murmured, walking forward again. "I certainly wouldn't want that."

Satisfied that I'd made my point, I followed him through the dining area and out the wide arched doors that led to the balcony. Several tables lined the stone terrace, but only one was occupied. A man sat at the table farthest from the door, his back to us, staring at the flickering flame of the lit taper gracing the table's centerpiece and drumming his fingers as if he'd been waiting less than patiently.

No, not a man. A male — something — that definitely wasn't a wind sprite.

The subtle perfume of the promised orchid teased my nostrils and killed my hope that this was all some elaborate mistake. This was Aaron, all right, and he was nothing like what he'd described.

Why the deception? What did he have to hide?

I allowed the satyr to seat me and shot him a glare when he tried to unfold my napkin in my lap. He dropped a couple of menus before us and bowed with a grin. "Enjoy your date, my Lord, my Lady," he said, and retreated back toward the archway, leaving me alone with my deceiver.

And I looked up and had to bite my tongue to keep from yelping with shock. I knew him. I'd known him forever — literally. His massive shoulders blocked my view of the satyr's retreating back, the black waves of his hair just brushing them. The impeccable Armani suit he wore couldn't disguise the raw power in that big body, power that glowed from his dark eyes. And by the look in those dark eyes, he wasn't any more thrilled to see me than I was to see him.

"Ares," I said when I could be sure my words wouldn't come out as a snarl. They still dripped with anger. "Well, this is certainly a surprise. Or would you prefer I call you Aaron?"

He narrowed his eyes at me. "Why on earth would I want you to call me that?"

"Oh, maybe because that's the name on your fake profile?" I shot back. "Tell me, why the 'wind sprite' thing? Any paranormal worth her salt would see through that the first time she felt your energy. Who exactly were you trying to fool?"

I knew exactly what I was doing as I unloaded on him. I was off-balance and feeling vulnerable. When in doubt, I prefer to attack. If he was on the defensive, maybe I could regain my footing long enough to figure out just what the hell had happened here.

But the God of War was nothing if not well-versed in battle, verbal as well as physical, and he didn't fall for it. "Fine, call me Aaron if it makes you happy," he said, leaning back and hooking one powerfully muscled arm over the back of his chair. "I'll just call you Theresa, shall I?" When I blinked blankly at him, his lips pulled back in a feral expression only a fool would take for a smile. "What, don't you remember your profile? I didn't think Artemis's acolytes were so forgetful."

This time it was harder to hold in the snarl, and the clear night sky dimmed with clouds as my temper started to affect the weather. "I do not worship your sister," I said through clenched teeth. Gods forbid I ever bind myself to the Huntress—I wanted to get *laid*, damn it, not follow a goddess who'd taken a freaking vow of eternal celibacy!

He lifted his wineglass and took a slow sip. I watched his throat move as he swallowed. I'd never seen Ares in a suit before, and damned if he didn't look better than ever in it—and he usually looked too good for any female's peace of mind.

Only when he spoke again did I snap back to the conversation at hand. "You're slow, Fury. Try again and let's see if you can figure it out this time."

I started to snap at him and shut my mouth instead. If he'd heard from an acolyte named Theresa and I'd been contacted by a sprite called Aaron, either there had been a coincidence of cosmic proportions that we were meant to meet our dates at the same place and time, or… "We've been set up."

He raised his glass to me. "Indeed."

# Chapter Three

Heat lightning sparked between the clouds and I made an effort to calm down, but, damn it all, I was so disappointed. Yet another male who didn't want anything to do with me. Still, I didn't much fancy the idea of a freak thunderstorm drenching me as I sat there, and if I didn't get a grip, that was just where this was heading.

"And who set us up?" I asked, reaching for my water goblet and wishing I had a glass of wine like Ares. Or possibly a triple-shot of vodka.

He shrugged. "Probably the website," he said, sounding as if he truly didn't care that he'd been manipulated. "Although I have no clue why they'd match me with you. You're pretty much exactly what I'm not looking for."

Ouch. I wanted to strike back, but that one had hit me a little too hard for a quick comeback. I opened the menu instead and stared at it with sightless eyes. Yeah, Ares really knew how to strike a disabling blow.

Suddenly his hand covered mine briefly. "That didn't come out as I intended," he said softly as his touch slid away. "I didn't mean to offend you, Thera."

"Of course you didn't," I said in a bland, unconcerned voice. "You know what I can do."

"Actually, I'm more impressed by what you don't do," he said, surprising me into looking up. His expression was no longer so furious, although still not pleased by any stretch of the imagination. "From what I've heard, you've never decimated anyone just for a misspoken comment."

Complacent bastard. "There's a first time for everything," I growled, letting my eyes flash red for an instant before looking at my menu again. "Stay or go, I don't care. I'm eating."

I heard his menu snap open. "Fine," he said, and his voice was tight enough to tell me that I'd offended him by refusing his apology. Good. "Just so you know, this isn't a date."

"And thank Zeus for that," I shot back. "I see more than enough of you on Olympus. You're the last person I wanted to spend an evening with."

If I'd struck him as he'd struck me, it didn't show. *Arrogant pig*, I thought, and concentrated on the menu again. Well, if he was staying, then he was buying, and I was petty enough to try to injure his wallet at the very least. It was difficult to figure out what the most expensive thing on the menu was, since this was the kind of place that didn't bother to put prices on the entrées, but I took a guess and decided on something with scallops and truffles and a few other things that sounded pricey.

When the satyr came back, he didn't seem the slightest bit daunted by the obvious tension at our table. I gave him my order without glancing at Ares, then asked for their finest bottle of champagne. Ares ordered a large hunk of meat and half the side dishes offered, and then glanced at me with a raised eyebrow before adding, "We'll both have half a dozen oysters on the half-shell."

"The hell I will."

He smiled again. "They're expensive, my dear. I had the impression you wanted the… best items they offered. Was I mistaken?"

*Mocking me?* The insufferable fool was actually mocking me now? I glared at him and spoke without glancing at the satyr. "We'll each have a dozen. Now go get my champagne."

Ares raised an eyebrow, still looking coolly amused. "A dozen each? Don't you want to save room for dessert? I hear their pastry chef has a specialty dish that will set me back a good fifty bucks."

I smiled sweetly—or at least, I tried to. I haven't had much practice at it. "I can always get it to go."

"Fairly pointless trying to exceed my credit limit, Thera. I'm just as obscenely rich as you are."

"Are you suggesting that we go Dutch?"

He laughed aloud. "No, I wouldn't want your sister to give me the clap or something."

I went rigid in my chair. "How *dare* you spy on us in our Temple!" I cried.

Ares stopped laughing. "You're joking," he said, but he finally sounded shaken. "You didn't really discuss—"

"Your castration by flesh-eating virus?" I interrupted. "We certainly did. Is that a problem?"

A cork sailed across the table between us, knocking over the candle and splattering wax all over the menus, before he could reply. We both turned to glare at the satyr. "Watch it!" we snarled in unison.

He froze, then regained his cocky smile. "Your champagne, my Lady," he said, pouring a glass for me before dunking the bottle in the ice-bucket I hadn't noticed him putting beside the table. "Your appetizers will arrive shortly."

Ares' arm shot out and blocked the satyr's retreat. "You," he said coldly. "What is your name?"

"Ceyx."

"Subtle," I remarked, shaking my head.

He grinned at me. "Subtlety is overrated, my Lady," he said. "I'll be right back with your aphrodi—I mean, appetizers." He ducked under Ares' arm and was gone in a flash.

"That satyr is up to something," Ares growled.

"Aren't they always?" I wasn't in the mood to talk about the damned satyr. In fact, I wasn't in the mood to talk about much of anything. Instead, I busied myself with the urgent task of draining my champagne glass.

He watched me drink it down, one eyebrow still cocked. When I reached for the bottle to refill my now-empty glass, he shook his head and covered my hand on the bottle, preventing me from lifting it. "I don't think that's such a good idea, Thera. Getting plastered in the mortal realm is rarely a good plan for a god."

"One glass of champagne won't do me in," I said, brushing his hand away. "And I need it if I'm going to deal with you all night."

"What makes you think you'll be with me all night?"

Ooh, he was really pissing me off now, but I was ready this time. "You ordered the oysters. You tell me."

And he actually blushed. I grinned and prepared to give him hell, but Ceyx was back again, dropping plates of iced oysters before both of us. I had to shake out my napkin and brush ice chips off my skirt, and I saw Ares had been similarly splattered by the satyr's less-than-suave serving skills. "Suck 'em into your mouth, roll 'em on your tongue, feel the slick juices running down your hot throat," he said, deadpan. "Enjoy."

And now Ares wasn't the only one blushing.

Our eyes met for a bare instant, both of us thrown off-balance by the blatant innuendo, and suddenly I laughed. After a moment, Ares joined me, his deep chuckle a bass counterpoint to the giggles I couldn't stop.

"Damn," he said as I wiped my eyes, trying not to smear my makeup. "That satyr is a walking 900 number."

"He definitely missed his calling," I agreed.

The oysters glistened on the plate, twelve perfect grey globs of raw meat, and I really regretted increasing the order from half a dozen. Yum, a dozen dead sea creatures, disemboweled and served in half their own exoskeleton. Now I'd have to eat all the damn things, and raw oysters were a taste I'd never much cared to acquire.

Ares had no such hesitation. Still smiling, he reached for a wedge of lemon and squeezed it over one of the oysters before bringing his glistening fingers to his lips and licking the juice away. He had great hands, I couldn't help but notice—large, square, long-fingered, and graceful. His tongue flicked over one knuckle to catch the last drop, and I realized where my mind was going and grabbed one of the oysters, downing it before I could think too hard about what I was doing.

*Ughhhh!* The slimy, cold glob quivered on my tongue for far too long before I could force myself to swallow. The feel of it sliding down my throat made me shudder. I dropped the shell in the depression on the side of the platter and fought to keep the oyster where it was, happily marinating in a champagne bubble-bath in my stomach.

And there were eleven more just waiting to jump in after it.

It'd be a real oyster party down there. Ick.

Ares sucked down his oyster with a lot more grace than I had. "You're doing it all wrong, you know," he said as he put the empty shell down. Pausing to lick his fingers again, a gesture that should've been hopelessly uncouth, not sexy, he met my eyes across the table. "Can I show you?"

What the hell. "Go for it."

He reached across the table and picked up one of my lemon slices. "You held it in your mouth too long," he said as he squeezed juice on another oyster. "If you don't eat oysters much, when you taste it, it's all over. You want to let it glide down your throat. The lemon juice will help disguise the taste until you get used to it."

He put the lemon aside and lifted the shell to my lips. The thought of licking the juice from his fingers as he had was way more tempting than it should've been. Luckily I could blame it on the alcohol, even though gods are fairly immune to the weak wines of mortals — it was a convenient excuse and I was clinging to it with both hands.

"Open," Ares murmured, and I couldn't look away from his dark eyes as I obeyed.

## Chapter Four

I'd like to say that the oyster slid right down this time. I'd love to tell you that his help made all the difference, that the rest of my oysters went down easy, and that I finished them off like a pro.

But the bastard had to wink as he tipped the oyster into my mouth, and that wink made me jump, which made the lemon juice shoot straight down my windpipe, which made me cough and shoot that damned oyster right back into his face.

Where it stuck for a split second, right between his eyes, before falling onto the table with a very audible *plop*.

Coughing violently, my eyes watering from the sting of the lemon juice, I started laughing. I couldn't help it. I positively *roared* with laughter. For a moment I thought I'd actually pass out from it, unable to get a breath in for the spasms of coughing and laughing so hard it hurt. Ares just watched me, his face as stony as one of his statues, and the thought of adding a stone oyster between the eyes of his bust in the Great Hall of Olympus was enough to get me going again.

Oh, I was so doing that on April Fools' Day, and screw him if he couldn't take a joke.

He waited until I'd wheezed to a stop before he moved, bending to hand me my napkin from where it had slid to the floor. I wiped my eyes, struggling to catch my breath, one arm wrapped around my aching stomach as dark spots danced before my eyes. Sweet Zeus, I couldn't remember the last time I'd laughed so hard.

"Are you quite finished?" he asked, his voice positively frosty, and it was a struggle not to start giggling all over again.

I managed it. "For now," I said, my voice quivering with suppressed laughter. His expression clearly showed that he didn't appreciate being the cause of such hilarity, and I tried harder to sober up. "I'm sorry, Ares," I said. "I didn't do that on purpose, I swear on my Temple."

He didn't look altogether mollified, but I decided his bad mood was no longer my concern. We glanced at the oyster lying innocently on the tablecloth, still glistening with lemon juice, and I had to bite both my lips to keep from getting absolutely hysterical again. He pinched it between his thumb and forefinger and flipped it over the railing.

I tried really, really hard not to picture some poor mortal getting slapped in the head with the thing when it landed. I might not have been thrilled to find myself having dinner with Ares, but I didn't want to totally offend him, either—well, no more than I already had.

But he winked again and leaned over the banister, watching the oyster fall, and I laughed again. "Three, two, one," he murmured, leaning a little further, "*contact!*"

And then he was laughing with me, reaching over to squeeze another lemon for me, and I knew my apology had been accepted. He held his napkin up like a shield when I lifted the shell and I inhaled the thing as fast as I could, not wanting to repeat the lemon-juice-in-the-lungs thing again.

*This* time, it went down easy, but the experience still wasn't anything to write home about. "I think that's about enough for me," I said, unable to face eating nine more balls of slime and feeling a little bad about wasting them.

But they didn't go to waste. Ares finished his off within minutes, then casually lifted my platter and set it atop his empty one to devour the rest of mine without even asking. "Twenty-one oysters?" I said, shaking my head in amazement as the last one disappeared. "That just can't be a good idea."

He grinned and leaned back as Ceyx arrived to clear the platters—which he simply dumped on a table a little further away. "Afraid I'll lose control and jump your bones?"

I snatched up my champagne glass to save it from getting knocked over as Ceyx served the soup course, sloshing a good third of it onto the tablecloth. He snapped his fingers and the stain vanished, then he tossed a basket of bread down between us and retreated again. "The service here doesn't exactly live up to its billing," I said, "and no, I'm not the least bit worried that you or anyone else will try to jump my bones."

He dipped his spoon in the soup—half his was gone, thanks to the satyr—before answering. "Why did you join the service then, if you're not interested in having your bones jumped?"

I rolled my eyes. "I never said I wasn't interested." I took a spoonful of my own soup. It was perfect, delicately seasoned and smooth as silk. I relished the flavor overriding the aftertaste of the oysters. "Just that I don't think it's very likely."

Ares frowned and took a few bites as he gave me a very thorough once-over. "I don't get it," he said at last. "You joined the site, you came here dressed for sex, and if those aren't fuck-me heels, I'll hire that damned satyr as my personal attendant. What's the deal?"

"Don't be obtuse," I snapped, staring down into my own soup, which now tasted like glue. "Why don't you want me? Because I'm a Fury," I answered before he could speak. "Every other male is the same. Even you went pale at the thought of my sisters going after you. Do you think a vampire or a selkie would want to chance dating someone a full-fledged god wouldn't touch with a thirty-foot pole?"

"I think you're overreacting a bit and putting words in my mouth too," Ares interjected when I stopped for breath. "You're not my type, Thera, but it's not because you're a Fury. You're... just not what I'm looking for."

I drained my second glass of champagne, wishing I had one of Bacchus's fine wines instead. "All right," I said, mentally steeling myself. I didn't think my ego could get much more crushed right now anyway. "Let's hear it. What are you looking for?"

Now it was his turn to toy with his soup. "Innocence," he said at last, and damned if there wasn't a hint of a blush on those killer cheekbones again. "It's really not you, Thera. I don't want *any* Olympian. I've known all of you for far too long. I'm tired of the games the nymphs play, the constant petitions for favors from the acolytes, the meaningless encounters with goddesses. That's why I joined the stupid website. Are you happy now?"

Definitely defensive, which probably meant he was being honest. Ares was just as skilled at deception as he was at out-and-out battle—both were tricks of war, and he was the master at that—but I didn't think he was lying now. And damned if he hadn't made me genuinely feel better too.

"I understand," I said, reaching out and touching his hand, which was strangling his spoon within an inch of its life. "Now eat. I'm afraid we'll end up wearing whatever's left in these bowls if they're not empty when Ceyx comes back."

"If he tries it, he'll end up wearing his heart on his sleeve—literally," Ares growled, and I laughed.

We finished our soup in a silence that was remarkably companionable. When the satyr returned to clear away the bowls, tossing them beside the discarded oyster platters on the other table, Ares shot him a glare that should have sizzled him where he stood. "Look, *Ceyx*," he growled, the name dripping with derision, "you might not have noticed, but you're serving a goddess tonight. How about working on your presentation before I'm forced to show you the error of your ways?"

Ceyx bowed low, but not before I saw him grin as if Ares' threat was just what he'd been hoping to hear. I didn't waste time wondering about it though. I was too busy being stunned and amazed that he'd protested not because the satyr wasn't treating *him* with the proper respect, but because his blasé serving style was insulting to *me*.

It was the first time in my entire existence that any male had been offended on my behalf. Even if it came from a god I'd never much cared for, I was determined to enjoy the novelty of it. I didn't think anyone had ever thought I needed defending.

When I tuned back into the conversation, Ceyx was serving plates of some kind of fancy salad with a tiny fried egg atop it. He set mine down with exaggerated care, dropped me a wink, and hesitated a moment—I could practically hear him thinking about it—before doing the same for Ares. The god looked ready to blow, so I blurted out the first thing I could think of to distract him. "What's this, Ceyx?"

He smiled and reached for my plate. "That's a fried quail egg," he said, flicking it with his finger. "These shaved white thingies—" he picked one up and held it under my nose, "are white truffles. And the black goo, naturally, is caviar." He dropped the truffle and flicked his fingers, sending caviar bits flying. "There's some kind of balsamic vinegar dressing on it, not sure exactly what. The chef keeps going on about the thirty-year-old vinegar like it's something special, but to old farts like you, it might as well be from five minutes ago. Anyway," he concluded, wiping his hand on the tablecloth, "eat it. And don't ask me what's in your entrée unless you want to hear about snails and duck liver. Bon appetit!"

We both gaped at him as he walked away. I looked down at my salad, now thoroughly picked-over, and poked it with my fork. "Well, at least I didn't ask him what was in the soup," I murmured.

## Chapter Five

Although Ares laughed, I could tell he was still pretty pissed off at the satyr. "He has no sense of self-preservation at all," he growled, confirming my suspicions. "I'll trade plates with you, if you want."

I shrugged and put my fork aside. "No, go ahead," I said. "I've heard of egg salad, but quail and fish eggs aren't what I would consider the perfect ingredients for one."

He demolished his salad within minutes and I helped myself to a thick slice of the bread. Soft, warm, and light, it practically melted in my mouth. I cut another slice and slathered it with the fresh butter again, knowing I was starting in on Ares' share of the bread and not really caring. I mean, he'd already seriously impacted the world's oyster population and finished two other courses, so he wouldn't starve if I ate his bread.

This time, Ares' glare seemed to have an impact on Ceyx when he came to add our salad plates to the growing pile on the other table. "Shouldn't you take those back to the kitchen?" he said, nodding pointedly at the mess. "This place has a reputation for a certain mood, you know. I can look at dirty dishes anytime."

"Whoops," the satyr replied, his eyes still twinkling even though he didn't smile. "I thought you two were mad about being matched up. I didn't realize you wanted the whole romance gig. I'll see to it at once."

And ignoring both of us as we sputtered incoherent replies about not wanting romance *at all*, he flipped up the edges of the other tablecloth and slung it over his shoulder, dishes, flowers, candles and all, before vanishing around the corner. There was a loud crash that told us he'd dropped it just out of sight, and I thought Ares was going to explode.

"Look," he growled, meeting my eyes across the table, "I know we didn't want to meet up with each other here, but I do apologize for this. I'll castrate him as soon as we're finished."

I grinned. "Oh, you're no fun. I was anticipating a little dinner entertainment, and now you've gone and destroyed my hopes."

He didn't smile, but I saw amusement in his dark eyes. "If I don't wait until we've gotten all our food, he'll just limp and whine," he said. "It'll be much better as an after-dinner show."

Ceyx returned with our entrées. As soon as my plate was presented to me, I knew I'd made a mistake. Ares' steak was still sizzling and smelled divine, his baked potato looked like something out of a gourmet magazine, his asparagus glistened with butter—in short, his plate looked like heaven, and everything was recognizable.

My plate, however… something was swimming in a creamy sauce at the bottom of the dish, and I wasn't sure if they were scallops or lumps of beige rubber. Lumps of brown, shriveled things lined the plate's edge—probably the truffles that cost so much. They looked like little turds. Pasta shells and various bits of vegetables I wasn't sure I recognized were arranged in an artistic pattern that could've been pretty, should the diner happen to be a big fan of Picasso.

Ceyx poured the wine—red for Ares, white for me—and bowed his way back into the main dining area with such exaggerated respect that I was fairly certain he'd heard us discussing his "tip." I glanced again at Ares' plate and couldn't keep the longing from my voice as I asked, "Want to trade?"

He grinned wickedly as he cut a bite of the steak—oh, sweet Zeus, he cut it with the butter knife, it was so tender!—and waved his fork at me. The bite of meat was cooked perfectly, nice and red in the middle, and I had to bite my lip to keep from leaning over and snapping it right off his fork. "Expensive isn't always better, Thera," he said, and popped the meat into his own mouth as I drowned in jealousy.

He closed his eyes with pleasure as he chewed. I glared at him, although I knew he couldn't see me, before scooping up a forkful of my own dinner. For something that looked more like the results of a food fight than an actual entrée, it tasted all right. I mean, I was never going to be a huge French food fan, but my uneducated palate could tell it was prepared to perfection, even if it didn't bowl me over.

I couldn't stop looking longingly at Ares' plate though, and after a few minutes of silence, he cut another bite and held it out to me. "Here," he said, and I didn't even think of refusing.

The steak tasted as good as it looked. I closed my eyes and moaned, savoring the flavors bursting over my tongue. Where my dish was perfectly mild and balanced, his steak was everything I could have imagined — tender, slightly spicy, and so damn good I was seriously tempted to arm-wrestle him for the rest of it.

As it turned out, I didn't have to. When I opened my eyes and found him staring at me, a strange expression on his face, I didn't even have time to ask for more before he offered another bite. I nudged my plate aside as he continued to feed me, his enormous meal providing enough for both of us. Every bite was incredible. He offered me a forkful of his baked potato, dripping in butter and sour cream, and I didn't hesitate to open wide for it. A droplet of butter ran down my chin, and I caught it with my finger before licking it clean.

Ares was looking decidedly flushed now, and I finally figured out that I was moaning with each taste of his food. A burst of excitement rocked me. Wasn't this what I'd wanted? A little flirtation with a gorgeous man, one who wasn't too awed by my powers to realize that I was a female as well as a Fury?

And even though he wasn't who I'd wanted to meet, I couldn't resist playing with him a little more, this time on purpose.

The next thing he offered me was a spear of asparagus, and instead of opening my mouth, I plucked the spear from his fork. The tip was tender, lightly glazed with a tangy lemon sauce. I sucked it between my lips and laved every drop of that sauce away before biting down. Daring a glance through my eyelashes at Ares, I barely stopped myself from laughing. He was so intent on my performance that he hadn't even noticed his elbow rested on his bread plate.

The spear wasn't long enough to really imitate the act I was thinking of—not that I had the confidence to imitate it properly—so I merely gave the rest of the vegetable a swipe of my tongue before engulfing it whole. Ares' eyes went unfocused and I leaned over, resting my elbows on the table in a move calculated to enhance my cleavage. "More," I breathed, opening my lips. He missed the steak twice before managing to stab it again with his fork.

Too soon the plate was empty, and Ares hadn't eaten much of it. I sat back as Ceyx came out to take our plates again, smiling and satisfied. "That was incredible," I said in a near-moan, licking my lips once more to make sure I'd gotten every drop. The satyr snickered and Ares glared at him.

"What are the dessert choices?" I asked before the god could decide to demolish our waiter. Full as I was, I still wasn't quite satisfied. After the satyr recited the desserts, I ordered the chocolate mousse cannelloni, and Ares chose the specialty cheesecake.

Somehow I wasn't surprised when my cannelloni arrived sporting two artistic dollops of whipped cream at its base and a distinctly phallic shape to the tip.

Ares was staring and I tried hard not to laugh. "This looks like just what I wanted," I said, and ran my fingertip over one of the dollops. The cream clung and I licked it clean before doing it again and offering my finger to him. "Want to try it?"

His dazed expression vanished in the blink of an eye. "No," he snapped, slicing into his cheesecake with a bit more force than necessary. "You'll have to take care of that yourself, Fury. I'm afraid I can't help you there."

And just like that, my own teasing mood evaporated. I wiped my finger on the napkin, feeling unaccountably hurt by his rejection. Why, I wondered? I knew he didn't want to date me any more than I wanted to date him, so why did it sting that he'd so firmly rebuffed my flirting?

But it did. I couldn't even laugh when I cut into the cannelloni and a spurt of white cream shot out the end. I drank more of the sweet dessert wine, hardly tasting my chocolate as I thought about the evening I'd dreamed of.

All my high hopes for nothing. Aaron was no more real than my dream had been.

When Ceyx came with the check, I excused myself to use the ladies' room, hoping to poof right back to Olympus and lick my wounds in private. It was far too crowded for that though. So after I reapplied my lipstick and washed my hands, I had no choice but to face Ares again.

Joy.

## Chapter Six

I found him standing outside the restroom, hands in his pockets and looking bored. "You didn't have to wait for me," I said, meaning it.

He shrugged, which only emphasized the width of his shoulders under the fine wool of the suit. Damned if he didn't look even better standing than he had sitting at that table with the candlelight playing in his dark eyes! "It started to rain," he said, and his bored tone told me he'd written this evening off as a total waste of time.

"Is the satyr still breathing?" I asked, trying to hide my own disappointment by returning to the lighter mood we'd shared at the table.

"For now," he growled, clearly not embracing the humor I'd been trying for. "I guarantee nothing beyond that. Now let's get out of here."

The elevator was waiting for us when we left the restaurant, and I made sure not to brush against Ares as I entered. He punched the button for the lobby as the doors slid closed.

"We could just leave from here," I said, staring at the floor indicator. "It's private enough." Then I wouldn't have to endure his company any longer than absolutely necessary.

He nodded toward the corner. "Cameras," he replied simply.

Naturally. I leaned against the back wall and waited to reach the lobby, no longer inclined to break the stiff silence.

Ares did, however. "You know, this wasn't completely unbearable," he said, turning and giving me a hint of his godly smile. "So it wasn't what I wanted—you were still a decent dinner companion, despite the snake-heads and temper tantrums."

That was the last straw. I straightened abruptly, so furious I was shaking. "What the hell do you mean, despite the snake-heads and temper tantrums?" I snarled. "I didn't start this, Mr. High-and-Mighty, so you can take your condescending attitude and shove it!"

Ares actually looked taken aback. "What's the matter with you? I meant that as a compliment!" he protested. "All I was trying to say was that you contained your real nature pretty well tonight, and I appreciate it. There's no reason to get all—"

"My *real nature?*" By now I was so angry that I could hear the thunder crashing as the storm built, even through layers of concrete and steel. "What do you know about my real nature? All the conversation you've ever had with me consisted of 'Thera, destroy this, maim that, strike down this general, sink those ships.' Where do you get off assuming that's all I ever think about?"

Now he was starting to get mad too. The lights in the elevator flickered as he closed the distance between us with one long stride. "You're a Fury," he said, biting off every word. "Your only purpose is to destroy and maim and strike down and sink. It's what you were created for, Thera, so don't bitch at me if you get a hard-ass reputation for it!"

"*I was not created only to destroy!*" I shrieked. And with an almighty crash of thunder, the elevator went pitch black and shuddered to a stop.

The sudden stop threw us both off-balance. I had the benefit of the rail to hold onto, but Ares ended up staggering to the side and crashing into the opposite wall. The dim light of the emergency phone provided the only illumination.

Ares steadied himself and glared at me. "Nice one, Fury. Maybe you should learn to control that temper of yours before the next time you decide to convince someone you're warm and cuddly."

I growled and launched myself at him, enraged because at least in part, he was right. He met me halfway, even allowing me to get in the first slap I threw at him before catching my arms and pinning them behind my back with altogether too much ease. I tried to head-butt him and only ended up hurting my forehead on his chest.

Damn, why had I thought it was a good idea to attack the God of War?

I struggled for a moment longer, holding onto my anger with both hands, hating him both for being right and for saying those things out loud. He laughed when I tried to kick his legs out from under him and I quit fighting, abruptly drained. "Let me go," I said, standing limp and defeated in his arms.

"Why, so you can hit me again?" The bastard didn't even have the decency to *pretend* he wasn't amused.

"No, so I can get the hell away from you and forget this night ever happened," I snapped back. Tears stung my eyes as I again remembered my high hopes. Well, my sisters would be glad to hear they were right. If nothing else, tonight had taught me that I was about as dateable as the Black Death.

Ares' grip loosened but he didn't let me go. "Don't try that pitiful poor-female tone on me, Fury," he laughed. "You're not going to catch me off-guard that way."

"Let me *go!*" I shouted, kicking at him again, hurt and furious and humiliated. I wanted to follow up with some hideous threat about what Maura and Odessa would do to him once I told them how awful our date had been, but my throat was so tight I knew he'd hear how upset I really was if I said another word. Despite my efforts to stop them, two fat tears trickled down my cheeks. If I didn't get out of here soon, he'd get to witness a hell of a lot more of them, and that would be the perfect finish to the night.

He released my wrists, only to catch me by the upper arms. "By Zeus," he said, no longer laughing. "You're not crying, are you?"

I kept my face turned away even when he tried to nudge my chin up and force me to look at him. "Let go of me so I can go home," I said, my voice very low. While he was touching me, I couldn't flash back to the Temple without taking him with me and that was the very last thing I wanted.

"Hey," he murmured, cupping my face in his hands. "Thera, talk to me. What's going on?"

I tried to bat his hands away. They stayed put, stubbornly unbattable. Finally I gave in to the inevitable and glared at him, not hiding the moisture on my cheeks. "There, are you happy now?" I snapped. "Want to make fun of me a little more? Maybe this will solidify your reputation as the Bad-Ass of Olympus — the Great Ares, the god who made a Fury cry. That'd be perfect for you, wouldn't it?"

"Shit," he whispered, but he didn't release me. His hands slid down to my shoulders, holding them in a gentle grip that was still unbreakable. "Thera, I — damn, I'm sorry. I thought... well, I mean, I assumed..."

"I know what you assumed," I said, trying to get hold of myself and failing miserably. The tears were falling in a steady rain now. "You assumed what everyone else does — Furies don't have feelings. We don't think of anything but destruction, don't want anything but blood, don't value anything but suffering. Well, guess what? You and everyone else forget one little fact — I'm a goddess, same as any other! Does Athena think only of collecting more wisdom? Does Artemis hunt all the time, forsaking everything else? Does Aphrodite spend her every waking moment screwing?"

Ares was looking at me like he'd never seen me before — and I suppose he hadn't. "With Aphrodite, it's close," he said, but he didn't smile. "I'm sor —"

"Yeah, you're sorry, everyone's sorry, big fucking deal," I interrupted, again trying to escape his grasp and again failing. "At least you've done one thing for me — I won't waste any more time trying to be something no one will let me be. Damn it, Ares, will you let me *go* already?"

He shook his head. "Not until you let me apologize properly," he said, and when I took a breath to yell at him some more, he stopped my mouth with his own.

I froze. His lips were firm, his tongue teasing; he tasted of the sweet dessert wine and a hint of spice, and I didn't have a clue what to do with him when he was kissing me. He nipped my lip, surprising a gasp from me and making me aware for the first time that I wasn't breathing. I jerked my head away as if waking from a dream.

"What do you think you're doing?" I snapped, trying for outraged and only achieving breathless.

"Apologizing," he murmured as he scattered little kisses over my jaw.

"I don't need a pity-fuck in an elevator to make me feel better," I growled, and tried to shut up every neglected part of my body that was screaming for me to take it back, that pity-fucks were just fine and they'd like one or two of them *right now*.

He nuzzled my earlobe, which immediately joined the chorus of body parts clamoring for a good fucking, pity-induced or otherwise. "Too bad," he whispered. He caught my hand and pressed it to the front of his slacks, molding my palm against the rigid length behind his zipper. "What about one to make me feel better?"

*Yes!* my body screamed. I told it to shut up and tried not to notice the thickness of his cock under my hand, the warm, hard size of it. I failed utterly. "Get off me!"

"No," he said, and this time when he kissed me, he was serious about it.

## Chapter Seven

His tongue didn't tease this time. He pressed a thumb against my jaw until I opened for him and then dove inside, conquering like the warrior he was. I whimpered—yes, I actually whimpered—and grabbed the railing behind me, unable to pull away and not entirely sure I wanted to. Experimentally, I met his questing tongue with a stroke of my own.

He rewarded me with a deep groan. His hands slid down to my waist and pulled me hard against him, away from the rail, leaving me with nothing to hold onto but him. His shoulders were perfect for steadying myself. He kissed me again, long and deep and so damn good I felt my panties getting wet even before he ground his hips against mine.

The hard length of his cock pressed against my belly, thick and insistent. I wanted nothing more than to feel its satiny strength in my hands.

Somewhere in the back of my mind, a voice was screaming that I was acting like an idiot and would really regret this in the morning.

My body told that voice very firmly to shut the hell up.

I melted against Ares and gave myself up to anything he wanted to do to me. The morning could take care of itself as far as I was concerned. For the first time in my life, I submitted and let someone else take control.

"Damn, you taste good," Ares growled, releasing my mouth to press a line of hot, open-mouthed kisses down my throat. He nipped the skin over my pulse and I jumped. "I've been wondering all night what you were wearing under this sexy little dress, Thera. Are you going to let me find out?"

My head thrown back to grant him full access, my heart pounding and my pussy getting more slippery by the second, it was a moment before I could find my voice to answer. "Try it and see," I whispered.

He growled and suddenly his hands were on my thighs, just beneath the hem of my dress. His mouth came back to mine as those big hands slid up my legs, disappearing beneath my dress, finding the lace tops of my stockings and dipping a fingertip beneath them. He shuddered as his fingers played. "Oh, hell yeah," he groaned against my lips. "I love stockings, baby. I want to see you in them and nothing else."

His words fired my own need and I could no longer stand not touching him. I grabbed his jacket and shoved it off his shoulders, mourning the loss of his hands for the moment it took him to drop the jacket to the floor. I kissed him this time, sucking his lower lip for a delicious instant before he took command of the kiss.

Dominant to the bone, and on some level I'd always known he would be. Here was a male who wouldn't be intimidated by me, who would control the pace and make me wait until he was good and ready. It excited me more than I ever thought it could.

When his hands came back, they pushed my skirt all the way up to my waist and cupped my ass. He groaned again as his fingers traced the line of my thong. The kiss deepened, quickened, became more desperate. I unbuttoned his shirt frantically, aching to feel him, to make him as hot as I was.

The warmth of his skin under my palms sent a jolt of hot lust through my entire body, bringing my nipples to aching peaks and shooting another wave of hot cream to my pussy. I broke the kiss to run my tongue down his throat, needing to know if he tasted as good as he felt. He responded by thrusting his knee between my thighs and backing me against the wall.

The rail made my back arch, thrusting my breasts forward, and he cupped them through the dress. I pinched his nipples, hoping he'd do the same to me, and was gratified when he yanked the bodice of my dress down and bared my scarlet lace bra. Instead of pinching me, he dipped his head and sucked my nipple into his mouth, bra and all.

I couldn't stop the cries of pleasure as he flicked his tongue over my aching nipple. Hotter than I could ever remember being in my entire existence, all I could do was tangle my fingers in his hair and pray he wouldn't stop.

He didn't. So focused was I on the incredible things his mouth was doing to me that I didn't notice him unfastening my bra until he pushed it aside and captured my other nipple, suckling hard.

The hot silk of his tongue against my breast, no barrier between us, was almost enough to make me come. My knees went weak and I would have slid to the floor if his thigh hadn't been between mine. The hard contact of his leg against my aching pussy was incredible. I ground against him, unable to stop myself as pleasure built and tightened deep in my belly.

"Oh, no you don't," Ares growled, grabbing my hips and stopping my movements. "You are not getting yourself there without me, damn it."

The next thing I knew, I was lying on the elevator floor, my dress bunched around my waist, looking up at Ares in the dim light as he tore off his belt and unzipped his slacks. The thick length of his cock sprang forward as he shoved his pants and boxers down. I instinctively spread my thighs, dying to know what it would feel like to have that gorgeous cock buried deep inside me, thrusting hard.

And then he was on the floor with me, his weight on his elbows as he kissed me hard, deep, and wild. I wrapped my legs around his hips to urge him on. He didn't need much encouragement. The head of his cock slid once against my clit, a delicious caress, and then found my pussy and sank inside.

The feeling of fullness, of impalement, was incredible as he sank deeper. "Ah, *damn*, Thera, you're so tight," he gasped, drawing back to thrust a little deeper. "So hot and slick and, by Zeus, so fucking good, baby."

I couldn't even remember words right now to answer him. I raised my hips for his next surge, loving the way his cock stretched me, filling me with his strength and heat. The incredible pleasure far outweighed the discomfort, and I rubbed my breasts against his chest. The added sensation was so damn erotic I had to do it again, and would've kept going if he hadn't growled with pleasure and thrust hard, sinking inside me all the way to the balls.

I cried out and stiffened—I couldn't help it. There was no barrier, of course—I'd taken care of that long ago with the first of a long succession of toys—but nothing could compare to the incredible fullness of a real cock buried inside me. As my body adjusted, I realized that I'd bitten Ares on the shoulder and dug my fingernails into his back. "Sorry," I whispered, loosening my grip and looking up at him.

The near-total darkness hid his expression, but I could hear the shock and confusion in his voice when he said, "You're—sweet heaven, Thera, you're a *virgin*?"

I gave an experimental wiggle as the pain faded and moaned as his cock rubbed me deep inside. "Not anymore," I said. I tightened my legs around him, afraid he'd pull away. "And if you stop now, I really will let my sisters have you."

He groaned and dropped his head to my shoulder. "There's no stopping now," he growled as his hips rocked gently against mine. "But you shouldn't have let me hurt you like that. You should've said—"

I shut him up with a kiss and wiggled my hips again, urging him to move faster. "Forget it. I'm used to pain," I told him between kisses. "But pleasure is something new to me and I want more of it. Now shut up and do me, Ares. I want to know what it feels like to come on a real cock."

"Christ," he whispered, and thrust faster.

Resting all his weight on one elbow, he kissed me hard and palmed my breast, pinching and plucking and rolling the nipple until I could hardly breathe. My moans filled the elevator. I ran my hands down his back and grabbed his ass, loving the feel of his tight muscles clenching with every thrust, loving the way his abs rippled against my stomach with every surge of his thick cock.

And when he broke the kiss to bite my other nipple, I came so hard I screamed his name.

His body went rigid and he groaned as he came, his cock swelling and throbbing inside me. I tightened all my inner muscles to milk him for every last drop. When he collapsed on top of me, I could hardly breathe and I didn't care. My body felt used, battered, aching and absolutely wonderful.

Who needed to breathe when I felt like this?

He stayed like that for a seemingly eternal time, both of us silent, trying to catch our breath. I slowly became aware that my zipper was digging into my back. Ares finally raised his head from my shoulder and cupped my face. "Are you all right?"

I laughed despite the fact that he was crushing the air out of me. "Are you kidding?"

He rolled off of me and I instantly mourned the loss of his hard body. Almost as quickly, my common sense, silenced by the demands of my libido, roared back to life and I realized how awful I must look right now. Lying on the elevator floor, skirt hiked up and tits hanging out, my hair a mess and the snakes exposed.

*I just fucked Ares!*

Okay, yeah, so that realization should've occurred before now. I know that. But as what I'd done really hit me, I was mortified. I'd actually fucked Ares! Was I insane? He didn't even like me—I didn't even like *him*—what the hell was I doing fucking him on the floor of an elevator? What would Maura and Odessa say when they found out?

Ares took a breath to speak, and I panicked. Rolling away from him so that we were finally no longer touching, I flashed myself back to my chambers on Olympus, too chicken to hear whatever he was going to say.

Yes, that's me, all right. Thera, the Fury of Cowardice.

## Chapter Eight

I managed to dodge my sisters' questions for three full days, quite an accomplishment considering Maura's innate ability to ferret out secrets. I was noncommittal, I was vague, I changed the subject with an utter lack of tact whenever they tried to ask me about the date. Maura kept popping into the office whenever I used the computer, asking leading questions about Aaron, and so far I'd been able to put her off with a muttered "he wasn't what I expected."

And if that wasn't the understatement of the eon, I didn't know what was.

Work took up all my spare time and I threw myself into it with abandon. Volcanoes erupted around the Earth's Ring of Fire, my favorite string of volcanoes ringing the Pacific Ocean, and set off a series of earthquakes—some minor, some a bit more fun. My emotional turmoil had already led to an abnormally busy hurricane season. As I looked down on the world from Olympus, stirring the clouds into ever-tightening swirls with a lazy finger, I let my mind wander.

This just wasn't as much fun as it used to be.

I couldn't get Ares out of my mind. Why had he kissed me in the elevator? Hell, why had he *fucked* me in the elevator? I couldn't figure it out. He had made it painfully clear that I wasn't what he wanted, and then when he'd succeeded in hurting me, he'd suddenly been all over me. Was he the kind of sadistic bastard who got turned on by making a woman cry?

That just didn't add up. I'd known Ares for more years than I wanted to count and if he was into shit like that, I'd know about it. There were no secrets on Olympus. The juicier the gossip, the farther and faster it spread.

So what was the deal? I gave up on the hurricanes and paced around the central courtyard, hardly paying any attention to where I was going as I chased my own thoughts.

I ran into Maura—literally. "Brooding about that stupid date again?" she asked, brushing an invisible spot of dust from her immaculate *peplos* and regarding me coolly.

"I'm not brooding, and for the last time, nothing happened on that stupid date," I replied, weary of repeating the same words over and over. "There's nothing to brood about. Will you give it up already?"

She snorted. "Sure," she said, her tone dripping sarcasm. "That's why we've had thunderstorms on Olympus for the last three days straight, there's a heat-wave in Siberia and blizzards in Death Valley, and even the sunspots have been extremely active. You can't lie for shit, Thera, so come off it. What happened and who do we need to kill?"

I silently cursed my affinity for the weather and opened my mouth to deny it all yet again, but at that moment a messenger sprite zoomed through the Temple to come to a fluttering stop between us. "My Great Lady Alekto," he squeaked, bowing in midair, "the Divine Lord Ares requests an audience and commands me to return with your reply."

"Tell him to go fuck himself," I snapped without thinking.

Maura's eyes widened as the sprite almost dropped out of the air in shock. I could have cheerfully bitten out my tongue. "Oh, you are shitting me," she breathed, clutching her chest. "*Ares*? We have to go kill the damned God of War? Thera, are you absolutely *insane*?"

The sprite was looking alarmingly close to heart failure, and I used him as an excuse to ignore my sister's question. "Sit down and don't take that message back," I told him, waving toward the nearest pedestal. "And take a breath, for Zeus's sake."

The little messenger gasped in a breath and plopped down on the marble. I almost felt sorry for him until I remembered who he worked for, and then I shot him a glare that sent him straight back into panic mode.

"Leave the poor thing alone and answer your sister," Maura snapped. "Tell me what happened to the wind sprite and how you ended up going out with Ares. And then I want to know exactly how he offended you so Des and I can plan his murder. Spill it, Thera. Now."

I transferred my glare to her and heard the ever-present thunder rumble outside. At least it hadn't rained today since I hadn't cried, but if I went back over every little detail like she wanted me to, we'd be having flash floods in no time. "The wind sprite was really Ares, but it wasn't his fault. It was the satyr who set us up. The food was good, the date was fine. I'm just pissed off that I got tricked. You don't have to maim or torture the God of War. Story time is now over, the end. Got it?"

Odessa stepped out from between two tall columns and shook her head. "Not the end," she began, but a booming voice cut her off before she could start trying to bully me too.

"You know, Thera, it really doesn't take this long to say yes and send my sprite back out."

All four of us spun around at the sound of Ares' voice. He leaned casually against a column at the head of the Temple, his long, muscular legs crossed at the ankle. I remembered how those legs had felt against mine and shivered before I could stop myself. He'd looked like sin in Armani, but now, wearing faded, well-worn jeans, a cream-colored button-down shirt, and black biker boots, he was a fantasy come to life.

He cocked his head to the side and smiled at me as the movement sent his hair sliding over one shoulder. "I refuse to believe you're speechless, Fury."

Odessa and Maura shrieked in unison as if his words had jolted them out of a spell. "How dare you disrespect our sister!" Odessa cried as she and Maura charged.

Before I even realized I meant to do it, I flashed across the Temple and materialized in front of Ares, determined to shield him from my sisters. As a result, I nearly got skewered as he drew his sword from nowhere to defend himself and missed me by less than an inch.

"Damn it, Thera!" he snarled, grabbing my arm and thrusting me behind him so I wouldn't get caught in the conflict.

"Stop it, all of you!" I shouted, infusing my voice with the power of the thunder that was mine to command and sending a cyclone-force gust of wind at my sisters, driving them back. I yanked Ares around to face me. "You will not draw your sword in my Temple. Is that understood?" I snarled, offended beyond measure.

He opened his hand and his weapon evaporated. "Your pardon," he murmured, ignoring the rage of my sisters as I used the wind to keep them away from him. "I came to ask your pardon for many things, not add to my list of offenses. Will you come with me and hear what I have to tell you?"

"She will not!" Maura hissed, the sound echoed by all the snakes of her hair. "Thera, strike him down for what he did to you!"

I whirled on her and knew my eyes were glowing red with the force of my rage. "And what the hell do you know about it?" I demanded. "From the moment I returned, you assumed the date was a disaster. I don't need your help in this, so just butt out!"

There was a tiny *thud* as the messenger sprite fainted, and we all ignored it.

Ares didn't even glance at Maura as she continued to scream threats at him. "I do not fear you, Thera," he said softly, meeting my glowing eyes, the eyes of an enraged Fury, without flinching. "And I do not need you to protect me from these two. Come with me, listen to me. If you wish revenge afterward, I will go with you to Dike and accept her judgment on me. All right?"

Odessa and Maura both objected vehemently, and that made up my mind for me. "Fine," I snapped. "But make it quick. I don't have all day to waste with you."

He smiled as if I'd happily accepted and offered me his arm. I rolled my eyes but rested my hand in the crook of his elbow, trying not to let the gallant act charm me, and followed him out of my Temple.

At the bottom of the marble steps, he reached down and scooped up a wicker picnic basket. "What's that?" I asked with a frown.

He turned that megawatt-smile on me again. "I wanted to make up for the dismal service at the Plaza," he said. "Since I can't guarantee that same satyr won't show up at any other restaurant I might take you to, I decided on a picnic. Is that all right?"

In truth, the gesture touched me more than I wanted to admit. Despite everything, he really had been angered by the satyr's lack of respect—not to *himself*, but to me. His effort to make amends was nothing I would have ever expected. I nodded, not trusting myself to speak.

*Don't read too much into this,* I warned myself. He might just be doing this out of guilt over what had happened in the elevator, not some deep and abiding affection. *One picnic lunch does not a boyfriend make, you know.*

Why did the voice of reason always sound just like Maura?

Ares led me down the hill, the Olympian grass springy under our feet. The sun was out now, peeking between stormy clouds, betraying my mood as always. He didn't glance up. Instead, he kept his eyes on me as he said, "I have a garden behind my Temple, much like yours, that is shielded from prying eyes. I give you my word of honor that nothing would happen there that you do not want to happen. Would you like to dine there, where we can be assured of privacy?"

"I wouldn't bet on Maura not being able to get in if she wants to," I replied, looking away after only a moment. His dark eyes were much softer than I'd remembered them, and much sexier. Damned if I wasn't suddenly figuring out the answer to the questions I'd been asking myself for the last three days.

Why had I let Ares kiss me? Why had I ripped his shirt off and licked his neck? Why had I let him take me on the elevator floor?

Because he was six and a half feet of the most gorgeous, incredible, tight, prime male flesh I'd ever seen, that was why. And when he looked at me like that, it was hard to remember any of the very good reasons why I shouldn't let any of it happen again.

I heard his answering smile in his voice. "Well, let her try then," he said, and with a faint *pop* we flashed away from my Temple and into his.

## Chapter Nine

I'd been in Ares' Temple many times before, and I was always impressed. Ancient weapons from around the world were displayed on the walls, each era separated by the thick marble columns common to all the temples on Olympus. I'd seen him in action enough to know that he was a master of all of them. As he led me past a full set of shining Roman armor, I couldn't help but remember the times I'd seen him in it, his long legs bare and golden beneath the skirt of leather pteryges that covered his hips and groin.

It was all I could do not to moan at the very thought.

Ares glanced my way, saw where I was looking, and gave me a grin that could only be described as devilish. "You sexist," he teased. "Drooling over a man in a short skirt. I could file harassment charges on you for that, you know."

I laughed out loud. "Dressed like that, you were just asking for it," I shot back.

His deep chuckle complemented mine, and then we passed through the stately columns at the back of the Temple and out into the gardens. "I could put it on for you, if you really want me to."

"Planning on doing battle?"

He grinned at me. "I'm always up for a little wrestling with a lovely lady," he said, and my snakes chose that moment to unravel from their loose twist and hiss at him. "Well, you might have a slight advantage," he added, reaching up to stroke one slithering head, and, to my surprise, he didn't get bitten.

Incredible.

I pulled away before the snakes could change their minds about taking a piece out of his finger and looked around his garden, which I'd never seen despite all the times I'd visited his Temple. Like the one I shared with my sisters, it was laid out around a long, shallow pool and surrounded by lush trees, but there the resemblance ended. His garden was filled with roses of all things — roses surrounding a splashing fountain, roses in neatly trimmed hedgerows, roses climbing in wild disarray over statues of entwined figures, loving and fighting and reclining in stone splendor.

This was no monument to war, Ares' garden. This was a refuge from it.

"Wow," I murmured, reaching out to touch a perfect, white blossom. "Not what I would've expected."

When I glanced up, Ares was looking at me with a strange intensity. "It's peaceful," he said. "I need that at times. Don't you?"

And I realized what the intensity in his gaze was — empathy. I felt the sting of tears in my eyes at the strangeness of it. Here was someone who truly knew what I went through daily, the savage nature of my work and the sometimes overpowering desire for a respite. I blinked and looked down at the rose, the soft petals under my fingertip. "Yes," I whispered. "I know just what you mean."

A gentle caress of my shoulder brought me back to the present. I smiled at him, suddenly unsure and trying to hide it. Ares smiled back and let his hand slide down to take mine. "Shall we dine, my goddess?" he asked, drawing me deeper into the garden.

All I could do was nod.

Ares led me through the statues to a small, marble gazebo, open to the sky. Roses climbed the pillars and entwined in multicolored splendor above our heads, a living canopy. Silk and velvet pillows were strewn over the plush rugs that covered the floor. Ares put the basket down and knelt, plumping a few cushions together and pulling me down to rest on them. "This time," he said when I was seated, "I will serve you, and I promise I won't spill half of it all over the place."

I laughed. "Then I promise not to spit any food in your face this time either."

His booming laugh filled the gazebo. I reclined on the cushions and watched him unpack the basket, content to just look at him. His big body was relaxed, comfortable in his worn, mortal clothes. The muscles of his arms rippled enticingly as he withdrew a bottle of red wine and crystal goblets from the basket. When he uncorked the wine and poured a glass for each of us, he dipped a fingertip into his glass and offered a few drops of wine to one of the snakes that slithered gently in my hair.

"You're going to win friends for life like that," I said, feeling the rest of them moving toward Ares' hand, hoping for some of the liquid. "Our acolytes don't tend to offer tidbits to my hair. They're afraid of the poison."

He dribbled a few more drops of the crimson wine into the waiting mouths, not flinching from the fangs that could kill even him within seconds. "I'm not afraid of anything about you, Thera," he said, meeting my eyes as he said it. A tight ball of nerves contracted in my stomach.

Zeus save me, but I was starting to dream of impossible things again. "Maybe you should be," I whispered. "Look, you were right. I'm not warm and cuddly, and I'm not always in control of what I can do. The storms that night, and the lightning—"

"Were because I acted like an asshole and pissed you off," Ares interrupted me. "You were right. I had no right to say the things I did to you when we were in the elevator, and I'm sorry for it. The Pantheon misjudged you, and I went right along with it even though I, of all the gods, should know better. I'm the God of War, and I long for peace. Why should you, a goddess of destruction, be any different?"

I blinked rapidly and took a sip of my wine to hide it. "You're going to make it rain if you keep that up," I whispered, not meeting his eyes.

He left the snakes and caressed my cheek instead. "I'm trying to bring the sun out," he replied, and leaned down to kiss me.

It was like I'd been waiting for this since the moment I'd flashed myself home, and I went off like gunpowder to a match. His lips were soft, the kiss gentle, soothing even. It was so close to what I wanted, and at the same time not nearly enough, that I wrapped both arms around him and held him tight, trying to urge him on to something more passionate.

Unfortunately, I'd forgotten the wineglass in my hand.

I smelled the sudden tang of wine in the air just as Ares jumped. When he pulled away, I saw the crimson stain running over his shoulder and down his chest. Several droplets splattered my *peplos* as I dropped the nearly-empty glass, mortified at what I'd done. "Oh, no," I said, grabbing the edge of my *peplos* and dabbing frantically at the shirt. "And here I just promised not to start another food-fight!"

Ares laughed and caught my hands. "You just gave me a very good excuse to take off both my shirt and your *peplos*," he teased. "You expect me to complain?"

And then he was kissing me again, deep and hot and dominant this time, pressing me back on the cushions and covering my body with his. I forgot about the stupid wine and tangled my fingers in his hair to hold him there for more. He was only too happy to comply. His tongue flicked over mine and drew it out to play as his hands found the clasps that held my *peplos* at the shoulders. I barely registered the faint thump as they fell to the carpets. I slid my hands over his shoulders and down his back, bare now — apparently he'd flashed out of the soaked shirt, and I heartily approved of it — and tried to silence the confusion that clamored for attention at the back of my mind.

But this time, I knew where this was headed and the questions refused to be ignored. "Why?" I gasped when he broke the kiss to lick a hot path across my shoulders. "I'm not what you want, Ares. You said it yourself. I'm not helpless or peaceful or any of it."

He didn't stop kissing my skin. "Maybe I didn't know what the hell I was talking about," he murmured, nudging the edge of my *peplos* lower, his breath warm on the swell of my breast.

"Maybe I don't need someone who doesn't know what war is, Thera. Maybe I need someone who understands me and wants me anyway."

He raised his head then and caught my face in his hands. "Maybe you're exactly what I want and maybe you're not. Point is, how will we know unless we explore the possibilities?"

My heart pounded so hard I was amazed he didn't seem to hear it. I couldn't even care what my rioting emotions were doing to the weather. "That's what this is?" I said, hesitant in spite of the hot desire flowing through my veins. "We're—you want to explore the possibilities?"

His thumb caressed my lower lip and I caught it between my teeth. "That's the point of dating, isn't it?"

A sudden burst of sunlight, lemon yellow and glorious, filled the garden. Ares grinned. "I'll take that as an indication you like my plan," he teased, and bent down to kiss me again.

It lasted only a moment though before he pulled away once more. "Ares!" I cried, trying to drag him back. "Don't tease!"

He reached for his wineglass and gave me a wicked grin. "Why not?" he shot back. "Teasing can be fun, sweet Fury. Very, very fun." He dipped his fingers into the wine again, but instead of offering the drops to my snakes, he let them fall onto my skin, collecting in the hollow of my throat. "Very nice," he whispered, setting the glass aside. "A good place to start, don't you think?"

## Chapter Ten

    His tongue flicked over my pulse and I moaned, understanding his game. He traced the path of every last droplet, suckling gently, occasionally biting and making me jump. When he reached the hollow of my throat, he opened his lips over the little puddle there and sucked, caressing the skin with his tongue as he eased my *peplos* down to my waist. "Ares," I whispered, running my hands through his hair, no longer wanting to rush him.
    This time, instead of sprinkling drops from his fingertips, he poured a thin trickle of wine over my breasts. The slight breeze chilled the liquid, making my nipples peak, making me yearn for the heat of his mouth on them. He didn't appease me no matter how I begged. Instead, he licked between my breasts, down my belly, over my ribs, chasing every stray drop and ignoring me when I tried to drag his mouth to where I wanted it. He chuckled against my skin and I growled impatiently as heat lightning flashed in the sunny sky above us.
    "Temper, temper," he chided, then dipped his fingertips in the wine and rolled my nipples between them.
    "Oh!" I cried, arching beneath him, wrapping my legs around his hips. He growled and kissed me hard. I opened without hesitation, wanting more, wanting anything he wanted to do to me, giving him lips and teeth and tongue as he plucked and rubbed my nipples, the wine slippery on his fingers. When he abruptly broke the kiss and sucked one nipple deep into his mouth, laving it with his tongue to get every last drop of the wine, I grabbed his hand and sucked his finger, wanting to taste the wine on his skin as he was tasting it on mine.
    His deep groan was my reward. He switched to the other nipple, giving it the same thorough attention he'd given the first. I slid his finger in and out of my mouth, running my tongue all

around it. His breathing quickened and the movements of his tongue became faster, almost frantic. When I nipped his fingertip, he groaned again and pulled his hand from my grasp.

"Damn it all, Thera," he growled, raising his head to meet my eyes, "you're making me forget why I wanted this to be slow and sweet. I wanted to make up for the way your first time was, and now you have me wanting to do you hard and fast all over again!"

I smiled with a surge of pure, feminine satisfaction that I could bring him to the edge of control. "Hard and fast now," I said, letting my hands slide down to squeeze that tight, hard ass. "Slow and sweet later."

"I like the way you think," he said, and then he was kissing me again and neither of us was coherent enough for any more words.

His jeans vanished and my disheveled *peplos* soon followed. The caress of the silk and velvet cushions against my bare skin was almost as intoxicating as the feel of Ares' hair-roughened chest against my breasts. I arched beneath him, rubbing my nipples on his chest as I had that night in the elevator, and it made me just as crazy now as it had then. He broke our frantic kiss to lick his way down my belly. When I realized what he intended, I bit my lip hard to keep from moaning aloud at the mere thought.

How many movies had I watched, how many books had I read that described the feel of a man's mouth playing with a clit, a man's tongue sliding deep inside a pussy? How many times had I touched myself and wondered what it would really feel like, if it could possibly be as good as the books said it was? I'd gone thousands of years without knowing. Now I couldn't wait to find out. As he took his time licking and kissing his way down my belly and over my thighs, I fought to keep from begging him to hurry *up* already.

From the first touch of Ares' lips on my labia, I shuddered with an almost violent rush of pleasure. He raised his head just enough to grin at me, clearly reading the anticipation on my face, before settling between my thighs and blowing a soft, warm puff of air over my wet folds. "I should really save this treat for dessert," he murmured, holding my eyes as he slid a finger through the crimson curls.

"Don't you dare stop now," I growled.

He laughed and caressed me again, this time just grazing my clit with his fingertip. "That sounds like a threat, sweetheart," he said, withdrawing the finger and flicking his tongue over it. I moaned at the look of bliss on his face as he tasted me.

"It is a threat, damn it," I said, positively shaking with need. My inner muscles clamped down on nothing, making me feel so very empty inside, throbbing and aching to be filled. "Don't tease me!"

He nipped my thigh, then soothed the sting with his tongue. "I like to tease you," he whispered, draping my thighs over his forearms, spreading me wide for him. "There are few enough firsts in an immortal's life, Thera, and I'm going to make this one incredible for you."

When his head descended this time, he didn't tease. I cried out again and again as he swept his tongue over my clit, humming a low note that sent the most delicious vibrations shivering down my nerves before his tongue licked deep into my pussy. I arched on the pillows, writhing, totally mindless with the sheer, unimaginable pleasure of it.

It was everything I'd imagined. It was more. It was... heaven.

He returned to my clit and slid two fingers inside me, thrusting them in and out as he suckled my clit. I came so hard I screamed, and he didn't stop until he made me come again, hard and fast on the heels of the first orgasm. Hands fisted in the cushions, my body drawn tight as a bow, I couldn't stop moaning as he licked me clean, taking his time and making a very thorough job of it.

"So, so damn good," he growled, giving my clit another teasing flick of his tongue. "I'm dying for you, Thera. Please tell me you're ready for me!"

I couldn't think of anything I wanted more than to feel his cock deep inside me, filling me up. "More than ready," I whispered, too breathless to demand, but it was enough for him.

Ares crawled up my body, still holding my legs over his arms, and kissed me as he slowly impaled me on his throbbing cock. I wrapped my arms around him, unable to get close enough, and as he started to thrust I was all but sobbing with the pleasure of it. He buried his face in my hair, uncaring of the snakes, trusting them not to harm him as he took me hard and fast, deep and so incredibly good that I came and came and came, unable to tell where one orgasm stopped and the next started.

When he finally went rigid in my arms, groaning as his cock throbbed inside me, I tightened my thighs around him and wiggled my hips, bringing another, louder moan from him at the delicious friction of it until he collapsed atop me, breathing hard, both of us utterly spent.

I loved his weight on top of me, even though he was crushing the air out of me, and I closed my eyes to better memorize the sensation of his hot body covering mine. For a long time we lay like that, arms and legs entwined, his face pressed to my throat, his softening cock still inside me.

I could've stayed like that forever, but when bursts of light flashed repeatedly through my eyelids, I reluctantly opened my eyes to make sure I hadn't inadvertently set fire to his garden in my mindless ecstasy.

Instead, I saw streaks of light tracing white fire across the blue sky. I grinned in mingled relief and amusement, and nudged Ares. "Look up," I said. "You've got to see this."

He lifted his head and saw the shooting stars through the tangled rose branches before letting his head fall back, laughing. "I think most of Olympus knows you just had a very good time," he teased.

I laughed too. "At least you can't accuse me of faking it."

Ares shifted, rolling to his side and drawing me into his arms. "I'll remember that," he promised. "Never stop loving my Fury until we both see stars."

# Paranormal Mates Society III — Stone, Jacobs, Elias, Marsters, Jordan

\* \* \*

Choose one of the following reasons for leaving Paranormal Mates Society:
\_\_\_Too expensive
\_\_\_I'm taking a break from dating right now
\_\_\_Found my lifemate! Please share your story with us in the box below

 I tapped the edge of the keyboard, staring at the screen and trying not to let the goofy smile take over again. *Goofy smiles are not becoming of a Fury,* I reminded myself. *Snarls, scowls, cold stares that freeze the blood...*
 It wasn't working. The goofy smile had become a permanent addition to my face lately. I supposed it was a side effect of regular, spectacular, utterly divine sex. If that was the case, it was an expression I'd just have to learn to live with.
 The box on the screen stared at me and I rested my chin on my hand, trying to marshal my thoughts. Finally I smiled and started typing.
 *I don't know what I expected when I signed on to this matchmaking site, but it's not what I got. What I got is much better than anything I could ever have hoped for. Just goes to show you that even the gods don't always know what they need. Thanks for not giving me what I asked for — thanks for giving me what I needed.*
 That'd have to do. Ares was waiting, and he'd promised to wear his armor today. I hit Send and ran out to meet him.

## Amelia Elias

Amelia Elias is the nom de plume of a Central Texas home health nurse and mother of ten—six cats, two dogs, and two monkeys who insist they're really boys. Amie was introduced to romances at the tender age of twelve by her late grandmother, who always packed a paperback for her to read during Bingo. After the last number was called, Amie would stay up late and, armed with a notepad and pencil, try to fill in those frustrating blank spots in the story when the characters closed the bedroom door. And yes, she still has those first clumsy attempts at writing the good stuff. Hopefully she's learned a thing or two since then. Learn more about Amelia by visiting her website at www.AmeliaElias.com.

# Paranormal Mates Society: Playing with Matches

## Cat Marsters

## Chapter One

Slurp. Slurp.

Nerissa gingerly attached the Virtual Mouth to her pussy and pumped the handle. It clamped on and sucked, and she tried hard not to laugh.

Slurp. *Sluuurp*.

She failed.

It was purple, for Aphrodite's sake. How many men had purple mouths? Or women, for that matter. There was a weird nobbly thing that kept poking her clit—a tongue? What sort of freak had a tongue like that?

Sighing, she put aside the Virtual Mouth and reached for one of her old trusted friends, Sid the Trouser Snake. Sid was a vibrator with some vague allusions to a snake shape, and he'd never let her down yet. She flicked on the TV to one of many adult films showing at any given time (Gods bless digital television!) and settled back to enjoy herself.

On screen, a busty wench in a rather alarmingly tight corset was bouncing up and down on the cock of a man wearing an eye patch. They appeared to be on a cheap pirate ship set. As Nerissa buzzed Sid against her clit, the wench pulled off her corset in one improbably easy motion and thrust her breasts at the camera.

"Nice," Nerissa said to herself, fondling her own nipples, "but fake as hell."

A second man strode into the shot, attired in a ludicrously fake pirate outfit.

"She can shiver my timbers any day," he declared, and the wench licked her lips a scant moment before the second pirate's cock was thrust between them. Impressive, Nerissa thought, sliding Sid into her pussy.

But something was missing. Cheap music, bad camerawork and even worse acting… the pirate scene wasn't doing it for her, and she only had one set of hands to please herself. Rising onto her knees, she grabbed Sid's friend Bob the Butt Monkey in one hand, and the remote control in the other, and changed the pirate movie to the DVD she'd been watching the day before. It was a ménage scene, her favorite. Back in the day, when Nerissa had rarely gone from sunup to sundown without some action, ménages had been a regular occurrence. She missed the hands and mouths all over her body, cocks thrusting, fingers diving, a ripe succulent nipple to taste here or there. The soft brush of a woman's flesh against her own, the hard scrape of manly stubble between her thighs. The men in these skin flicks were always so shaved and plucked, and Nerissa preferred a little natural hair on her lovers.

Onscreen, some lucky girl was getting cock action in every orifice of her body. Nerissa smeared lube all over Bob and started to work him inside her ass, but she'd hardly got him in half an inch before a loud 'ding' echoed from the next room.

She paused, frowning, and turned off the sound on the TV. That wasn't a standard e-mail ding. That was a special ding. A new ding. A ding she hadn't heard before.

*Ding.*
*Ding!*
*Ding!*

Was it her imagination, or were the sounds getting more frantic?

Nerissa slid Sid and Bob out, grumbling under her breath, and padded naked to the bathroom to wash the lube from her hands before she tackled the computer. Before she'd even got through the door, more dings sounded. And they were definitely getting louder.

The computer, always on, was flashing frantic messages into the dark of her office.

**Error**
**Error**
**Unauthorized Command**

What the fuck? Unauthorized? Who the hell had managed to get past her firewall, her state-of-the-art designed-by-demigods guaranteed-impenetrable firewall?

And what the fuck was he doing?

Sid, Bob, and bad porn forgotten, she swung into her desk chair and grabbed the mouse. The error message was as incomprehensible as they always were, but she checked the system and found that someone had tried to delete a file.

A profile.

Sitting back in her chair, Nerissa tried to figure out what was going on here. Someone had gone to all the trouble of hacking into the system just to remove their profile from the ParanormalMatesSociety.com site? Why do that? Why not just contact her and cancel the subscription?

She cleared the error message, frowning, and checked her inbox to see if anyone had tried to cancel. No, there was nothing there she didn't expect. A lovely e-mail from a werewolf and vampire who had found love on the site. She smiled. Sometimes making bets with the devil paid off.

Leaving the computer, confused but not panicking any more, she went back to the ménage DVD, fantasizing that she was the woman onscreen with one fat cock in her ass and one between her lips, the lips of a beautiful woman suckling her nipples. Nerissa was mostly straight, but there was something about a soft woman's body that made for really great sex.

Later, after a long bath with her waterproof toys, she wrapped herself in a silk kimono and wandered onto the terrace outside her villa, overlooking the lake. She'd moved to Tuscany fifty years ago, lured by the warmth and the beauty of both the land and the people. Small wonder the Romans had done so well for themselves with splendor like this behind them. Who could doubt their own supremacy when the gods had gifted them a land like this?

A sound from her computer drew her attention. A regular e-mail sound, this time. Wondering if it was another happy Paranormal Mates Society couple, she drifted back inside to check.

And stared at her inbox in horror.

"When filling out my application, I specified deities only, and you have matched me with a vampire..." "I am a fourteen inch tall water sprite, and you have matched me with a seven foot yeti..." "What makes you think a sorcerer who can't cross running water would make a good mate for a mermaid?"

Vampires and gods? Sorcerers and mermaids? What the hell was going on? Nerissa had spent a long, long time working out the kinks in the system that matched potential mates. The software had been designed to read the client's profile and work out exactly what he or she wanted. Or didn't want. Part of the extensive application process was determining which characteristics, and even species, each member of the site wanted.

Water sprites and yetis? Surely that wasn't even physically possible!

The computer dinged again, and Nerissa opened a terrifically scathing e-mail from a vampiress who'd been matched with an acolyte of Helios.

What the fuck was wrong with the website?

She brought up the homepage of Paranormal.com and glanced it over.

Welcome to Paranormal Mates Society! Where finding the love of your life is supernatural, super easy.

Tired of squeamish humans passing you over because blood is your beverage of choice? Do you long to indulge in intimate moonlight jaunts with a potential Pet Smart Companion? Are your fins fed up with the goldfish bowl of dating? Did the devil make you give up on ever finding your soul mate? Long to soar to the heavens with the match of your dreams?

Fill out our in depth entry form. Browse thousands of profiles from paranormals just like you! Make new friends—find the immortal man or woman of your dreams in just one easy click.

Let us help you find the paranormal match of a lifetime at www.paranormalmatessociety.com!

Where meeting the perfect match can be out of this world!

It looked fine to her. She clicked through a few profiles. Also fine. So what had happened?

She started going through the code, bit by bit, but it made very little sense to her. She hadn't written it, after all. Maybe she'd get Hermes or someone to take a look at it for her. Was he doing computers these days? She should check up and see if a new god had been assigned to the task.

She'd just got up to make herself some coffee when the back of her neck prickled, and she whirled around to see an astonishingly beautiful woman flash into the room. Attired not in a traditional *peplos* but an Armani suit, her abundant blonde waves had been fastened into an intricate braid. Her lush mouth was tight, and her delicate brows were drawn down.

"Nerissa," she said tightly, "what the fuck have you been doing?"

Nerissa winced. Aphrodite had got so uptight lately, what with all the lawsuits and bureaucratic crap heaped on her. It was the same for all of the pantheon nowadays—if it wasn't some mortal suing them, it was a deity from another team.

"I just had Freya flashing into my temple, laughing like hell at the mess you've made. Hephaestus nearly wet himself when he heard."

"I didn't do it," Nerissa said. Hell, it worked for Bart Simpson.

"But you do know what I'm talking about," Aphrodite said, narrowing her eyes.

Nerissa swallowed. "Was it the yeti?"

"The what? I don't even know what that is," Aphrodite dismissed irritably.

Ahh, the narrow-mindedness of the gods.

"Do you have any idea what you've done to Ares?"

Ares? Oh, hell. "I knew it was a bad idea when he signed up," Nerissa muttered. The god of war, on a dating site? "What happened?"

"What did he ask for when he signed up?"

Nerissa went back to the computer and brought up Ares' profile. "Innocence," she said. "Peace. After an eternity of war he wanted peace."

Aphrodite said nothing for a moment. Of course, the gods all knew she'd carried a torch for Ares for centuries. But peace had never been part of their relationship.

"You want to see what he got?" she asked, and curved her hand in the air. An image appeared where her hand had passed, and it showed a man and woman at a candle-lit dinner table. Ares she recognized instantly, but it took a few moments to figure out the woman sitting opposite him.

Red hair and stormy eyes. As she glanced closer, Nerissa made out a tiny movement in the woman's hair. A tiny, tiny little ophidian head peeped out of her classy up-do and waved at her, before diving back in.

Nerissa went cold. "A Fury?"

"Mmm. The most brutal of them all. She's flattened cities in less time than it takes me to put my mascara on."

Nerissa swallowed. Fuck.

As they watched, Ares fed the Fury an oyster, and she spat it back out at him.

Fuckety fuck.

"He's going to have your ass, Nerissa," Aphrodite said, erasing the image.

"If she doesn't first." Nerissa made a fevered mental note to check her home insurance for Acts of God.

"They can take one cheek each. I thought you said this thing was foolproof?"

"It is. And it has legal disclaimers on it."

Aphrodite snorted. "They only work for mortals."

Before she could say any more, there was another flash and a second woman appeared in the room, looking more than a little angry. She had dark hair and features and wore a Babylonian robe that left one shoulder bare.

"Ishkhara," Nerissa said weakly, recognizing one of her counterparts. "How nice to see you."

"You really screwed up this time," Ishkhara said. "Ishtar is pretty mad."

"Ishtar is completely mad," Aphrodite said with studied distaste. "Am I the only one who remembers Gilgamesh?"

"What did I do to your lot?" Nerissa asked helplessly.

"You messed up a whole load of matches! There are hundreds of immortals who still pray to us, you know," Ishkhara said, a touch defensively.

"Hundreds?" Aphrodite said with mild scorn. "Ahh. How sweet."

Nerissa sent her a speaking look, and turned to the Babylonian. "I'll fix it," she said. "I promise. I just need to figure out what caused all this."

"Oh, I can tell you that," Aphrodite said, and brought up the image again. As Ares and the Fury glared at each other over the dinner table, a black-suited waiter approached their table. He moved with such grace, his muscles flowing beneath his impeccable suit, every movement smooth. He moved like a cat, fluid perfection, and heat built low in Nerissa as she watched him. Sex oozed from his every pore.

"I know him," Ishkhara said, watching. "He used to work for Ninkasi, before he defected for the Egyptians."

"Ceyx?" Aphrodite said. "I didn't know he came from them."

"Yes, he went to Shesmu for a while. But I think it was too violent for him. Dionysus was much more his style," Ishkhara said.

Nerissa said nothing. Ceyx, was he calling himself now? His name changed with the wind. He'd been one of Dionysus' satyrs for years and years, surviving the regime change and the move to Rome. But he hadn't lasted long after the Barbarians moved in. In fact she recalled he was out of the place five minutes after Rome fell.

He turned, and she saw his face. Like most of the deities, his appearance changed with the times. Being that Ceyx was something of a jobbing satyr and he'd worked for all the big pantheons, he looked different every time she saw him. But appearance was nothing. She knew it was him like she knew the business-suited woman next to her was Aphrodite. Right now, Ceyx looked like a rock star in a tux, all long black hair and designer stubble. The little goat horns on his temples only added to the image. A sort of filthy sexuality wafted around him.

Ishkhara whistled. "Looking good," she said, and Nerissa glowered at her.

"He ruins my business and all your love matches, and that's all you have to say?"

Ishkhara scowled at her, and vanished. Aphrodite erased the image and turned to Nerissa.

"You going after him?"

"Are you kidding? I am going to fucking slaughter him. That is, if Ares and his girlfriend don't get here first."

## Chapter Two

The girl across the dance floor definitely wanted him. Ceyx took a sip of his beer and sent her a wink, and she convulsed with giggles, leaning on her friend. She wasn't bad, he thought, raking her over with his gaze. Nice ass, great rack, shame it was fake. Big pouty lips and long blonde hair. That was also fake, but Ceyx wasn't picky when it came to mortals.

Alive and willing was about all he looked for these days.

Bored, he turned back to the bar. She'd do if no one else caught his eye, but to be honest he was getting kind of bored with the mortal scene. For sex, anyway. Causing mischief was always fun, no matter the species.

Like that little stunt with Ares and Thera. Well, they were asking for it! A dating site, honestly. What the hell was that about, anyway? He couldn't believe it when those lesbian sprites told him they'd met online. Paranormal Mates Society? Geddoutatown!

But after a few bottles of ouzo and a round of enthusiastic boinking with the sprites, they'd convinced him to put his own profile on the site. Well, not in so many words, but he figured if they were getting so much great sex, he might try it out too.

The morning after he'd realized what he'd done, he immediately tried to reverse it. Which hadn't exactly worked…

A prickling at the back of his neck told him someone was near. Someone immortal. Someone godly. He turned slowly, and scanned the bar. A dark, throbbing, sexy beat started up, and then he saw her, leaning against the bar a few feet away.

Whoa.

*Whoa.*

There was nothing fake about this one. Her long, tumbling blonde curls were real, the color of honey, gleaming in the light from the bar's optics. Her lashes were so long they brushed her eyebrows, topping deep, beautiful eyes. Blue, maybe, though it was hard to tell in the dim light. He took his shades off for a better look.

What wasn't hard to tell was what a gorgeous body she had, because it was wrapped around by a dress so tight it was pretty much a full-body condom. Short, white, a deep halter that framed a perfect golden cleavage, a short stretch of fabric that came close to being an engineering marvel.

She shifted on her heels and tossed that glorious mane over her shoulder, surveying the bar. Then her head turned, her eyes on his the whole time, searching him with an intensity he hadn't experienced in a long time.

For a second, the rest of the bar fell away, and it was just him and her, staring at each other. Then sound returned, and she straightened in one fluid move, and walked away.

He watched the sway of her hips, the perfect movement of her curvy little backside, as she made her way to a table on the terrace, gliding into the seat with astonishing grace.

Ceyx found his feet following her without the prior knowledge of his brain.

"Is this seat taken?"

Her eyes flashed up at his. Blue. Fathomless. "Does it look like it's taken?"

Her voice was smooth, accent-less, clipped. She didn't seem amused, but she didn't look annoyed, either.

"Can I buy you a drink?"

"Shouldn't you have asked me that at the bar?"

"I didn't think of it at the bar."

"You were standing there with people buying drinks and you didn't think of it yourself?"

"I was distracted."

"By?"

"By?" He allowed a smile. "By your beauty."

Her shoulders twitched with what might have been a tiny laugh. She blinked slowly. "Cognac," she said.

He ran his gaze over her again, then nodded and went to the bar, thinking. She was a nymph, he was sure of that. One of Aphrodite's handmaidens. He hadn't seen any of them in years—would she recognize him now? When he went back she was staring over the balcony, her hair falling over one shoulder, baring golden skin that gleamed in the bar's subtle lighting.

He put the brandy glass down, and she didn't move.

"I love the street theatre in Rome," she said, still looking out at the piazza below.

Ceyx took the other chair and glanced over in the direction she was looking. Nothing special was happening, just people walking about in pairs or small groups.

"People talking and laughing and drinking," she went on. "Falling in love. The air smells of sex."

"That's probably the couple who were fucking in the bathroom earlier," Ceyx said. He picked up the matchbook sitting on the table and flicked the cover open with one hand.

"Rome hasn't changed much."

"Neither have you."

She turned then, looking at him, and settled back in her chair. "Since when?"

"Since the last time I saw you."

"And when was that?"

"I don't remember."

"You don't remember? But you remember that I was different."

"You were different."

"How was I different?"

"You didn't ask so many fucking questions."

Her eyes gleamed a second, and she smiled minutely. There was a hint of satisfaction on her smooth, golden face. She sipped her brandy. Ceyx tore a match from the book and lit it.

"You ditched the *peplos*," he said.

"About nineteen hundred years ago."

"And the toga?"

"Fifteen hundred years ago."

"The Romans had less staying power."

"Sure. That's why they call this the Eternal City."

"No, that just explains how long it takes to serve a meal here." The match burned down to his fingers, and he tossed it over the balcony. The nymph—damn, he really should figure out her name—inhaled her cognac, sipped, and exhaled. The movement of fine muscles under her skin had him entranced.

He really had spent too much time with mortals if five minutes with a nymph had him drooling.

"What have you been doing since last time I saw you?"

"When you don't remember how different I was?"

He didn't smile. She shrugged.

"I've been settling down."

"Settling down? What, husband, kids?" Ceyx joked.

"Yeah. His name is Kevin."

He stared for a long second before he realized she was joking too. Well. Joking implied some kind of mirth, and so far she'd yet to crack a proper smile. She just sat there, leaned back in her chair but with every muscle tense, radiating sexuality.

"And the kids?"

"George and Louise. We live in Michigan." She swirled her cognac. "What about you?"

"Paris. My wife's name is Gina. She teaches schoolchildren."

"Kevin is a salesman."

"What sort of sales?"

"I really don't care." She put down the glass, clearly bored now. "What are you calling yourself now?"

He eyeballed her, the tight curves of her dress and the brush of her hair over her bare skin. "Ceyx."

A flash of something, not jolly enough to be amusement, flashed across her face. This was one pissed-off nymph.

"Come on, it's a little funny. What about you?"

"Nerissa."

"Meaning nymph."

"Less funny than yours."

"And what have you really been doing?"

"I've really been settling down."

"With Kevin in Michigan?"

"No, with a business in Tuscany."

"So this is local to you?"

"More local than Michigan."

"What kind of business?"

She shrugged. "I'm a nymph. What kind do you think?"

He frowned. The elegant line of her bare shoulder as she shrugged it notwithstanding, she was getting a little annoying. "You own a brothel."

She rolled her eyes. "Satyrs."

"What do you do? Marriage counseling?"

"Matchmaking service."

He raised his eyebrows. "And that's a business now? Time was, we weren't so formal about things."

She drank a little more brandy. "Well, time was, we weren't getting sued all the time."

He winced. "Bureaucracy getting to you too?"

"I have to file business plans now."

"Tell me about it." Was she finally warming up? "Last year I had a couple sue me for breaking up their marriage."

"Did you break it up?"

"Well, sure, but not on purpose." He flashed her a never-fail grin, to which she didn't respond. Maybe she wasn't warming up. "I may have supplied the alcohol and the dancing girls, but I didn't make anybody sleep with anybody."

"He slept with a dancing girl?"

"They both did."

That earned a raised eyebrow from her.

"Humans these days are so litigious," she said.

"They sue at the drop of a hat," Ceyx agreed. "Or they just stop worshipping. Whatever happened to the good old days of smiting?"

"They realized no one was listening when they prayed, so they stopped caring about retribution."

"I remember when Ares had his hands full of favors," Ceyx said fondly. "Waging war on anyone who'd offended the gods."

"Good times," she said, taking another sip. "Of course, his hands are still full now. There are more wars than ever."

"True," Ceyx said, thinking with glee of the private war he'd caused between Ares and the Fury.

"And all he wants now is peace."

"Is it?"

"Yeah." She finished her cognac. "He came to me looking for someone peaceful."

"To you?" Ceyx opened his mouth to ask why he'd come to her, and then it hit him. Matchmaking service. Paranormal Mates.

Oh, *fuck*.

She was watching him like a cat. Ceyx closed his mouth and smiled weakly. "Fancy that."

"Yes," she said, eyes narrowed. "Fancy."

"And, ah, who'd you find for him?"

"Well," Nerissa said, tapping one nail against her brandy glass, making it ting, "here's the thing. Ares wanted someone peaceful. Someone innocent. Someone unlike all the scheming goddesses and nymphs," she tapped the glass especially hard, "in the pantheon. He put this in his profile. He ticked all the boxes. Clicked all the buttons. Embedded his choices in the computer program's algorithms."

"Did he, now?" Ceyx tapped his beer bottle, and it refilled itself. A little trick he'd got from Dionysus. Only he wasn't filling it with beer, this time.

The absinthe hit the back of his throat and made his eyes water.

"The computer should have chosen matches for him."

"Amazing things they can do, those machines…"

"Don't you want to know who he got?"

"Uh," Ceyx gulped his 150-proof beverage. "Sure."

She lifted her brandy snifter and ran her finger around the rim. It hummed, and then an image appeared inside the glass. Ceyx shrank back in his chair as Ares' disastrous dinner swam into vision. He watched the red-haired Fury spit an oyster in the god's face, and tried to melt into the wood of the chair.

It didn't work. Nerissa was staring fixedly at him, her expression frighteningly neutral.

"You know, it's weird," she said. "Thera is a natural disaster Fury. She controls storms and the like. Brutal, powerful. She's not known for her innocence and peaceful qualities."

"Good job she's hot, then," Ceyx croaked, and Nerissa's eyes flashed.

"So I wondered how the hell my computer system had managed to set them up together," she said. "Because, you know, they'd have to have e-mailed each other once or twice before they met. Don't you think? I mean," she gave a sudden smile that lit up the entire balcony like bright daylight and nearly knocked Ceyx off his chair, "let's face it. I know the pantheon are randy fuckers but the Furies aren't known for being easy. And it's not like any of the Olympus crowd ever matched us for casual sex, right?"

Her sudden confiding tone had him worried, but the way she leaned across the table, her cleavage so softly rounded and gorgeously tempting, a warm scent rising from her golden skin, made Ceyx lean forward too, just to be closer to her.

"You remember the good old days, Ceyx," she said, her voice rich and warm, like good wine. "Playing tricks on mortals, the ever-full wineglasses, playing chase with us nymphs. We always let you win, you know that? The chase was just a little bit of fun before the fucking. You remember the fucking, Ceyx?"

He could only nod, speechless. His cock certainly remembered it.

"Yeah, I remember it too. It's not the same any more. I mean, the pantheon are so dispersed, always busy with other concerns. Last time I saw Aphrodite she was wearing a *suit*. You trick half a dozen mortals into a ménage and the next morning they're suing you for sexual harassment or moral defamation or something. And all you wanted was the comfort, the pleasure, of warm skin and soft mouths. A soft breast in your hand. A hard cock in your mouth."

She licked her lips, and Ceyx went light-headed. All the blood in his entire body had headed to his rock-hard cock.

"But it's so hard to come by now. You have to have permission from mortals before you can even set them up any more. It takes skill to do it, Ceyx. It's not just the computer program. I personally approve of every match that thing spits out."

She leaned back abruptly, leaving Ceyx stretched so far over the table he was almost in her lap.

"Until it started doing things all by itself and allowing my members to contact each other and set up dates without apparently having ever read each other's profiles. Now that's weird, Ceyx. That's really weird."

He swallowed and made a strangled noise in reply. She didn't seem to notice his discomfort.

"I once read in a mortal newspaper that if you bought a computer and let it run by itself it would never need maintenance and never break down," she said. "It's only when people start interfering with the program that it all goes wrong. *Cogito ergo corrumpo*," she added.

"I think, therefore I corrupt?"

She flashed another smile. "Or as the help website put it, 'To err is human, but to foul things up completely requires a computer'."

Ceyx relaxed a tiny bit and smiled. She didn't know it was him. She didn't know who the hacker was. Then Nerissa held up the brandy snifter, and every nerve he had screamed in horror.

There he was in the little moving image, spilling soup all over the table in front of Ares and Thera.

She *knew*.

He was *so dead*.

Nerissa tapped her nail against the snifter and it immediately filled with cognac, which she dashed in his face, then grabbed him by the horns and yanked him forward over the table until his face was half an inch from her own.

"You will fix my computer program," she said with deadly quiet vehemence, "you will fix the mismatches you made, you will refund all the vampires, werewolves, selkies and demons you pissed off, and you will apologize to me. Now."

"You want me to do all that now?" Ceyx spluttered.

"No. I want you to apologize to me now."

"I'm sorry!"

She twisted his left horn and he tried not to yelp. "Apologize harder or I will yank out both of these horns and ram them up your ass. And," she ran her thumb over the screw curve of one horn, "I'll twist."

He swallowed. "I am sorry," he said. "And I will fix it! I swear!"

She dropped him suddenly, sighing. "Yeah," she said, "fix it. You're a fucking satyr, you don't fix things. You just break them even further."

With that she vanished, leaving Ceyx dripping, confused, and for the first time since the dawn of time, rather ashamed.

# Chapter Three

Nerissa flashed back into her villa, irritated as hell. Why she'd bothered to go after Ceyx she didn't know; what was she going to get out of him? He was a satyr, his purpose in life was to cause havoc. She'd done a little investigating before she left, and found out he'd worked for all the gods of chaos there ever were. His last employer had been Loki, who very much enjoyed messing with mortals and gods alike.

She tossed her handbag on the floor and kicked one foot in the air. The strappy gold sandal that had been fastened there by means of intricate knots vanished, to materialize in its place in her wardrobe. The second shoe followed, and then her dress melted away.

She'd been naked beneath it. Underwear would have shown, and besides, she didn't really care for it.

Annoyance gathered around her, she grabbed her handbag from the floor and hurled it at the bedroom door. It didn't do much to make her feel better.

But the naked couple lounging on her bed did.

Nerissa stopped in the doorway and stared. The woman had long dark hair, high breasts, and dusky skin, while the man was pale of skin with dark hair and bright blue eyes. Both of them were naked.

"Roman slaves?" Nerissa guessed, but they didn't seem to understand what she said. She stepped over to the bed and ran her hand over the man's stomach. His skin was hot and smooth, the muscles of his abdomen perfect ridges. He was real, all right. And he enjoyed her touch, from the look of the large cock rising between his legs.

She touched the woman, felt the soft fullness of her small breast, the silkiness of her hair.

Hmm.

It was a little too much to expect a gorgeous couple of apparently willing sex slaves to appear ten minutes after she'd been telling Ceyx how much she missed warm bodies in her bed, but right now Nerissa didn't really care.

"Do you speak?" Nerissa asked. "Do you understand me?"

The woman shifted sensually on the bed, thrusting her small breasts at her. The man stroked his growing cock. Nerissa took that as willing assent, and dived in.

Ahh, the bliss of it! They enfolded her in their arms, cuddling her between them, so hot, the contrast of smooth skin and rough hair delicious as they rubbed against her. Nerissa closed her eyes as soft lips nuzzled her neck and warm hands trailed over her body. If she thought about it, she could tell which hands were his and which hers, but she didn't much care. She'd wanted this for so long now, and it felt so good.

A hand touched her breast, cupped and molded it, and she sighed in pleasure. When a mouth touched her other breast, she opened her eyes to see the woman's head resting there, her soft pink lips latching onto Nerissa's nipple. She held the woman there, burying her fingers in the soft strands of her hair. The man continued nuzzling her neck, his hand busy at her breast, but soon he replaced his fingers with his mouth, and Nerissa moaned as both her nipples were sucked into hot, wet heat.

This was what she'd been missing. Sid and Bob were all very well, but they didn't have hands, they didn't have hot skin to brush against hers, and they didn't have mouths. The least said about the purple sucker, the better.

Fingers trailed down her body, over her stomach, her hip, stroking her. Nerissa turned her body slightly to face the woman, who slid one hand up Nerissa's back, one leg between hers, and held her close. It meant she lost the man's mouth on her breast, but she gained the all-over warmth of a body both in front and behind her.

Her thigh between the dark woman's, Nerissa felt the wetness of a real female pussy against her thigh. Sex toys didn't have those, either. She worked her thigh against the pussy, and was rewarded with a soft sigh as the woman switched breasts.

Behind her, his stiff cock growing against her back, the man nuzzled at her neck once more, kissing her sensitive skin, nibbling on her ear. His hands roamed her body, caressing her stomach, her hip, her thigh, before finally dipping between her legs and parting her slick folds.

Nerissa let out a moan as he stroked her slowly, teasing her labia with his fingers, dipping inside her, coating his fingers with her wetness and circling her clit. Panting, she reached down for the other woman's pussy and mimicked his movements.

The woman moaned her appreciation and redoubled her efforts at Nerissa's breasts, licking and sucking enthusiastically, stroking and tweaking. Nerissa closed her eyes and fantasized about sliding that big hard cock into her pussy while a soft little mouth sucked on her clit. Hey, they could trade places. She hadn't eaten pussy in a long time.

The thought was so appealing she grabbed the woman paying such devoted attention to her breasts, and wriggled down her body. With the man's hand still doing marvelous things to her pussy, she rolled the woman onto her back, slithered on top of her, and licked her stomach.

The woman shuddered.

Nerissa kissed her inner thigh. The woman let out a soft moan. Then Nerissa went for broke and licked her pussy, savoring the salty taste and the softness of the flesh beneath her hands. A soft pair of thighs cradling her face, the wonderful bit of skin just beneath her lover's buttocks, the hot, slick flesh on her tongue.

This was fabulous. She didn't really care where Ceyx had found these two. She wanted to keep them.

When the lover behind her started kissing down her back and licking between her buttocks, Nerissa shuddered. There wasn't a sex toy in the world that could give a decent rim job. With his fingers still plunging into her pussy, he ran his tongue around her anus, and Nerissa nearly sobbed with pleasure. She buried her face in hot, sweet pussy, dipping her tongue in deep, so engrossed she didn't see the flash of light behind her.

In fact she wouldn't have known Ceyx was in the room at all if it hadn't been for the sudden cessation of pleasure between her thighs. When she raised her head to see what was going on, she saw him standing there, his black shirt open to the waist, tight jeans hugging his considerable erection, his eyes glued to the scene on the bed.

"I was going to ask how you were enjoying your apology," he said, his voice husky, "but I see you're getting on pretty well."

The bulge at his crotch seemed to get bigger. Nerissa concentrated her powers, and his clothes melted into a puddle of cloth on the floor.

Oh, my.

As all movement on the bed ceased totally, she found herself staring at the most gigantic cock she'd seen since — well, since last time she saw Ceyx naked. Which had been many centuries ago. She'd add them up but she was far too horny to use her brain for anything other than figuring out the best ways to use the two cocks, one pussy, six hands and three mouths now available to her best advantage.

Her clit throbbed. Her pussy tensed. She straightened up, her eyes on Ceyx's face, and he took off his shades with one hand as she knelt between her lovers. His eyes were dark and glittered with raw sexuality.

Nerissa held out her hand to him, staring at that monster cock, her tongue darting out to lick her lips. He came to her as she fell back on the bed, kneeling between her legs and driving himself inside her.

She cried out as he filled her, absolutely filled her up inside. He went so deep she swore she could feel him in her throat. Never in the mortal or divine world had she ever met a man to match a satyr. No one had a cock as big. They'd been known to drive mortal woman away, screaming, at the sight of the gigantic throbbing member swaying between their legs.

But not Nerissa. She was a nymph, made for fucking, made for giant cocks. He pushed inside her up to his balls, and she grabbed his butt with both hands to hold him there.

Ceyx grinned down at her, gleaming eyes and dark stubble, and started to move.

Nerissa closed her eyes. So maybe she hated the man, so what? He felt damn good inside her. Really damn good. She planted her feet against the mattress and pushed up as he thrust into her, taking him as deep as he'd go and then some. Heat built in her, pounding higher and higher as Ceyx rammed into her harder and faster.

She screamed when she came, and still he kept on thrusting, shoving pleasure into her as fast as she could take it. She thought she'd go on orgasming forever until finally he pulled out, leaving her limp and wet, splayed open on the bed.

She opened her eyes to see him grinning at her, his hand on his gigantic shiny cock, still hard and dark with arousal.

"I think someone painted you like that once," he said, tweaking a strand of her hair, stroking her slippery pussy lips. "A nymph ruined, or something."

"I was ruined when I was made," she said, stretching luxuriously, and he grinned and flipped her up into his arms.

This close she could smell his sweat, feel his breath on her face. His dark eyes flashed at her, and then he kissed her, his tongue sliding deep, his fingers firm against her flesh as he held her.

"I remember the old days," he murmured against her mouth, and then he had her in his lap, his back against the headboard, sliding his cock into her again, this time from behind.

He felt even bigger that way.

"I remember the hands." He cupped her breasts and stroked her nipples. "I remember the mouths," he added, licking her neck. "I remember the thrusting cocks." He punctuated this with a thrust inside her. "I remember them all in plural."

Silently, the dark-haired woman, who Nerissa had totally forgotten about, climbed on the bed and settled between Nerissa's spread legs, where she proceeded to return the favor and lick Nerissa's pussy as Ceyx's cock glided in and out.

"Ohhh," she moaned as Ceyx plucked her nipples. "Oh *hell*, yes."

"Don't you mean Hades?" Ceyx murmured in her ear, and she'd have lambasted him for being far too coherent while having sex, if it hadn't been for the other Roman slave kneeling up in front of her and presenting his cock to her mouth.

"A breast in your hand," Ceyx guided her fingers to the breast of the woman between her legs, "a cock in your mouth. Remember the fucking, Nerissa?"

She had the feeling he was making fun of her, but with his huge cock embedded inside her and the woman's soft mouth and clever tongue playing on her pussy, she really didn't care. She took the other man's cock in her mouth and sucked it deep, her whole body writhing with pleasure.

He came in her mouth, just before she came around Ceyx's cock. He carried on pumping into her while the small dark woman carried on licking. Nerissa knew she was licking Ceyx's cock and balls as well and came again from the thought of it.

Then Ceyx, who seemed to be able to go for hours without coming, directed her to lie on her side while he fucked her deep, one leg over his shoulder, with the two slaves licking at her from before and behind. She came twice more before he did, filling her up as she convulsed around him, and then he sank into her arms, his head on her breast, lazily licking at her nipple.

Cocooned in warmth and sex, a tangle of arms and legs, soft breasts and semi-soft cocks pressing against her, Nerissa felt a completion she hadn't in years.

"This doesn't mean I like you," she murmured as she fell asleep, and felt Ceyx chuckle and tighten his arms around her.

"Then I don't think I want you to."

## Chapter Four

Ceyx woke alone in Nerissa's big, comfortable bed. The Roman slaves, borrowed from Dionysus for a night, had been whisked home hours ago—thankfully after Nerissa had fallen asleep.

Nerissa...

He stretched, feeling pretty satisfied. Fucking the nymph had been like driving an Aston Martin all day after years of puttering around in a series of ancient rusty wrecks that lasted five miles then conked out.

Nerissa had been made for sex. Love and sex. Her body was amazing, a perfect instrument to be played upon. Soft, round breasts, large enough to fill a man's hand but not so huge they got in the way. Rosy, plump nipples. A small waist, rounded hips, her skin soft and her flesh firm. Long thighs, soft enough for a pillow, strong enough to clench tight around him. That halo of blond curls, like a veil tangling around his shoulders.

She was perfect.

Where the fuck was she?

The room was made up like a Roman villa, with warm-hued tiles and mosaics patterning the walls and floor, simple furniture and drapes of soft fabric on the bed. A fan turning lazily on the ceiling and recessed spotlights reminded him he wasn't in the fifth century any more.

French doors led to a balcony overlooking a terrace, and he padded out to see if she was there. She wasn't; but he spied her through a row of columns that separated the terrace from a pool area beyond it.

He flashed down to the terrace and moved over the smooth terra cotta tiles, lingering behind a bay tree to watch her.

The pool was surrounded by tall columns in the classical style, like the spas at Baden or Bath, totally private, enclosed even while it was open to the air. Ceyx remembered idly when every city had elegant public baths like this, centers of gossip and high society. Nerissa looked totally at home here, a lady taking the waters, taking slow steps down the stone stairs that led into the pool.

Her hair floated wide around her as she ducked under the surface and swam a lap without coming up for air, the early morning light flickering through the water to dapple her skin.

A breeze whispered past, chilling Ceyx, and he flashed himself into his clothes of the night before, leaning there against a pillar, watching her swim. She was so graceful, a nymph of the water. He tried to remember if water had been her element, but in truth there had always been so many nymphs around that he'd never really distinguished them all that well.

Eventually she surfaced, her back to him, and said, "Where did they go?"

"Back to Dionysus. They were only on loan."

"You must owe him a favor."

"I do now."

A pause, then she said, "Why?"

"You said you missed it."

She turned then, leaning back against the edge of the pool on her elbows, her breasts just coming free of the water. "Why do you care if I missed it?"

Ceyx paused to admire her a moment before answering. "I wanted to apologize."

"Bullshit."

"I did!"

Her eyes narrowed. "You didn't just want some ménage sex?"

"Well, I..." He trailed off under her cynical gaze. Well, of course he wanted the ménage sex. "You didn't have to invite me in."

Her gaze dropped. "You'd have invited yourself anyway. What else did you flash into the room for?"

Ceyx sighed, straightening up. Two steps forward and he'd be in the water. The pillars left no room to walk around the edge of the pool. He could be a gentleman and walk the length of the pool on the terrace side, take a seat on the bench overlooking the water by the steps... or he could just do what Ceyx always did.

He could act on impulse, and have some fun.

He leapt into the pool from a standing start, still fully clothed, sending up a tremendous splash as he bombed into the water, whooping and yelling.

When he surfaced, Nerissa still hadn't moved, and she didn't look impressed. "You're such a child," she said.

"You didn't think so last night."

She looked away, and Ceyx swam over. "What happened to you, Nerissa?" he asked. "You never used to be so censorious. The nymph I knew used to frolic and fuck all day long. The drinking and the orgies, Nerissa, remember?"

"I remember," she said, still looking away.

"Why did that all have to end?"

"Because it all ended, Ceyx," she said. "Not all of us jumped ship like you. We didn't all quit Rome and go play with the Celts—" he opened his mouth to protest and she amended, "—or whoever. Some of us stuck around. We were loyal. We stayed with the pantheon through the hard times, and we adapted. Some of us posed for portraits," she said, and he smiled a little, because he was damn sure he'd seen those portraits. "Aphrodite took care of us and we stayed loyal to her. We set up love matches."

"As I remember Aphrodite, she preferred setting up sex matches."

"Well, yeah, that too. But she stopped because she got into trouble for it. The mortals got pissed off with her. And you know if you piss off a mortal, they stop worshipping you. And once they stop worshipping..."

"You lose," Ceyx said. "Yes. I know." How to kill a god. Just stop believing in them. He'd seen the start of it in Rome, which was why he'd gotten out. And just in time, too. Unlike Nerissa.

"So we had to adapt," she said. "Keep mortal favor. Bring things into the real world. Even on Olympus we were still getting sued."

"Can you believe mortals? Trigger-happy lawyers. At any given time I have half a dozen lawsuits stacked up against me."

She cocked her head and said with mild sarcasm, "And you seem so unhappy about it."

He shrugged. "I'm a satyr. I live for havoc."

She sighed, and he wondered what had happened to the fuck-happy nymph he'd left on Olympus. Where had this tense, closed-up, irritable woman come from?

At least she still enjoyed a good fuck. Then again, Ceyx preened, he'd never fucked a woman—or a man—who hadn't enjoyed it.

"I will fix it," he promised.

"No, you won't."

"I will!"

"No, you won't. Or you'll make it worse. I remember satyrs, Ceyx."

He couldn't think of anything to say to that, so he said nothing, and for a moment they were silent.

"It was good though, wasn't it?" he said eventually, grinning, and a small smile curved her lips.

"You know it was."

He moved closer, felt the heat of her body through his wet clothes.

"You're soaked," she said, and he ran a finger down her face, making her shiver.

"So are you."

"Yes, but I'm not wearing anything."

He grinned at her, then flashed his clothes away. She tried to groan, but she didn't hide her smile very well. Ceyx leaned in until her body was pressed against his, every warm wet inch of her, her nipples hardening against his chest.

"Neither am I," he said in her ear, and felt goose bumps come up all over her. All over every inch of her. He smiled against her skin, chilled by the morning air, and kissed her ear. She shivered.

"Is this you trying to get in my good books?"

He licked her neck, and she let out a soft moan. "No, this is me trying to talk you into more head banging sex." He lifted one of her legs to prop it on his hip and rubbed his cock against her pussy, slick even underwater. "How'm I doing?"

Her breathing quickened. "Disgustingly well."

Ceyx smiled, wrapped his arms around her, and went in for the kiss. But several seconds later a flash of light made them both jump, and he lifted his head to see a young man standing by the pool, dressed only in old jeans, his chest bare and his blond hair tousled. Even in modern guise he was easy to recognize. He was extraordinarily beautiful, and looked extraordinarily pissed off.

Eros. Fabulous.

Nerissa pulled away from Ceyx slightly, and inclined her head. "My lord," she said. Ceyx sketched some sort of deferential nod, wondering what the hell Eros was doing here. Wasn't Nerissa under his mother's control? What say did Eros have in what she did?

"*You*," Eros growled, "are in a lot of trouble."

Ceyx swallowed. "Sorry," he said, "but—"

"Not you," he said in disgust. "Her."

Nerissa shrank against the mosaic wall of the pool.

"She didn't do anything," Ceyx said.

"No? But she's the site administrator of the website that's been fucking things up. Mismatches, nymph, and don't think I haven't noticed. They're coming to me in disgust. One of Psyche's dryad friends signed up for your site. You matched her with a lumberjack werewolf."

Nerissa winced. Dryads were tree spirits. The werewolf had probably killed hundreds of her friends.

"I am not happy, nymph. Not. Happy."

"I'm sorry, my lord," Nerissa began, her skin cooling, her body tense in his arms. "There—" she paused for a microsecond, then went on smoothly, "there was a problem with the computer program. I'm working on fixing it."

"No, you're working on fucking this satyr. You nymphs! You're all the same! All you ever think about is sex. All of you, obsessed with having sex. You have a job to do. My mother lets you get away with far too much. And you know, she's pretty pissed off with you right now too."

"I'm sorry, my lord," Nerissa replied again.

"Well, you will be." Eros's blue eyes flashed like a storm. "Fix this, and fix it soon, or I will have your head, nymph. You're only immortal until someone kills you."

With that, he flashed out, and Ceyx was left with a very stiff, tense nymph in his arms. She trembled a little, and he wrapped his arms around her, trying to warm her.

She let him for a second, then she pushed him away and rubbed her arms. "Right," she said. "Well, I have work to do."

Ceyx stood there in the calm water of her bathing pool, watched the play of emotions on her face. Fear, determination, resiliency. She lifted her chin, terror still shaking her body slightly, and leveled her gaze at him. "I think you ought to go," she said. "You've done enough damage."

He opened his mouth to say something, anything, but no words came. Here stood this beautiful woman with a body to die for, the only nymph he'd even seen in years, perfect and wounded. And he'd wounded her. He'd put a death sentence on her head. He had to fix it.

He caused mischief. He didn't get people killed.

"I—" he began. She squared her shoulders. "I—" She raised one brow. "I'll go."

She nodded, her face tight, her eyes guarded.

"I'm sorry," Ceyx said, and then he flashed out.

\* \* \*

Nerissa slumped against the pool wall. Eros wasn't some two-bit one-temple demi-god. He was the real thing. He was ancient. His father was the fucking god of war! If he threatened death, then death would indeed be forthcoming. Ares himself seemed to be pissed off enough with her—although he hadn't made a personal appearance. Probably didn't want it known he was using a dating site. But he'd stick by his kid, and if Eros was hurt, Ares would act.

If Nerissa didn't fix this then Eros, or Ares, would end her.

She flashed into her office, sat down as the computer, and started untangling the program Ceyx had mangled. But it was like shoveling falling snow. For every line of code she fixed, another popped up, twisted out of shape. The segments she thought she'd fixed came back broken, or refused to mend. Half her commands weren't heeded at all.

She put her head on the desk and cried.

\* \* \*

Ceyx pushed away from his computer with a growl. The stupid thing wasn't playing along with him. Had he pissed off Hermes, too? Every time he tried to fix one of Nerissa's broken codes, it broke again. Half of them he couldn't even access. It hadn't been so hard to break the program. Why was it so hard to fix?

He leaned against the doorway and glowered at the machine. It glowed back.

"Stupid piece of crap," he said. The cursor winked at him.

He swung back into the seat and opened up the website. Logged on as Administrator, he could see who the computer had matched with whom. Deity and vampire? Water sprite and yeti? Sorcerer and mermaid? Ceyx grinned. Well, he'd caused chaos all right. Look at this mess! It was fantastic!

His smile faded. This mess was causing Nerissa a huge amount of trouble. The sort of trouble that could kill her.

He started making notes, sending e-mails, and finding contact addresses. He'd made the mess, he could clear it up.

## Chapter Five

Three days later, Ceyx put the phone down on a Brazilian fire serpent who had found true love with a yeti. Ceyx, who'd always thought yetis were fictional, had listened to Sinna's cock-warming tale of love and sex, and rung off rather confused.

He'd thought they were one of his mismatches. Maybe not.

Then there was the werewolf who'd specified a werewolf lover only, and ended up happily boinking a vampire. The sandman? Who in the hell would knowingly screw someone that caused intense sleepiness? A pair of vampires who were both into dominating each other. It was insane. How had these people managed to fall in love and not kill each other?

In desperation, he turned to Ares and Thera, and found them cuddled together in an oversized armchair in his temple, feeding each other grapes and giggling like teenagers.

Ceyx peered closer. She was feeding him grapes, and he was giving bits of fruit to the snakes in her hair. And they were letting him. No biting at all.

He flashed in. "You have got to be kidding me."

Thera sucked in her breath and he found himself battered back against a wall covered with medieval battleaxes. Ares glowered at him. "I don't remember inviting you, satyr."

"You two are meant to hate each other!"

"Well," Thera glanced at Ares and bit her lip, grinning, "we changed our minds."

Ceyx slid down the wall to the floor and put his head in his hands. "I don't understand. The computer said you two would hate each other."

"So it was you who tampered with it?"

"And there are all these other matches that should have been terrible. I thought it was my computer prog—er, the bad, broken computer program," he amended, flashing a weak smile at them, "but it turns out they contacted each other from the site. And look at you two! Your profiles said you wanted people exactly the opposite of what you are!"

"Well, everyone makes mistakes," Ares said, and both Ceyx and Thera stared at him. "Everyone but me, of course," he amended. Thera rolled her eyes, laughing.

"You are so full of shit," she said fondly.

"So how am I supposed to tell who's a good match and who isn't?" Ceyx asked, more to himself than anyone else.

"Well, the ones who are having lots of sex and calling each other pet names are, clearly, the bad matches," Ares said, standing up.

"Yes, and the ones who fight all the time and insult each other on an hourly basis are the great ones," Thera said, stretching in the chair.

"Bitch," Ares said.

"Asshole."

"Shrew."

"Jock."

They grinned at each other, and Thera pulled herself up by Ares' body to kiss him. Ceyx averted his eyes, hearing slurping. How was it possible that two people who wanted such different things in a partner could fall in love? So quickly? Probably it was just sex, he told himself. After all, Thera was a Fury and most of the pantheon was fucking terrified of her. Who'd want to shag that?

He heard footsteps and saw Ares walk past, out of the room. Thera remained, lounging in the big chair, wearing what was clearly one of Ares' shirts and not much else. Her cheeks were flushed, her hair tousled, and the snakes that peeked from her tresses hissed lazily at him, sated. She looked Ceyx over, then spoke.

*"In faith, I do not love thee with mine eyes, For they in thee a thousand errors note; But 'tis my heart that loves what they despise, Who in despite of view is pleased to dote."*

He blinked. "Shakespeare?"

"I'm glad you've had a rounded education."

"What does Shakespeare have to do with all this?"

"Maybe your education wasn't that great. What the poem means is that you can't always reason who you're going to fall in love with. The heart isn't reasonable. It doesn't pick someone because they seem like they're compatible. It picks them because it can't imagine being without them."

Ceyx stared dully at a Viking axe on the far wall. "So all this matchmaking shit is just… shit?"

She laughed. "No, it's not shit. Nine times out of ten people are predictable in love. But there's no accounting for taste. Sometimes the person who seems the most unlikely is the person who captures your heart."

He looked at her in mild disgust. A Fury waxing poetic about captured hearts? Gods save him.

"So," he wiped his hands over his face, "what, you thought you'd never love a guy like ol' Ares, but the moment you saw him you fell madly for him?" He narrowed his eyes. "'Cos I know that's not true."

"No," Thera's usually stormy eyes looked dreamy, "it was probably sometime around the elevator incident."

"The—"

She smiled to herself. "Mmm. The elevator broke down," she said. "We were trapped, and… oh, you know." She giggled.

The Fury *giggled*.

Merciful Zeus.

Ceyx flashed out of there, but not before Ares had come back in, bringing roses for his lady. Roses, for Loki's sake! Had the world gone mad?

Lounging in a Paris nightclub in the Latin quarter, nursing a glass of cognac, he watched the beautiful people of the world writhe past in a smoky haze. Once upon a time he'd have jumped right in, caused some major hormonal havoc—the best kind—and taken a girl or two home for the night. Or a guy. Ceyx wasn't strict about that kind of thing, and after a drink or two who knew what could happen?

Well, he could post his profile on a dating site, for one thing. And then panic and try to remove it, and when such a thing proved impossible, change all the match protocols so no one would ever choose him.

And in doing so, endanger the life of an angel.

Okay, she wasn't an angel. Angels didn't make for such fantastic bed sport. But she made him look like a devil—horns notwithstanding—and Ceyx wasn't sure he liked that.

If you didn't count the fall of the Berlin Wall, which to be honest he'd thought might cause more havoc than it did, he had been at the root of rather too many of the world's evils. Hell, the Berlin Wall might not have gone up without a little help from him, although he'd vociferously deny all knowledge of it. Computer viruses were his bread and butter—and also his largest source of lawsuits—as were stealing letters, e-mails and important memos. Some of them were totally inconsequential. Some caused wars. Some caused deaths by the thousand. By the million.

One day, he'd probably cause them by the billion.

Ceyx shifted uneasily in his seat. The Cold War was one thing, but all those souls being ferried across the Styx because of him was another, and he wasn't sure he was comfortable with it. No, in fact he was sure he wasn't comfortable.

*When did I start getting people killed?* he wondered.

His mind flashed back to Nerissa, trembling in the pool, under a death sentence. What had she done but try to help people, and try to help them find love? What could be more noble than that? And where was it getting her?

She was stupid, that's all there was to it. Love always was. It was a pointless waste of time. Look at Paris and Helen! Look at Romeo and Juliet! Okay, all right, Romeo and Juliet were fictional, and Paris might have lived quite happily with Helen if Ceyx hadn't tipped off Menelaus; but that wasn't the point. The point was that she was a silly girl, doing silly things.

And she was going to die.

Because of him.

Ceyx knocked back his brandy at a speed that would make a connoisseur faint, and refilled his glass. Nerissa dying wouldn't usually make any difference to him, of course, but she was a damn good screw. So he ought to save her, so he could carry on having sex with her.

Yes, save her.

Although she might not let him carry on having sex with her if she was still mad at him. The other night she'd been desperately horny and lonely and she'd probably have fucked anybody. Given a choice now, she probably wouldn't choose him.

He had to make it up to her. Had to apologize somehow.

He needed a plan.

\* \* \*

The little e-mail icon in the corner of Nerissa's screen blinked, and she stared at it wearily. Another complaint? A final reminder from Eros? For the first time in her life, she found herself wishing it might be spam.

**Automatic e-mail generated by www.paranormal.. rockyourworld@. has removed his/her/its profile.**

Great. Fabulous. That was Ares, and he was so pissed off with her he was leaving the site.

**The user has chosen the following reason for leaving the site**: Found my lifemate! **and left the comment**:

Well, you screwed up on the 'finding me a peaceful woman' front, nymph, although I will admit she's innocent. Or at least was. And you're still in trouble for letting that fuck-headed satyr hack in and arrange such an idiotic date. But since Thera did actually turn out to be the best thing that's ever happened to me, I'm going to let you live. For now. But only because killing you will eat into my busy schedule of licking Thera all over. Ares.

She stared, read it again, then stared some more.
A second e-mail popped up.

Automatic e-mail generated by www.paranormal.com. funlovinfury@paranormal.com has removed his/her/its profile. The user has chosen the following reason for leaving the site: Found my lifemate!

Funlovinfury? That was Thera.
This was weird.
Cautiously, Nerissa checked the rest of her inbox. Two more testimonials from happy couples, and one from a threesome. Remembering her foursome just a few nights ago, Nerissa blushed a little. She opened the next e-mail. It was a mildly snarky missive from a vampire who objected to the term 'lifemate,' but who had nonetheless found love. With a werewolf.
Curiouser and curiouser.
Nerissa opened the next e-mail.

Thank you for your prompt refund, but after reading the testimonials on the site I have decided to remain a member. A promising date with a water sprite has been set up. Signed, GraniteMan192.

Nerissa blinked. Unless she was mistaken, GraniteMan192 was a troll. A very large troll. And water sprites were not known for their size.
She leaned back in her chair, eyeing the screen doubtfully. There was a possibility that all was as well as the e-mails suggested… and then there was a possibility that it wasn't. That fuck-headed satyr had messed up her system once before. He could just be playing a prank on her again.
She concentrated, and found him in a large hotel in Houston. Probably at a convention, messing with the price of oil. Channeling Aphrodite, she dressed herself in a red power suit and fearsome heels, whisked her hair into a chignon and added a pair

of designer specs for extra formidability. Then she flashed herself to the hotel and prowled into the lobby, seeking Ceyx.

\* \* \*

He saw her across a crowded room, ferociously sexy in fire engine red, and watched as all motion ceased and every pair of male eyes turned to her like iron filings to a magnet.

She worked those heels like a catwalk model, striding across the lobby, people scattering to get out of her way, an angel in a deeply bad mood, and Ceyx wondered for the briefest second what he'd done to annoy her this time.

Then he decided he didn't really care, because her skirt was tight and she was just the hottest thing he'd ever seen, and she was headed straight toward him, and every other man in the place was drooling over her.

"Hey, baby," he said, flashing her his trademark rock star grin. "You look great."

"You look like a man who is going to get his horns shoved up his ass," she replied, and Ceyx nervously checked in the reflection from the elevator doors to see if his horns were showing. They weren't, which was a relief—he'd been chased with pitchforks before when he'd forgotten to hide them.

"Is it anything in particular you're punishing me for," he asked, "or does inflicting pain turn you on?"

Her eyes flashed. "No," she said, "unlike some people." She brandished a piece of paper at him and he took it, read it. It was an e-mail from a mermaid who'd found her true love through Nerissa's web service. It was followed by one from the fire-serpent he'd spoken to the day before. And another from Ares.

"I am not fuck-headed!" he protested.

She raised her eyebrows. "You're so fuck-headed I'm continually amazed you haven't grown a dick on your face."

"Make oral sex great, wouldn't it?" Ceyx said, and had the enormous pleasure of watching her blush. He waved the letters at her. "So your business is back on track?"

"So it would seem," she said, not looking particularly happy about it.

"Well, smile then."

"Did you send me those e-mails?"

Ah, so that was her problem. Ceyx's good humor dimmed slightly as he realized she thought this was all still part of his prank.

"On my honor," he said, "I swear I did not."

She rolled her eyes. "Your honor? Swear on something that's vaguely important to you."

"All right, I swear on my gigantic cock that I didn't send them. I did, however, contact all the mismatched clients and offer them a full refund, out of my own pocket. And I apologized to them all. And I fixed your computer program."

She looked at him warily.

"Ask them!" Ceyx said.

"You fixed it?"

"Yeah. Wasn't easy — my skills lie more in the breaking than the mending of things — but yeah, I fixed it. Although, you know, there were a couple of matches from the chaos."

"Ares and Thera?"

"Yeah." Ceyx re-read Ares' testimonial. "I'd swear he was making it up but I've seen them together."

"Really?"

"Yeah. She was quoting Shakespeare."

"'Is this a dagger I see before me?' 'I'll be revenged on the whole pack of you'?"

"No," Ceyx said, grinning, "the sonnets."

"Sweet Olympus," Nerissa said, her eyes wide.

She looked so good standing there in her vixen suit, every curve of her delicious body subtly tailored to, her long legs made even shapelier by her vertiginous heels, her immaculate coiffure and spectacles making her look like some fantasy from the business pages of a snooty newspaper.

But under all the modern, harsh trappings she was still the long-haired, soft-skinned, big-eyed nymph who'd frolicked with him on Olympus and welcomed him to her bed four nights ago. Her perfect breasts moved subtly beneath her suit as she breathed, and Ceyx licked his lips, wanting her quite suddenly, and quite desperately.

He glanced toward the elevator. Hell, it'd worked for Ares.

"Look," he said. "Come and have dinner with me. There's a restaurant on the top floor. We can talk about old times."

She hesitated.

"I'll apologize to you between courses," he said. "You can kick me under the table for being an ass."

She tweaked his horns, visible to her but not to the mortals around them. "Asses don't have horns."

"This one does." He gave her his best pleading look, and she shrugged as if it was a great chore, and nodded.

Ceyx smiled his most charming smile, and offered her his arm.

## Chapter Six

He was up to something. Nerissa was sure of it. Of course, he was a satyr. He was always up to something. What she had to figure out was whether it was going to get her in more trouble or not.

She allowed him to lead her to the elevator as if they were a normal couple. As if she wasn't wearing a suit and fuck-me heels and he didn't look like a particularly dissolute rock-star. At least he wasn't wearing his shades today. She had a feeling he'd worn them before to cover up his hangover.

He leaned past her to press the button for the top floor and he smelled good, a hint of spice rising from his hot skin. Her nipples puckered under her suit as she inhaled, and as he drew back Ceyx grinned at her. She had a feeling he knew what kind of effect he was having on her.

There was one other couple in the elevator, and the thought flashed into Nerissa's mind that this was a big hotel, and it would undoubtedly take them a long time to get to the top, and how inhibited were Texans these days, anyway…?

No. She needed to stop thinking like that. It wasn't fair to snare an innocent couple, who were more than likely just business associates, not lovers. And there was no Stop button on the control panel, anyway. Probably just as well, she told herself. It wouldn't do to get too addicted to Ceyx's rather intoxicating brand of sex.

He ran a hand through his hair, and his scent wafted over again. He wore a black t-shirt and faded, torn jeans over scuffed biker boots. A cigarette packet was rolled in the sleeve of the t-shirt, which clung lovingly to an extremely impressive set of muscles. She remembered how those muscles had felt flexing against her back as he'd fucked her from behind; how glorious the friction of his chest hair against her nipples had been when he took her the first time.

Her eyes traveled downwards. The old denim of his jeans outlined his lean thighs and was worn thin over the bulge at his crotch. Truly, she'd never seen anyone with a cock as big as his. Not even the other satyrs. How could a mortal man please her at all, once she knew what it was like to have that monster pulsing inside her?

She licked her lips, her palms sweating and her pussy dampening hotly as memories flooded her. Recent memories of Ceyx, his eyes dark and glorious as he plowed into her, his thick, hot cock filling her up and making her sob with pleasure. Old memories of warm sunlight and pretty meadows, a tag team of satyrs chasing her as she leapt, naked and laughing, over tall flowers and fallen logs before falling, captured, into the hot grass, surrendering to their pleasure. And what pleasure! Two, three, four of them at a time or more, licking and sucking at her tender flesh, rubbing and pinching with careful fingers, thrusting with eager cocks.

She'd always loved being taken by more than one man at a time, but she did recall Ceyx's attentions being more consuming than the others'. When it was just him inside her, she forgot about everyone else. The power of that huge cock, that skilled mouth, those clever hands, wiped away all other experiences.

The elevator pinged, and she blinked and stepped out of the way of the couple exiting. Ceyx hit the Close button on the doors, then their floor again, his finger clicking the button repeatedly as if he was nervous. It was mildly adorable.

"Stop," she said, "you'll break it."

And as if on cue, the elevator slid upwards for half a second, then jolted, shuddered, and was still.

Nerissa froze, her eyes on Ceyx.

"Did you have to say it?" he said.

She hit the Door Open button, but nothing happened. A light flashed on the control panel. Panic rose in her. "It won't open."

"I think we're stuck between floors."

She jabbed the button again, repeatedly, but nothing happened. Ceyx grabbed her hand.

"Stop it," he said, "you'll make it worse."

"You broke it!"

"Oh sure, blame the satyr."

Nerissa stared at the control panel and tried to calm herself. He was right, of course. Things like this did just happen. Electronics weren't reliable, not all the time. Computer programs could break all by themselves.

She offered him a smile. "Sorry."

"It's okay. It is what I do, after all."

He still had her wrist in his hand, and his thumb began drawing small circles on her skin. Nerissa shifted, and felt the dampness between her thighs as she did.

There came a crackle of static from the control panel, and a tinny voice asked, "Hey, anyone there?"

"Yeah," Ceyx said. "Two of us."

"You okay?"

"We're fine."

"Okay, folks, looks like a problem in the computer program that controls the elevator. Sit tight and we'll have someone to fix it."

"How long will that take?"

"Oh, not more than an hour or two, I should think."

"Two hours?" Nerissa said. "To fix a computer program?"

"We'll have to get an engineer in," the voice said, and as if he feared their complaints, he clicked off.

Nerissa met Ceyx's eyes. "We could just flash out of here."

"Yeah, but then wouldn't they wonder where we'd gone?" He flicked his eyes to a tiny lens set in the ceiling: a security camera. "First rule of the mortal world—"

"Never let them see anything out of the ordinary," Nerissa said. "Yeah, you're right." His thumb was still stroking her wrist. Her nipples were still puckered. "So… what could we do for two hours, on our own, stuck in here?"

Ceyx licked his lips, and gave her a slow smile that made her pussy contract.

"I like your plan," she said breathlessly, and he grinned and yanked her into his arms and kissed her. Sweet Eros, the man could kiss!

"You don't mind that they're watching?" Ceyx murmured against her lips.

"I've had sex in front of half the pantheon," she said, sliding her hand over the hot muscles of his back, under his thin t-shirt, feeling his smooth skin. "A couple of security techs don't bother me."

"You like being watched," he said, biting her lower lip and making her moan.

"Mmm," she agreed. "Foursome sex is difficult without it."

He laughed and started unbuttoning her jacket, halting in surprise when he slid his hands inside and realized she wasn't wearing anything under it. Nerissa looked up, met his eyes, and he exhaled, shaking his head.

"Damn, woman," he said, "you really know how to take a guy to full throttle at the speed of light."

"Should've been a motorsport engineer," she agreed, shucking the jacket. Ceyx let out a pained groan and palmed her breasts, weighing them, stroking his thumbs across her nipples.

"You," he slid one hand around her waist, across her hot bare skin, "are so," he pulled her against him, her nipples chafing against his t-shirt, "hot."

"And you're kind of burning too," she said, nuzzling his neck, licking a long path up to his ear.

"I meant to look at," he panted.

"Yeah, me too," Nerissa said, and nibbled on his earlobe.

He found the zip at the back of her skirt and quickly pushed the garment away. Underneath it she was wearing nothing, and stood there in just her red high heels, eye to eye with him. His cock pressed against her, a huge bulge behind his fly, so big she thought it'd burst the fabric. No wonder his jeans were so worn in the crotch.

"Fuck, I want you," he breathed, and leaned her back against the elevator wall, dipping his head to lick her breasts as she unfastened his fly and took his cock in her hands. He bit down on her nipple when she stroked his tip, sucked her flesh into his mouth when she grasped the thick length of his cock in her hand. When she reached down and cupped his balls, he moaned and the vibrations rippled through her.

"Fuck me, Ceyx," she panted, "fuck me really hard."

From the control panel came the sound of someone clearing his throat. "Ah, folks, we've fixed the problem."

They both froze. The elevator gave a jolt, then started moving again.

"It seems someone got into the program and set up a piece of malignant code. Hitting the buttons in a certain order would cause the elevator to stop. Seems one of you must have... inadvertently... hit the buttons in that order."

Her nipple still in his mouth, Ceyx became so still she couldn't even feel him breathe.

"Are you, uh, still okay, folks?"

Nerissa found her voice and replied, "Yes. Thank you. We're fine."

"Okay then." The intercom clicked off, and the elevator was completely silent. Ceyx gave her nipple a hopeful lick and she swatted him away, all lust replaced by irritation.

"Accident, huh?" Nerissa said eventually, and he winced.

"I never said I didn't do it," he defended, and she gave him a look. "Well, I didn't."

"And if I'd asked...?"

He made a face, and she knew that meant he'd have lied. She sighed, yanked her clothes back on, and glanced at the display above the door, which merrily counted up the floors to their destination.

"Why?"

"I thought," he began eagerly, then caught sight of her face and continued in a more apologetic tone, "I thought it might be romantic."

"Romantic?"

"Well, Ares and Thera got together in an elevator."

She threw up her hands. "And Rhett and Scarlett got together in the siege of Atlanta! Were you going to create a gigantic civil war next?" He looked thoughtful, and she hurriedly added, "Don't, by the way. That's really not romantic."

Ceyx looked unusually bashful, twiddling his thumbs nervously.

"Why romantic, Ceyx? It's not like I'm playing hard to get. You did me three times in one night. With attendants. Little tip: I'm a sure thing. Or at least I was until you started being so stupid! What is wrong with you?"

"I thought," he began again, then trailed off.

"I don't think you did, Ceyx," Nerissa said. "I think that's the problem."

\* \* \*

So she left him, choosing the ladies' bathroom to flash out unobtrusively. Ceyx leaned on the bar of the rooftop restaurant, scowling at the room. Stupid woman. If she was going to be so ungrateful he wasn't going to bother with her any more.

"Can I get you anything?" the overtly camp barman offered.

He'd saved her business, and probably her life, too! And all she could do was insult him and vanish on him. It was meant to be a little bit of fun, some excitement in her dull, dull life. Ceyx wasn't entirely sure when he'd decided it was his mission to bring Nerissa back to the sexy nymph he'd once known, but his goal seemed pretty concrete now.

"Sir?" the barman said. "A drink?"

"Scotch," Ceyx said. "No, cognac."

"Cognac, coming right up."

"And scotch too," Ceyx said irritably.

The barman winked. "Bad day?"

"Idiot woman."

"Ah. Well, if you don't mind my saying, she must be an idiot to get on your bad side."

Ceyx gave him a brief smile and snatched the cognac as soon as it was poured. Downing it far faster than was recommended, he slapped the glass back down and said, "Keep it coming."

The guy was right. She was an idiot. He could wreak massive havoc on her, and she was just blowing him off? What was wrong with her? The wrath of the gods wasn't enough? Granted, Eros wasn't a particularly terrifying god, but a god he most definitely was, with all the rights and privileges thereof. He could turn her to a smoking pile of ashes in an instant.

Ceyx downed the scotch next, then gestured for a refill.

And what had he done? He'd tried to help. Gone against his very nature and undone all his chaos, just to help her. To make her happy again. He didn't seriously believe Eros would actually kill her, but there was no denying Nerissa'd been severely depressed at the prospect of it.

It was just that she'd gotten so uptight. Nymphs shouldn't have to worry about lawsuits and mortal outrage. A nymph, Ceyx was pretty certain, was created for enjoyment. Her own, and that of others. He'd certainly enjoyed her many a time. And now look at her! Just like... like... like a *human*! It was pitiful.

Well, she could stay like that. He'd fixed the mess he made, and he wasn't about to go any further to help her. Let her be miserable. Let her have her sex toys. He didn't care any more. It was not his problem.

Ceyx drank the second brandy a little slower than the first and felt the warmth slide through him. The bartender, clearly seeing Ceyx didn't want to talk, silently refilled it, and he swirled the brandy in its snifter, remembering how she'd done the same that night in Rome. Dear Loki, she'd looked good. That tight white dress, her shimmering golden skin, the caress of her hair on her bare shoulders. His cock ached at the prospect. She'd turned him on more in that half hour than he'd ever been in the thousands of years preceding it.

"She's such a prick-tease!" he burst out, startling the bartender.

"A lot of women are," the guy agreed.

"Dressing up like that and then walking out on me. Twice! Bloody women," Ceyx grumbled, drinking more cognac. He found he was developing a taste for it.

"Mind you, men can be prick-teasers too," the bartender said. "God knows I've met my share of them."

"Hmm," Ceyx said darkly. Men were usually much more straightforward, in his experience. Have cock, will fuck. Simple.

"And I just heard there was this guy in the elevator here who programmed it to stop so he could indulge in a little—you know—" The bartender made an appropriate gesture, and Ceyx straightened. "Right in front of the security monitors."

"Some people like being watched," Ceyx said.

"Well, yeah. But it's a little inconsiderate to break the elevator just for some horizontal mamboing," the bartender said. "There was a huge crowd in the lobby waiting for it."

"There are other elevators," Ceyx said.

"All full. We're a busy hotel. Anyway, she went along with it until the controller told them someone had broken it on purpose, then she got kinda mad and left."

"Well, see, that's stupid. He was clearly just trying to be romantic."

"But why is that romantic? Sounds to me like he was just trying to get his rocks off."

"Well, she was hardly complaining."

"So he could have done—er, seduced her anywhere. Maybe if the elevator had actually stopped by accident and there was all the excitement, yeah, it could be romantic."

"I know a couple who got together that way," Ceyx told him triumphantly.

"But actually engineering it? It's kind of unimaginative. Not very personal. If you ask me, he should have thought of something personal to her if he really wanted to do something romantic."

Ceyx downed the rest of his brandy, scowling. Was that why she was mad? Because he was copying someone else's romance? Well, how many original romances were there in the world? None whatsoever. Everything was a copy these days.

The bartender moved away to serve someone else, and Ceyx glowered at his empty drink. So what was he supposed to do to be romantic? Find something personal to Nerissa. Saving her life wasn't enough?

He drummed his fingers on the bar. What did she love? What gave her joy? Apart from sex, obviously. She used to love being chased across flower-strewn meadows then group tackled and licked all over until she screamed. She'd certainly enjoyed the group sex he'd arranged at her villa in Tuscany.

Group sex? Was that romantic?

He had a feeling it wasn't.

Frowning, Ceyx reached over the bar for the bottle and poured another drink while he thought about it.

## Chapter Seven

The website was running perfectly. In the last week, Nerissa had heard of two more dates being arranged and one mating ceremony taking place. The angry e-mails had stopped. Eros didn't seem in any hurry to kill her. Aphrodite had IM'd her yesterday and never mentioned the incident at all.

Which meant Nerissa was out of trouble. Everything was back the way it had been, and her life was great again.

Well, her life was good, anyway.

It was at least okay.

It wasn't horribly bad, at any rate.

She flopped on her bed, bored out of her mind. Ceyx had been unpredictable and annoying as hell, and he had nearly gotten her killed, but she had to admit life was more fun when he was around. Certainly sex was more entertaining.

She idly flipped on the TV to watch a skin flick, watching dispassionately as a couple frolicked by a big, sparkling pool. It wasn't a turn-on. It was boring.

Everything about her life was so boring.

She was just about to switch the TV off when a figure sauntered onscreen, a man with impressive biceps, long messy black hair, and the hugest cock she'd ever seen.

She stared.

He turned to face the camera, while behind him the couple carried on fucking enthusiastically.

"Nerissa? Hope you'll forgive me for messing with your TV, but I had a feeling you'd be switching onto this eventually. I wanted to apologize for the stunt in the elevator. I was trying to be romantic, but I guess that's your gig, not mine."

She blinked. Ceyx?

"Either way, I wanted to invite you out tonight. To Rome — again — the Temple of Venus. After midnight." He grinned. "That's when these things take place in fairy tales, right?"

Nerissa stared some more.

"Just bring yourself," he said. "I'll be waiting."

With that he walked away, and she was left watching a woman on a sun lounger get enthusiastically shafted by a man with a deeply fake tan.

She blinked, and shook her head. Looked at her watch. It was only a little after ten.

Not that she'd be going anyway. Whatever scheme he had cooked up, she didn't want to be any part of it.

She reached resolutely for Sid, and tried to enjoy the rest of the movie, which was appalling. By the time the credits rolled she was bored to sobs, and was just about to switch the TV off when she saw the credits roll.

Candy Kane, Zane Everhardt, Ceyx Toye.

He'd actually been in the movie.

Nerissa stared at the screen a while longer, then got up off the bed and ran a bath. She washed and oiled herself carefully, in the Roman tradition, before dressing herself in a silk *stola* girdled with gold cord, wrapped several times around her body from her waist to below her breasts. She piled her hair on top of her head and secured it with a gold circlet, letting a few curls trail loose. She outlined her eyes with kohl, darkened her brows and added a touch of lipstick, grateful that modern cosmetics came in neat little packages and didn't spill ochre powder all over the place.

She left off the *palla*, the large wrap that covered most of the *stola*. The fabric she wore was so fine as to be nearly transparent, and she couldn't see the point of covering it up. Back in the day, clothes had just been a sort of decoration, a distraction to her. In the modern world there were all sorts of tiresome rules about public decency, so she had to cover herself up when she left the villa. But not tonight.

Checking her reflection in the mirror, she wondered what the hell she was doing. Why was she going to see Ceyx? Why was she taking such care over her appearance? He was an irritating, stupid, mischief-making drunkard who had nearly gotten her killed.

And yet—

He made her laugh. He made her body sing. Before Ceyx had catapulted into her life again she'd been so bored with her life she was reduced to watching bad porn and playing with sex toys.

Why not play with Ceyx Toye instead?

The clock by her bed read 00:16. Nerissa checked her hair once more, and flashed herself to Rome.

The Temple of Venus had once been a stunning structure, but it was now almost entirely ruined. Grass grew where the floor had once been and the graceful columns of the colonnade were now just a few sticks of stone silhouetted against the night sky.

The Coliseum glowed, brightly lit, beyond the ruin of the temple, and across the still-busy street the fallen columns of the Forum lay crumbled. Cars darted by, music thumping, lights flashing, another reminder that she wasn't in the ancient world anymore.

But up here in the calm shadow of the temple's ruins, she didn't care. Torches had been lit all around and tiny flames flickered from the ground and high up inside the arch that had once housed a giant statue of the goddess. Lounging on the grass, on blankets strewn with flowers, food, and wine, were couples and groups, talking and laughing, but she didn't see Ceyx anywhere.

She did see Ares though, Thera in his arms, looking more relaxed than she'd ever seen him. She saw a pair of vampires feeding each other from goblets of dark red blood, and recognized them from Paranormal Mates Society profiles.

In fact… Nerissa narrowed her eyes. The vampire couple were Erica and Tony and she'd thought they lived in Atlanta, Georgia. Not far from them a group of merpeople were frolicking in what looked like—a paddling pool? A beautiful man put his head above the surface and she recognized him as Taine, a selkie who had recently withdrawn his profile after finding love with a mermaid.

The Sandman and his boyfriend. A werewolf and his beautiful Chinese dragon mate, laughing with a tall dark guy who had his arms round a big beautiful woman with fangs. Sinna the fire serpent, relighting the torches her yeti boyfriend was blowing out. A genie and a psychic. And the devil.

Nerissa blinked and moved a little closer, but she wasn't mistaken in the slightest. There under the statue's arch stood Paranormal Mates Society's former owner with his not one, but two lovers. The three men stood with their backs to her, obscuring the fourth, but as she walked toward them two of the men broke off and went to join the festivities. They smiled as they passed her, but Nerissa hardly noticed, because under the arch stood one devil talking to another.

"Nerissa!" Ceyx cried when he saw her. "I'm so glad you're here. I was terrified you wouldn't come."

She glanced between him and the devil. "What's going on?"

"Your satyr here wanted to prove that he's not the most evil man in the universe," Scratch drawled.

"At least acknowledge he's a close second," Nerissa said, and the devil laughed and walked away. She turned to Ceyx, and was dismayed to see him looking crestfallen.

"Do you really think I'm evil?"

"What?"

"I mean, I know I messed up, but I was talking to Ares earlier and he says Eros isn't really all that mad at you any more. Aphrodite's forgiven you. And look, all these people—"

She put a finger over his lips, silencing him. All those people had found each other through her site. They were all happy. "I don't think you're evil," she said, and felt some of the tension in his body fade. "I think you're stupid, and reckless, and you're far too attached to creating havoc to ever exist in any sort of stable environment—but I don't think you're evil."

He appeared to be considering this. "Not the best compliment I've had in a long time," he eventually said, and she laughed.

"Sorry. But you do have the biggest cock I've ever seen and I am mightily impressed with your lovemaking skills."

He waved a hand. "I get told that all the—mmph!"

Nerissa kissed him, tasted his lips with her tongue then delved inside, winding her arms around his hot, strong body and melting herself into him. Ceyx kissed her back with vigor, his hands sliding down to cup her bare backside through the sheer *stola*. When he let her go at last they were both breathless, and she could feel his erection butting at her through the jeans he always wore.

She caressed one of his horns and he closed his eyes, moving into her hand like a cat being stroked.

"Did you really organize all this?" she asked softly, and he nodded. "Why?"

"I wanted to do something for you. Something that was important to you. And I know your site is, that matching people and making them happy makes you happy. So, I thought… and the temple, you know, to Venus—Aphrodite might drop in later—and I sealed us off from human eyes, too. And I wanted to apologize for making such a mess of things for you, and getting you into trouble with the gods and stuff. And…"

"And?" Nerissa said, more touched than she'd ever been.

"And I wanted to make you happy."

She blinked, her eyes stinging with tears.

Ceyx winced. "Clearly, I failed…"

"No, you idiot." She smiled, a tear falling down her cheek. "You didn't fail. This is the most romantic thing I've ever seen. I am happy," she insisted, sniffing.

Ceyx wiped her tears gently with his thumb. "Really? I'm forgiven?"

"Yes," she laughed, throwing her arms around him.

"Does this mean we can have sex again?"

"I really hope so," Nerissa said, and he grinned and kissed her again, a kiss with benefits as his hand slipped between them to cup her breast and stroke her through the thin fabric.

"Right here?" she murmured against his mouth.

"Mmm. Yes. Right here, right now. Well," he amended, glancing back at the picnickers on the grass, "maybe not *right* here…"

"Why Ceyx, your modesty surprises me—*eeeee!*" Nerissa squealed as he threw her over his shoulder and marched behind the archway to set her down on a fallen pillar, out of sight of the other revelers. He knelt between her legs, pulled her into his arms and kissed her again, his skin warm through her thin tunic.

"Nymph," he said against her lips, "I am determined to thoroughly destroy this human veneer of civility and turn you back into the charmingly degenerate creature you once were."

"And do it with all your heart," Nerissa said fervently. "I'm so bored with being… bored!"

"Oh, sweetheart, I promise you never will be again."

With that he flashed her *stola* away, his clothes rapidly following, and kissed her breasts all over, licking and sucking at her nipples as she writhed in his arms. Here, not twenty feet from a busy main road in Rome, not entirely certain she trusted Ceyx's word that they were invisible to mortal eyes, she threw back her head, spread her legs and thrust her breasts closer toward the magic of Ceyx's mouth.

Her hand reached down to find his cock already swollen to gargantuan proportions and she stroked it lovingly, caressing the awesome length, seeing how far she could stretch her fingers around its impressive girth. She needed two hands to completely encircle it, but when she did Ceyx groaned and bit on her nipple, making her gasp in pleasure.

She stroked away the drop of moisture on the head of his cock, caressed his balls, pumped her hands up and down his shaft until he started to tremble, and pulled away.

"You're going to make me come, and I want to be inside you first," he said, lifting his head and looking at her with hugely dilated pupils.

"And here I thought you had awesome stamina," she teased.

"I do. But you have awesome hands."

She laughed at that and slid from the pillar to lie on the cool grass, her legs bent and apart, beckoning him. He dived between her thighs and gave her pussy one long lick before capturing her clit and sucking on it.

"Oh, sweet Aphrodite, that's good!"

Ceyx slipped a finger into her cunt, then two, pumping in and out, stroking her from the inside. Nerissa moaned as he added a third and fourth, fucking her with his hand, sucking hard on her clit until her body shook and her fingers grasped helplessly at his thick hair and she completely lost the ability to form words. Sobbing with pleasure, she came, her body thrashing on the cool grass, her hips bucking toward Ceyx's hot, wicked mouth.

She opened her eyes to see him above her, his eyes glittering as he lifted her hips and drove into her with one long stroke that nearly made her come again. She wrapped her legs around him, holding him deep inside her, keeping him still for just a second while she concentrated on remembering the feel of him filling her up completely.

"Can I move yet?" Ceyx whispered in her ear, and she smiled, then laughed, and wiggled her hips to make him groan. He slid out, almost all the way, then pushed in again, his balls brushing her dripping pussy.

"Fuck me, Ceyx," she told him again—maybe this time it'd come right—"fuck me really hard."

"My pleasure," he replied, then proceeded to do just that, slamming into her harder and faster until she came again, then rolling her on top of him to watch her move, his hands on her breasts, on her hips, urging her on, looking up at her with those dark eyes of his as he thrust deep, violent pleasure into her.

She broke first, crying out her orgasm so loud she was sure the whole of Rome could hear it, and he followed half a second later with a roar loud enough to wake all of Italy.

Nerissa collapsed against his chest, slick with sweat, feeling his rapid heartbeat pound against her breasts. He wrapped his arms around her, held her close and kissed her temple as she snuggled her head under his chin.

"We definitely have to make that a regular habit," he said after a while, and she laughed and snuggled closer.

"Fine by me." She breathed in the scent of hot, sexy male and sighed contentedly.

"Except, you know, I wouldn't want you to get bored again," Ceyx said. "We'll have to vary it. Try lots of different things."

"Mmm." She licked his neck. "Lots."

The cool night air kissed her skin, making her shiver. Ceyx ran his hand up and down her back in a way that was probably meant to be warming, but instead just got her hopelessly aroused again.

"Oh, and I meant to tell you," he said. "I've been looking up new recruits. Members for your site. Some of Aphrodite's girls. And a couple of sileni and quite a few satyrs were interested, too."

"Really? Wow." Nerissa entertained a memory of quite a few satyrs holding her down in a meadow and fucking her six ways to Sunday while she shrieked with laughter and pleasure. She shifted a little, feeling Ceyx's thick cock rub delightfully against her rapidly dampening pussy.

"You, er," Ceyx began, "um. A couple of them were looking for a ménage relationship."

Her nipples hardened against his chest. Nerissa licked her lips, then lifted her head and licked his.

"And I was just wondering if, you know, you might want to invite one of them over at some point, occasionally, to have the odd night of, er…"

"Mindblowing threesome sex?" Nerissa said, already extremely hot from just thinking about it.

"Or foursome," Ceyx suggested, his eyes glinting, and Nerissa bit his lower lip.

"I thought you'd never ask…"

# Epilogue

**Automatic e-mail generated by www.paranormalsociety.com. Partyguy69@paranormalmatessociety.com has removed his/her/its profile. The user has chosen the following reason for leaving the site: Found my lifemate! and left the comment:**

Apologies to anyone waiting for a response from the site administrator. I'm afraid I can't allow her out of bed. She's not ill, I just have to shag her on a regular basis or I get withdrawal symptoms. In fact it's been at least twenty minutes since we were last naked together, so I'll have to go. All the best, Ceyx.

## Cat Marsters

Cat lives in a village in southeast England, which, while not quite a fairytale setting, is nonetheless very pretty and was mentioned in the Domesday Book of AD 1087. She shares a house with only slightly batty parents who hardly ever tell her to get a real job, and a musician brother who knows there's no chance she'll ever get one if he doesn't. Life is kept from being boring by the often hilarious antics of three geriatric cats and a dog who thinks she's Marilyn Monroe.

Cat has been writing all her life, but in order to keep herself rich in shoes and chocolate, she's also worked as an airline check-in agent, video rental clerk, stationary shop assistant, and laboratory technician. She's aiming for a fairytale cottage, and asks all potential Prince Charmings to apply in writing with pictures of themselves and their Aston Martins.

Visit Cat's web site at http://www.catmarsters.com.

# Paranormal Mates Society: The Midnight Hour

Isabella Jordan

# Chapter One

Spencer Kingston struggled to breathe, lifting himself from the exhausted woman who'd been sandwiched between him and her smiling husband. Grace had lasted for hours, taking both of their cocks into her curvy body, burning them with her sexual fire. They'd made her beg for more time and again, driving their cocks into her until she screamed.

Grace yawned and stretched, sleepy now. Carter Annis shifted her to snuggle against his side, allowing her the rest they'd denied her through the night. Her hair was a shining river of black that flowed down her back and over her husband's arm.

As much as Spencer admired Grace's raven locks, he was thinking about hair that was much different.

A beautiful shade of red.

Sitting up, Spencer pressed a kiss to Grace's shoulder and winked at her husband, Carter. His cousin's eyes swung to the clock on the bedside table and back to Spencer. It was only a couple of hours until dawn.

"Are you leaving?"

Spencer was already out of bed and pulling on his slacks. "I had a great time." Spencer always enjoyed being invited for a ménage a trois with his cousin and his wife. Last night's had been one of the most arousing ever. They'd pleasured Grace until way past midnight, tormenting her and pushing her to unimaginable heights of ecstasy, and she'd drained each of them several times.

Yet this time was different, unsatisfying in a way that was neither Carter nor Grace's fault. Spence felt restless. He wanted more.

"Get some sleep, old man," Carter told him, closing his eyes.

Spencer snatched up his shirt and the rest of his clothing. "You too," he threw over his shoulder as he headed out of their bedroom and down the hall to the room he always took when he stayed with them.

It wasn't sleep that he was interested in. No, Spencer wanted to know if *she* was out there.

Leaving the lights off, he dumped his clothes on the floor. He'd left his binoculars on the table by the window. Snatching them up, he used them to search the night for her. Was his mystery woman out there? Had she been watching him with Carter and Grace?

His cock hardened at the thought. He certainly hoped she had.

When he'd first arrived at their summer home in Cornwall Grace and Carter had told him that someone was watching them. Carter seemed uninterested. Grace believed it was someone from the mysterious group she'd once been a part of. They'd want to know how she fit into her new life and surroundings, she supposed. Neither of them believed there was any threat.

Spencer hadn't liked the idea initially. So what if they didn't pose a threat? He didn't want or need someone watching his ass and he wouldn't tolerate it. The stupid humans had to realize that their kind—werewolves—could easily sense their presence no matter how cleverly they believed they'd hidden themselves.

The first night Spencer was aware of this watchful party, but they weren't there for very long. The second night, whoever it was had lingered until Spencer wanted to tear down the walls to find them and rip them apart. The third night, he'd deliberately gone out on the grounds to search the shadows and put an end to this nonsense already.

And that's when he first saw her.

Granted, she was only a human, but Spencer had wanted her from the moment he spotted her, crouching in the darkness and trying to make her way off the property, a black cap covering her hair. Spencer had excellent night vision. Even in the dark he could see that the skin tight black cat suit she wore did nothing to conceal her lush curves. This lady was long and sleek with full breasts and a heart shaped ass that he'd love to sink his teeth and cock into.

He'd only caught a fleeting glimpse of her beautiful face that night. She was a fair beauty with large eyes and full lips that he had no trouble imagining wrapped around his cock.

Needless to say, he hadn't slept a wink that night.

The last two nights, Spencer had joined Carter and Grace in their bed. They'd invited him because it heightened their pleasure and he enjoyed it as well. Yet he'd derived something else from the encounters. It gave him release from the fierce storm of lust that had consumed him since the little spy had entered his awareness.

Carter shared Grace with him as he often did. Only Spencer hadn't seen Grace as he ate her pussy or pushed his cock into the tight ring of her ass. No, he'd seen the woman from the shadows in his mind.

Spencer *wanted* this woman and he meant to have her. He just needed to find some way to draw her out.

Ah, there she was. Spencer watched her climb into her small, black car just outside the gate in front of Carter's home like she'd done the night before. Not a bad idea since people often parked there for a short walk to the beach. It was also secluded enough if they wanted to stay in the car for a romantic rendezvous.

She yanked off her cap and her glorious red curls came spilling out. Spencer's fingers itched to sink into that hair, to spread it across his pillows as he drove his cock into her.

*Are the curls covering her pussy the same color? Or does she shave?* He couldn't wait to find out.

What was she doing now?

Spencer grinned, watching her shift behind the wheel of the car that she hadn't started yet. Her full lips fell open as he watched her hands working in her lap. Spencer could only see her from the waist up but he had an idea he knew what she was doing.

His little beauty was masturbating.

Spencer's cock turned to stone, watching her squirm and toss her head in the car. Oh, this was too good. So she'd like what she'd seen, had she?

Even though Grace had warned him that members of the group she'd once belonged to were not allowed to approach their subjects, Spencer was confident he could get this little lady to bend the rules. After all, Grace herself had done it. Wasn't she now married to Carter and part of their pack? She'd made the choice to meet him. Otherwise the prophecy that had predicted that she'd come to them to determine the new alpha and be his mate wouldn't have been fulfilled.

Spencer wasn't a big believer in fate and prophecy. He made his own way. If he wanted something, he found a way to get it.

And he would find a way to get his beautiful redhead.

## Chapter Two

Helen Slade simply had to convince the Thoth Agency to give her another assignment. She'd been assigned to watch former agent Grace Shaw for the last month. Unlike the other projects she'd been given, this one was slowly driving her insane.

As quietly as she could, Helen pulled the car door closed and slumped behind the steering wheel. Okay, so part of the reason this case was driving her nuts was her own fault. It had started when they'd sent Grace Shaw's computer to her flat from the London Motherhouse. All she needed to do to retrace the other agent's steps was to look at the files relevant to the case and disregard the rest. That was all she *had* to do.

And what had she done? She'd gone snooping through Grace's personal items on that computer too, all of her files and bookmarks. She could tell herself it was part of her job, but it really wasn't necessary to go through *all* of Grace's stuff. It hadn't taken her long to discover that Grace had initiated contact with Carter Annis through the Paranormal Mates Society website, a dating site for werewolves, vampires, and the like. Her notes on the case had been stored in a text file on the desktop—again an easy find.

It had really shocked Helen that the other agent had broke with agency policy and made contact with the notorious werewolf.

*Why?*

That was the answer she knew she wouldn't find in any manila folder or on the computer. The other agent's personal files had been pretty ordinary stuff. Spreadsheets with her budget, her tax records, recipes. Then Helen had gone through the sites that Grace had bookmarked and, well, that's when the problem began.

Being a member of the Thoth Agency was a solitary life and every member knew that going in. It was unavoidable, considering the rules they had to follow when they were sworn in as agents. Agents couldn't talk to anyone about the agency except possibly with each other. No intimate relationships were allowed outside of the agency. And agents were to conduct themselves at all times in an appropriate manner.

Basically, you couldn't talk and you couldn't get laid unless you fucked one of the geekazoid guys who worked for the agency and most of them had the personality of a sheet of paper. Plus, you had to act like a nerd. Since Helen pretty much was a nerd, most of it wasn't a problem. The only time she had to be careful was when she returned home to New York for the holidays to visit with her family. She wasn't allowed to answer all the damned questions even if she'd wanted to, which she didn't. When was she going to meet a nice man and get married? She was thirty-five, for Christ's sake. Why didn't she take a job closer to home so she could see her sister's children grow up? Why didn't she call more often?

Helen really wasn't looking forward to the holidays coming up for that very reason. Plus, she wasn't sure she'd be finished with this assignment in time to get back to the states for the holidays anyway.

She'd been given the responsibility of observing Grace Shaw who, in a totally unexpected move, had resigned from the agency to marry the very werewolf she'd been investigating for the murder of Francesca Woods. Of course, Carter Annis hadn't been the murderer. One of his former lovers had hired another werewolf to kill the senior agent. The whereabouts of the woman behind the murder, also a werewolf, were unknown.

Helen's job was to study how Grace now fit into this notorious pack of werewolves. That was a little bit of a challenge considering Helen had never met the other woman and Grace's personnel file had vanished along with her.

It was an odd assignment and it wasn't. Rarely were agents sent to observe subjects without some reason—world domination plots, kidnapping humans for breeding purposes. That the subject had once been one of their own was probably the only reason

Helen was sent. Yet she couldn't shake the feeling that there was a motive that had not yet been revealed to her.

Grace Shaw had been an agent with a flawless track record within the agency. It was no surprise that someone like her had been brought from the states to investigate the murder of Francesca Woods. It had been a big deal.

Always striving to be a better agent herself, Helen just wanted to see what sort of websites interested a fellow agent, one with a sterling record. She shouldn't have been surprised to find most of the bookmarks took her to porn sites, but she was. And not just any porn sites. These all had the same theme—threesomes and orgies.

*There's a big surprise.*

If Grace's favorite sites had shocked her, 69isfine.net, Gangbangsrus.com, Nudegroups4u.com, it was nothing compared to what she'd discovered when she'd caught up with the couple at their vacation home in Cornwall.

The first night they'd arrived, they'd headed straight for the bedroom and had gone at it. If Helen got all hot and bothered about that, well, it was her own fault. It wasn't part of her job to watch the subjects she studied fuck and she knew it.

But watched she had. Like some sort of pervert, she'd stayed in the tree just beyond that bedroom window and watched Grace's new husband fuck her six ways from Sunday. It had gone on for hours and Helen had stayed for a long time, her pussy aching with each step she took back to her car. She'd gone back to her flat that night and broke out the jackrabbit while she checked out some of Grace's porn sites.

The next night had been much worse. That night a second man had joined in their bedroom activities and it had almost been too much for Helen to take. She recognized him from the photos in the case file as Spencer Kingston, first cousin to Carter Annis and a notorious London playboy. The gorgeous man with his blond hair and impossibly sexy body made Helen ached to have his hands and mouth on her, to have him slide that enormous cock into *her* aching channel…

Grace already had one. *Let's share the love, huh?*

And tonight? Tonight she wasn't going to make it back to the Cornish hotel where she was staying. She'd watched the three of them going at it again until her entire body shook with lust. Grace had taken those magnificent cocks in all of her passages until Helen was ready to break into the house. She needed relief and she needed it right now.

Then she apparently needed to find a twelve step program for voyeurs because that's just what she'd become.

Safe now in her car, her thoughts drifted to Spencer Kingston and her lower body throbbed with arousal. The fire that had started in her pussy the first night she'd watched at that bedroom window was impossible to ignore now. It was pulsing in a heated, hungry need for satisfaction. She'd never been this bad off physically in her entire life and she'd had a few lovers even after she'd joined the agency. They'd never said anything about one night stands, after all.

Helen ran her hands over the sleek spandex of her shirt at her stomach. Her fingers left a trail of wicked sensation in their wake as she slid down a little in the leather seat. The thick cream in her panties dampened the slick material of the snug pants she wore.

Helen's fingers ran over her mound, her breath a hiss of desperation. She thought about Spencer's cock now. It was long and thick, even at rest. Trembling with desire, Helen moaned as her fingers slid inside her panties. His thick column of flesh would be more than enough to fill her greedy pussy and bring her to orgasm over and over again. Spencer would be more than enough to fill her cunt. He'd stretch her until she begged for more.

Her fingers slid around her clit, skimmed down the slick passage between the wet lips until she reached her aching entrance. Her head fell back and she spread her thighs wider as she gave into the lust she'd been battling for days now.

Helen had always had a strong libido but this was the first time she'd physically *needed* it. Usually her work for the agency dominated her thoughts and her time. She could get by with the vibrator.

Since she'd begun this assignment, sex crept into her mind and her awareness with unrelenting persistence. When Spencer Kingston entered the picture, it had only gotten worse. Now all she thought about was him and fucking him in every way imaginable.

Her tongue swiped across her lower lip and she whimpered as she pressed two fingers inside her body. Her pussy quivered in a spasm of pleasure as it stretched and parted. It had been so long since she'd been laid and she was so tight in there. She struggled to breathe as she pushed her fingers deeper, stroking sensitive nerves that hadn't had attention in some time.

Her other hand had wandered up inside her shirt and underneath her bra. With her thumb and forefinger she tweaked and pinched one hard nipple. The small bit of pleasure/pain combined with the third finger she slid into her cunt had her moaning out loud. Her thighs strained and her muscles tightened as she fucked herself with her fingers as deep and hard as she could.

She was going to come any second. The pool of heat in her belly exploded, sending sizzling sparks of ecstasy spreading from her pussy to the rest of her body. The wet sounds of her thrusting and her breathy cries filled the car around her.

Helen closed her eyes, imagining that Spencer Kingston was between her thighs, working the thick length of his cock up into her greedy channel, stretching her and devastating her with one delicious stroke after another.

With her thumb she began to work her clit as she began to thrust her fingers in and out with increasing speed. That was all it took to send the orgasm ripping through her body, devastating her flesh with fiery streaks of pleasure. Her hips jerked as her cunt milked her fingers, coating them with the hot juices of her release. Her body arched, her sharp cries rang in her ears as she rode it out, wanting it to last.

When the last of the spasms faded, she pulled her fingers out of her body and slowly put herself back together. Her fingers were hardly a replacement for a huge cock, but it had held off the hellish desire that hounded her until she got back to the hotel and to her vibrator.

Then she was going to say every prayer she knew that the agency pulled her off this case very soon.

# Chapter Three

The clock said it was four in the morning but Helen couldn't sleep. Maybe it was just sexual frustration, but she couldn't for the life of her understand why there was a need now for the agency to watch Grace Shaw. The former agent had agreed not to divulge any of their secrets when she'd resigned and had even given them the name of Francesca Woods' murderer. Why now was there a need to keep an eye on her?

And why the hell did it have to be her that did it?

Shit, now she was dreaming about Spencer Kingston. Only there'd been nothing sexual about the dream. No, she dreamed that she was dancing with him and he was wearing a black mask with a tuxedo. It was a masquerade party. She would have known him anywhere with his blue eyes glittering and the lights shining off the blond locks of his hair. It felt so good to be in his arms, to hear the deep sound of his laughter as they spun around the crowded floor.

Then all at once, as it happens in dreams, the lights went out and a strong wind blew through the ballroom. The sound of screams erupted around them and Helen knew that some great evil had come on the scene. Turning around to see what everyone else saw… Helen woke up.

Now she couldn't go back to sleep.

Turning on her laptop, Helen pulled up a web browser. At first she looked at the news sites to see what was happening in the world. Then, with no other ideas, she decided to take another look at the Paranormal Mates Society site. She didn't know what she could have missed there, but what the hell? It was a cute, pink site full of images of happy couples and attractive singles, all waiting for that special person.

*Well, it had certainly worked out for Grace.* Grace was a paranormal herself according to rumor, though what type Helen didn't know.

Helen began to browse through the site, through the categories. Bite Me/Vampires. Wings and Things/Angels. *Cute.*

And Wild Thang/Werewolves and more. Ah, that was the category where Grace had to have found Carter Annis. According to Francesca Woods' notes, he was supposedly posting on the Internet looking for a woman outside of their pack to fulfill some obscure prediction. Apparently he'd decided Grace was that woman once she contacted him through the site. She must have agreed because she left the agency to be with him.

Out of curiosity, Helen combed through the listings in the werewolf category. Were these people for real? Well, creatures. Looking for someone to share a deer with? Someone looking for a howling good time? *Please.* To narrow the entries, she got specific with her search. She entered "Female seeking Male for a date."

Okay, there *were* some nice looking guys here. Some way too young, some older. A couple of the older ones didn't look bad at all. When she clicked to get to the next page, the first listing nearly had her heart leaping out of her throat.

*Spencer Kingston.*

What the fuck?

The entry had been made on today's date which meant he'd posted it in the last four hours. The email and description he'd posted stopped her cold.

> luvsredheads@paranormalmatessociety.com
> Virile alpha male seeks curvy lady with a thing for voyeurism. Did I mention I like redheads? If you'd like to have your every fantasy fulfilled, why not come in out of the shadows? You know you want to.

Oh shit. *Oh shit! He's seen me!*

Helen tugged on one of her stubborn, red curls nervously, rereading the entry. She'd compromised herself, pure and simple.

If she hadn't watched the marathon fuck fests or stopped last night to masturbate in her car, maybe he wouldn't have caught her. Shit! How could she have been so fucking stupid?

Leaping out of her chair, she began to pace.

Now what? She'd compromised her position, right? She needed to call the Motherhouse and get the hell out of Cornwall. They could send someone else to watch Grace get sandwiched. That's what she'd wanted anyway, right? Off this particular case?

Problem solved.

But it would look like shit on her record. The better agents never got caught on an assignment, ever.

Grace Shaw had probably never been caught.

Stopping to look again at the screen, she gazed at the simply gorgeous photograph that Spencer had uploaded of himself. His handsome face was all hard planes and angles, his nose straight, his mouth strong but sexy. He wore a navy blue pullover sweater and his blond hair, neatly cut, gleamed.

It was his eyes that had her mesmerized. His eyes were the clear blue of the sky over the ocean and there was a hint of laughter in them. The asshole was laughing at her? Challenging her to reveal herself to him?

*It's a trap.*

All the more reason for her to call the Motherhouse and get out of here.

*But my record...*

Helen went back to pacing. It all came down to one question. What was more important to her? Her record and her career? Or the fact that she wanted Spencer Kingston to fuck her into oblivion?

No, the latter was impossible. What the hell was she thinking? Agents weren't allowed to have outside relationships. If she allowed that to happen, she had no career.

*Not if it's only once. One night doesn't count as a relationship.*

Helen stopped in her tracks at that thought.

Couldn't she have the best of both worlds? What if she contacted Spencer Kingston? She could meet up with him, scratch her itch. Then, the morning after, she could call the Motherhouse and let them know that she *thought* her position might have been compromised. They were too busy with thousands of cases around the world to go digging for evidence, right? They'd reassign her, she'd have the whole Spencer thing out of her system, and life would back to normal.

Oh, but she was a horrible liar.

Yet she almost had to do it. She could wing it. The worst case scenario was the agency would find out her position was definitely compromised. Then it went on her record. That wasn't so bad. It wouldn't end her career or do much of anything except disqualify her for certain awards or recognitions.

Now any other cons?

*It's a trap.*

Was it a trap or an opportunity? After all, this pack of wolves hadn't harmed Grace. And Francesca had been murdered by a jealous ex-lover of the pack leader, to prevent him from finding the woman meant to be his mate.

What if Grace had been protected from harm by their belief that she was the woman from the prediction?

And Grace had been a paranormal.

Oh, crap. Dashing back to the computer, Helen was unable to stop herself from clicking on the instant messaging icon on Spencer's entry. The message she half expected, but hoped wasn't there appeared.

You must be a member to access this feature.

Crap.

She couldn't sign up, could she? She wasn't a paranormal.

The hell she couldn't!

Throwing herself back down in the chair, Helen clicked on the link to join and filled out all the information she could using one of her lesser known aliases. Then she got to the one question that she knew would stump her.

Species.

Well, hell.

Helen eyeballed the categories again. Vampire? No. She didn't even want to try to do the dead thing or the goth thing. Ghost? Um, no. Angel? Demon? Mermaid? No, no, no. Witch?

That would work as long as he didn't expect her to be able to twitch her nose and make shit happen.

She entered witch. Her username? How about hocuspocus@paranormalmatessociety.com? She typed in the username, completed the registration and paid for the heavenly membership. That entitled her to use all of the features, including instant messaging.

Now she was in business.

Getting comfortable in her chair, Helen clicked on the instant messaging feature to see if he was possibly there.

# Chapter Four

It took Helen over an hour to decide if she was really going to meet Spencer Kingston for dinner and another hour to decide what to wear. When she arrived at the restaurant, she had to talk herself into getting out of the car.

Somehow she made it to the door where the hostess flashed a friendly smile. "Miss Leads?"

Helen smiled and nodded at the name she'd given Spencer, an anagram of her actual surname. She'd given him her real first name though. She wanted to remember him yelling Helen when he came, not some alias.

"Mr. Kingston is waiting. Follow me, please."

Helen followed the leggy blonde hostess through the restaurant, trying to remember to keep her pace slow since she had a tendency to walk fast. She kept her shoulders back. The slinky, red dress she wore had spaghetti straps that slid off easily when she slumped and she tended to do that too.

She'd taken pains with her appearance, pinning up the unruly red curls of her hair. She'd taken her time with her makeup and waxed. She'd even painted her nails which she rarely did. She felt sexy and when the hostess stopped at Spencer Kingston's table, his slow, appreciative grin had her insides heating in record time.

Rising from his chair, Spencer held out his hand. Damn, he was tall. Well over six feet.

"Hello, Helen." His clipped British accent was cultured. "I'm so pleased you could join me for dinner."

Okay, now she was nervous. She'd thought that dressed as she was, confident as she tried to feel, that she'd have the upper hand here. When she lightly placed her hand in his, she knew she was in way over her head.

Spencer Kingston exuded confidence. He lifted the back of her hand to his lips and pressed a warm kiss on her skin. His blue eyes were intent on her as he slowly released her. The man looked incredible in his black suit and silver colored tie. His hair was lightly rumpled from the breeze outside and it made him look even more appealing, if that were possible. Just seeing him this close had the muscles of her belly tightening in excitement, making her fight for breath.

"It's nice to meet you, Spencer."

"You're American."

Helen nodded. Many people, women in particular, rambled when they were nervous, offering lots of information unnecessarily about themselves. She wasn't going to. Her training from the agency did her a service here. The less she told him, the better.

"Please have a seat."

Helen took a seat at the small, candlelit table and Spencer pushed her chair in for her. A perfect gentleman. If she hadn't already known what he was like in the bedroom, she might have made the assumption that he was just another boring Englishman. Ah, but she knew better than that. Beneath that polished exterior was a man whose sexual preferences apparently ran to the extreme.

"You look beautiful, Helen. I love your dress. The color is very becoming on you."

Helen's felt her face warm. "Thank you."

"Of course, I like your black suit too."

Helen swallowed hard. She started shaking inside. "I'm not sure I know what you mean."

The waiter stopped at their table. Spencer rattled off a wine order and sent him on his way. "I'm sure you do know what I mean, Helen. I've seen you outside my cousin's home five nights in a row."

Shit. Now what did she say? Did she deny it and play the game? Or did she just give up the ruse?

Well, Spencer was being direct. Why shouldn't she?

"Let's be frank," she began.

His smile was a flash of white teeth that made her pussy convulse and her nipples draw up into tight, hot points. "Please."

"Why did you post to the dating site this morning?"

"Because I knew you'd find it." There wasn't a hint of apology in his voice. "I wrote it just for you. And it worked quite well, don't you think?"

"Well, I'm here." She'd give him that. "Anything else I can't guarantee."

"I see." Spencer tried to suppress his smile but wasn't altogether successful.

That confident, was he?

"What do you want with me?" Helen had to ask. "Another conquest? I know of your reputation."

Spencer leaned toward her, his blue eyes narrowed dangerously. "I want to know why you were watching outside the window at my cousin's house. Do you really just enjoy watching? Are you really a voyeur, Helen? Or do you want more?"

Easy answer. "I'm not at liberty to discuss my investigation."

"Are you with the authorities? If you aren't, you should know that you could get into a lot of trouble for trespassing."

"I'm aware of that."

One of his blond brows lifted. His eyes were now glittering mischievously behind his thick, dark lashes. "You didn't answer my question."

"I don't have to."

"Tell me, did you like what you saw? What we were doing to Grace?"

He damn well knew she did. Would she be here otherwise? Helen shook her head at him. She wasn't going there with him. At least not right now. Not here.

"Are you done yet?" She tried to sound nonchalant.

His charming smile was back. "Oh, Helen, I do love your spirit. I can't wait to see what you're like in my bed."

That took the breath out of her as effectively as a punch to the gut. Juices collected between her thighs, coating the swollen folds of her pussy.

"What did you say?"

"I said that I can't wait to see what you're like in my bed, Helen." Spencer didn't lower his voice, didn't care that the waiter had arrived with their wine. "I think you want to be there too."

Helen waited until the waiter had served their wine and was out of hearing range before she said anything. No doubt her face matched either her hair or her dress after that.

She had no intention of discussing the fact that she'd watched the three of them having sex for hours, anymore than she wanted to talk about masturbating in her car last night. As casually as he was talking about everything else, it would be her luck that he'd conveniently bring up what she did in her car last night when their appetizers had arrived.

Helen knew where she wanted this to go and he'd just told her he wanted the same thing. What was the point of continuing this verbal sparring match? "Spencer, here's the deal. I can't talk about the case. I shouldn't be talking with you at all."

He nodded, sipping from the glass of red wine he'd ordered. He kept his face a mask of calm and composure. Yet she sensed so many emotions brewing just underneath that polished, polite veneer. "Then why are you here?"

"You know why I'm here, Spencer. You know what I want."

Did he actually growl softly?

"I want just one night with you. That's all. Considering that's the duration of many of your affairs, you should be quite pleased. After that, you'll never see me again. That's the deal."

Helen couldn't believe that she'd said it. It wasn't in her nature to be so straightforward about what she wanted. And her work at the agency certainly hadn't encouraged her to pursue anything for herself.

Yet it felt so damned good to sit there with the man who'd haunted her dreams day and night for the last week and tell him she wanted him for a night of wild, sweaty sex. Her heart was racing in her chest and sexual tension was whipping around the table like a storm warning while she waited for his answer.

Spencer gazed at her over the rim of his wine glass. His expression darkened with sensual intent. He was very good at playing the polished socialite, but the intensity of his gaze reminded her that there was a beast inside him, one that could easily devour her at any time. "You can have anything you want from me, Helen. May I ask why I'll never see you again after tonight?"

Helen lifted her glass of wine and took a healthy sip. She was going to need it.

"No, you can't," was the only answer she'd give him. "Do we have a deal?"

His blue eyes searched her face. "We do."

# Chapter Five

Spencer had offered to drive Helen to the Annis estate, but she didn't want to leave her car. She wanted to be able to leave whenever she liked and he'd agreed to that.

Conversation during the rest of dinner had been a tense affair for Helen and she was really surprised that she hadn't developed heartburn as fast as she'd eaten. Spencer, on the other hand, had seemed to be in no particular hurry. He'd enjoyed his meal at a leisurely pace and he spoke with ease about a variety of subjects. Not only was he sexy as hell but he was intelligent and charming too. Both qualities Helen really liked in a man.

It figured. It would only make it harder to leave in the morning.

The half moon hung high overhead as Helen walked around her car to take Spencer's hand, allowing him to lead her into the enormous estate. It seemed strange to be able to just walk right in as opposed to creeping along in the shadows. She knew every inch of those darkened spaces around the house now, every good hiding place.

Spencer guided her through a wide hallway with pictures of ancestors hanging on the walls. Had they been werewolves too? Had she stopped at any time to think about that fact that she was about to fuck one? Not a sexy man, a *werewolf*. Her pace at his side slowed as her minded started buzzing. Grace was a paranormal. Maybe that's why she could hold her own with Carter Annis or in a wolfie sandwich.

What if this tore her apart?

Spencer's hand tightened around hers and his pace didn't slow. He was literally dragging her behind him until he turned a corner and stopped abruptly before a wide wooden door. He turned to face her, his gaze heavy with avid hunger as he studied her.

Then his face split into a wide grin. "What's wrong, my little witch? You look like you'd like to find the nearest broomstick and fly away into the night."

Spencer had a way of stripping away all illusions and bullshit. Even though it was her bullshit, she had to respect that. "As sharp as you are, I would've thought you'd figure out that I'm just your average, everyday human."

There was a knowing look in his eyes as he nodded. That heated gaze swept over her body and his tongue snaked out over his full bottom lip as it slowly came back up. "I'm glad actually. And there's nothing average about you, Helen."

Helen's nipples beaded hard, her lower body flooding with fire under his intense scrutiny.

"You do know what *I* am?" he asked.

"Yes." She went for confident. *Think vixen, think smart, confident woman.* Yet she was so far out of her experience it all went to hell. "This isn't going to hurt, is it?"

Spencer chuckled at that. A warm rich sound that jarred her with a sense of déjà vu. That was exactly how his laughter had sounded in her dream. "No, I'm not going to hurt you." Spencer opened the door to the enormous room beyond. "Unless, of course, you want me to."

Letting him pull her into the room, Helen looked around at the well-lit suite. It was like a really nice penthouse suite, all clean with gleaming lights, a bar and immaculate white furniture and carpeting.

Spencer closed the door behind them softly. "Helen," he whispered, coming up close behind her. His fingers caressed her bare shoulders before trailing down her arms. She shuddered as he breathed in the scent of her hair. "Trust me. I'll give you what you want. Everything you want."

Helen's knees were shaking when he turned her around. His fingers sank into her hair, freeing the pins from the thick locks until it was a wild tumble all around her head.

"Your hair is so beautiful." Pressing a tight curl to his lips, he breathed in again. "Now I want to see the rest of you. I want to touch you, to taste you. I'm going to get to know every inch of you, Helen, until you beg me to take you. Then I'm going to fuck you for the rest of the night, until you wonder if you'll ever be free of me."

There was no fight or resistance in Helen when he covered her mouth with his. It was what she wanted, what her body needed. Lust reclaimed her body like a fever as his tongue sparred with hers intimately. Sparks of desire ran through her body now, awakening purely carnal sensations that she hadn't felt before.

Mimicking him, Helen breathed in his scent as she wrapped her arms around him. The smell of male combined with a fragrance she was unfamiliar with, something wild and untamed. His lips stroked over hers, claiming her mouth with an insistence that made the walls of her pussy quiver. Her hands slid up into the silky, fine locks of his hair and Spencer hauled her up against his body hard. His cock was a fiery ridge, nudging at the heat between her thighs. The little thong she wore beneath the dress was wet now with her juices and excitement curled hard in her belly.

"You're so aroused, aren't you, Helen?" His breath was hot in her ear. His tongue darted into the sensitive shell, making her squirm in his arms. "I can smell it."

His teeth lightly closed over her lobe and she shivered, clinging to his body which was all straining muscles beneath the expensive suit he wore. His hands roamed freely over her body and his touch was hot, creating trails of fire through the thin, silky dress she wore.

"Lovely as it is, I want this dress off," he told her, even as fingers found the zipper behind her and slowly began to pull it down. His finger slid back up on the flesh he'd revealed, and just that lightest touch had her body blazing to life in the most carnal way. Her pussy clenched, demanding satisfaction. Her entire body was filled with an aching need that begged for relief. For him.

His eyes had darkened to the color of the late evening sky as they locked with hers, his movements slow and graceful. "So soft." His hands slid down over her ass and squeezed gently. "What's under here?"

His hands slid inside the back of her dress and found her thong, pulling on it gently. Helen's low moan filled the room and her grip tightened on his shoulders as she fought to remain standing. When his fingers slid down between her buttocks, she thought she might just pass out.

"No one's ever touched you here, have they, Helen?" His finger circled the tight little hole there, in slow, maddening circles. "You wonder what it feels like to have a man take you there, don't you?"

"Yes," she whispered, beyond shame now.

His low growl had her panting against his chest. When that teasing finger slid a little further down to the entrance of her pussy, she thought seriously about dragging him to the floor and begging him to fuck her right now. His finger slid on the wetness he found there, drawing more circles around her aching channel.

"This is where you had your fingers last night, wasn't it?" Spencer's accent was a little thicker, his voice rough. "What were you thinking about when you fucked yourself in the car? Did you imagine my mouth between your legs? Did you want me inside you?"

"Yes!" Shit, she just knew he'd seen that, but at the moment she didn't give a damn.

His fingers left her and she watched as he sucked them into his mouth, tasting her juices on them. "Then let's get to it."

Before she could take a step, he scooped her up in his arms and headed out of the lovely parlor they'd been standing in. Easily he carried her into an immense bedroom decorated in neutral colors. He carefully laid her on the huge four poster bed there, climbing onto the high mattress after her.

The drapes on the huge window next to the bed were wide open.

"W-would you close those?" Helen pointed at the window. That's all she'd need, to have another agent out there she didn't know about watching *her* bare ass.

Spencer's eyes twinkled with amusement. "I don't mind being watched."

"Well, I do," she told him.

Spencer laughed as he climbed off the bed and made his way to the window. He enjoyed calling her bluff immensely. She might have been really pissed about it had she not been in such a sorry state.

When he came back to the bed, he pulled off the silver tie and dropped it on the floor. The jacket went the same way, but he took his time unbuttoning his shirt, giving her a show as his gaze fastened on her. And what a show it was. When he undid the last button and he took the shirt off, she was treated to an up close view of his powerful upper body. His chest was a hairless wall of solid muscle, holding up wide shoulders and ending in a taut abdomen that disappeared into his slacks.

Damn, he was gorgeous. Helen waited on the bed, panting as his hands worked at his pants. He took his time with the zipper, too, before pulling open the material and pushing the slacks down the hard trunks of his thighs.

She knew from watching him the last few nights that he wouldn't be wearing underwear and she loved that. His cock was long and thick as it jutted out from the curls at its base that were just a shade darker than the hair on his head. Her heart began slamming against her ribs as he climbed on the bed once again to join her.

"Now it's your turn, little minx," he whispered on his knees by her feet. "Come here."

Helen was shaking as she rose up onto her knees so that Spencer could pull the dress over her head. She wore no bra. So it was the easiest thing in the world for him to fill his hands with her breasts, his thumbs brushing over her nipples until they turned hard as little stones. Her cunt was throbbing now, craving attention.

"Is the real thing better?" he asked.

"Oh, hell, yes," she said aloud.

And it was. Watching from the cold outdoors was nothing compared to the feeling of him pressing his lips to hers. When his tongue slid into her mouth to entice hers with tantalizing strokes, she shook from the heat of lust that threatened to consume her.

Spencer bent to take one of her nipples into his mouth and she cried out sharply. He licked her slowly like candy, smashing her sanity with gentle lashes of his tongue. His thumb was still teasing her other nipple when he caught the aching bud between his lips and teeth, tugging on it. It was a struggle for Helen just to hang on in the storm of powerful sensation she found herself caught up in. She felt ready to come any second and he hadn't even made it back to her pussy yet.

Spencer was in no hurry. When he was done with the first nipple, he started on the other even though her fingers were clutched tightly in his hair and her cries echoed through the room around them.

He pushed her back on the bed and climbed up to settle himself between her thighs which were trembling fiercely. He smoothed his hands over that quivering flesh, leaning forward to nuzzle against the red thong that covered her pussy.

"You shave," he pointed out as he kissed her through the transparent material. "I love that."

Okay, so now she was glad she'd gone to the trouble.

That was the last rational thought she had as he settled himself there, his head between her thighs. His tongue began to trace the slim line of the thong. He started at the area that covered her anus and traveled slowly up to the spot where the material concealed her mound. Over and over he did this, the teasing and tickling sensation of it making her lose her mind.

His finger hooked around the string and he pulled the garment out of his way. When his tongue curled around her clit, her hips shot off the bed. That's how needy she was. His tongue flicked for a fleeting second against her clit, and she almost came.

To her surprise, Spencer pulled himself up. "You're not going to be a bad little girl, are you Helen?"

She swallowed hard, wondering what he meant by that.

"I don't like being denied anything, particularly in bed. I'm going to eat your pussy now and you're going to make it easy for me."

Helen gasped when he roughly flipped her onto her stomach and pulled her ass high up into the air. She jerked her head around to look at him. He rewarded her with a sharp slap to her ass that made her hiss in pleasure as much as from pain.

"Head down, Helen, and keep it there unless you want to be spanked until your ass matches your lovely hair."

Oh, shit. She didn't do know what to do. She'd never been spanked before but the heat from the blow heightened her pleasure immensely. Yet she wanted his mouth too.

Another slap stung her other ass cheek and she moaned. Helen dropped her head back onto the pillows.

"That's my girl."

He shifted behind her and she jerked when she felt his hot tongue slide over the soft folds of her pussy. He moaned and the vibration of the sound against her cunt nearly had her climaxing. The only sounds in the room aside from their harsh breaths were the wet sounds of his tongue as he lapped at her juices, teasing and circling her weeping entrance until she was pushing herself back at his mouth.

She wasn't sure how long she could last. Her ass was up in the air and his mouth was buried in her pussy. His long tongue slid down between her swollen lips to find the throbbing nub of her clit and he began to flick against it, devastating her. Angling her head so she could see, she nearly came undone at the sight of his chin bobbing just beyond the shaved lips of her mound as he licked her. When his tongue began spearing in and out of her pussy like a cock, it was more than enough to break her fragile control.

Helen's fingers dug into the pillow she clutched as the powerful release shook her. Wave after wave of intense pleasure crashed over her, leaving her panting and trembling. The room spun around her and she fought for breath against the strongest orgasm she'd ever experienced.

She collapsed on the bed before she stopped to consider whether or not he wanted that. She had her answer when she felt him stretch out next to her and turn her toward him until she was in his arms. She could smell herself on him, and it made her feel wild, made the muscles of her stomach tighten again, as he rose above her.

When his cock jerked against her thigh, she realized that they hadn't gotten to the good part yet. And she wondered how she'd ever survive it.

# Chapter Six

Spencer knew it was frowned upon by the pack when he took human women as lovers and he couldn't care less. He hadn't found a human woman yet who interested him for more than a night anyway or had the stamina to keep up with him.

As he gazed down into Helen's flushed face, he recognized pure desire there, lust as she waited for him to continue what they'd started. She was more than willing. She wanted him and he was going to have her.

*After that, you'll never see me again.*

Spencer shouldn't have cared that she only wanted one night with him for whatever reason. She hadn't been exaggerating when she'd told him that one night was how long most of his affairs lasted. Spencer liked a variety of women mostly because he just hadn't found one that truly held his interest.

Ah, but his little spy had captured it. She'd thrown down a challenge with her stubborn refusal to reveal anything about herself. It pricked at his pride that she thought she could just waltz into his life for a night of fun and be done with him.

He was going to give her something to think about.

Her bright, green eyes searched his face and those full lips he liked so much were parted. His balls knotted hard when he thought about them wrapping around his cock. No, she wouldn't be getting away from him without doing that.

He didn't like the idea of her getting away from him at all. It was a ridiculous notion, but it was how he felt nonetheless.

Spencer's breath hissed out when he felt her reach between them for his cock, wrapping her fingers around him as he fought the urge to transform. He growled with the need to possess this woman, to mark her as his. His blood boiled in his veins and his cock throbbed as she began to move her hand over his shaft.

Then she reached down to massage his balls and he knew he wasn't going to last with her touching him that way. She knew what she was doing. The speed of her strokes were just right and she knew exactly where to apply pressure. She was destroying him.

Grabbing her hands and pulling them around his neck, he lowered his body onto hers, pushing her thighs wide with his own. He couldn't wait any longer. He positioned his cock at the warm, wet entrance of sweet pussy, groaning at the hot juices coating his cock head as he slid it into her heat. Helen bucked beneath him, her sheath grabbing him as he slowly worked his cock into her.

He'd never seen a woman, werewolf or otherwise, *this* turned on and so desperate to fuck. Spencer wanted to make this last as long as he could, but as he slid even further into her tight pussy, he knew it wouldn't be easy. Her cunt closed around him like a fist, threatening his control.

Growling, he sank his hands into her hair and began moving against her, loving the way her cunt closed around him, trying to hold onto him as he withdrew.

"Spencer!" Her hands clawed at his hair, scraping down his back. Spencer liked the light pain. "Oh, God, that's good!"

Helen seemed to know instinctively what he liked as she lifted her hips to meet each of his thrusts. He liked to fuck hard. He liked to play rough. This little lady was giving as good as she got. Spencer pounded as hard as he dared inside her. How he would have loved to put her on her hands and knees and have taken her from behind, sinking his teeth into her skin and marking her as his, but he knew he'd scare her if he did that.

Spencer focused instead on the way her cunt squeezed around him and how she whimpered when he stroked the right spot within her. Her nails carved trails into his back and he growled, thrusting into her. "Yes, harder!"

Grabbing her buttocks, he pulled her so tightly against him that he was able to grind against her clit. Helen screamed his name, her thighs tightening about his hips and her head thrown back. Her face was flushed as only a redhead could be and her hair looked like streaks of lava across his pillow.

Reaching beneath her, Spencer coated his finger with cream from her pussy and slid the tip into the tight ring of her ass. Helen went wild beneath him, her anus closing around his finger as he pushed deeper. The walls of her pussy began to quiver around him and Spencer thrust faster, harder, wanting to push her over the edge.

Helen's entire body went taut, her screams filling the room. It went on for the longest time while Spencer pulled back to watch her beautiful face, transformed by exquisite pleasure.

Spencer waited for her to come down, continuing to stroke himself within her, stretching her ass just a little. As he pleasured her to the point that she was going to come again, he knew he wanted more than this one night. There was so much he'd enjoy doing with a woman this passionate…

The color rose again in her face, her body tightening. He knew she was about to let go and he went with her. Pushing his finger to the hilt in her ass, he exploded within her, shooting his come into her body with a little less restraint than he'd been using. She screamed and held onto him, her hips pumping wildly to meet his until they were both sated.

Spencer stretched out beside her as they both struggled for breath. Helen felt so good snuggled against his side. He loved her softness pressing against him. The smell of sex floated on the air around him and for the first time in days, he felt peaceful. Free of the demon of desire that had been riding him hard since he'd first laid eyes on this woman.

Normally this was the part where he started thinking about a nice rare steak and what apologetic parting would work best the next morning. Instead, he was thinking about what he planned to do with her next. Having her give him a blowjob and fucking that beautiful ass were high on his list of possibilities.

"Wow." Helen's voice was low, breathy. "The night's off to a great start."

Spencer chuckled in delight. A woman who thought just like he did. Most of them were wanting to cuddle, or worse, talk by now.

Not his little spy. No, she showed the promised of having a libido to match his own.

And she was leaving tomorrow.

Helen dozed off and Spencer thought about that for a long time.

# Chapter Seven

Spencer scowled at the door, the sharp rapping sound jarring him from a sensual dream of the flame-haired beauty sleeping soundly by his side. He didn't know what the hell was so urgent but he wanted to stop them from knocking again. He didn't want Helen awakened just yet.

Jumping out of bed, he grabbed his robe from its peg in the bedroom and pulled it on as he marched to the door. Yanking it open, he found Carter standing on the other side. Spencer frowned at his cousin. "Yes?"

Carter was dressed but he didn't look well rested. He looked like hell. The concern he read in his cousin's expression let him know there was a good reason for the visit. "Spencer, we need to talk."

"Come in then," Spencer bid him, opening the door wider for his cousin's entrance.

With Helen's assurance last night that he wouldn't see her again, he wasn't about to go anywhere else to talk. She might actually try to slip away from him, and Spencer was surprised to realize that he wouldn't like that. He wanted to be there to talk to her when she woke up. How that was going to go, he had no idea.

Actually, he wanted to do much more than just talk to her.

First, he had to deal with Carter. "What's going on?" Spencer asked.

Carter sank into one of the armchairs in the parlor, his elbows braced on his knees. "We have a little problem, Spencer," Carter began. "A werewolf has turned up dead in Devon."

"Who?"

"We don't know his name. We're just pretty damned lucky that the Hannahs are staying at the same hotel as he for the masquerade. He apparently got drunk to the point of illness in the hotel bar last night. James Hannah, you know how he is, went to check on him and found his dead body in wolf form. They alerted us and secured him before the humans found him."

Spencer shook his head. Luck indeed. Thank goodness everyone was coming down for the ball Carter and Grace were holding for Halloween. Having the human world find that kind of evidence of their existence was one of their kind's biggest fears.

"So they have the body?"

Carter nodded. "I've got someone coming to take care of it."

"Any idea what happened to him?"

"He was shot in the head. We don't know by whom. Grace thinks he might have been dead several hours before he was found. But she'll be the first one to tell you she's no forensics expert."

That meant anyone could have killed him. Still, the unthinkable hadn't happened. The Hannahs were part of their pack. If they had the body and help was on the way, the danger was mostly thwarted. "Did anyone else see the body?"

"They didn't think so." Carter raked a hand through his dark hair until it was literally standing on end. "Grace and I drove up there early this morning to take a look after we got the call."

"And?" There was obviously something more than just a dead werewolf that they didn't know.

"Grace noticed that one of his teeth was broken. That's important because she actually saw the crime scene where Francesca Woods' body was found. She remembered bite wounds on the woman's body that suggested a tooth was broken or missing."

"So there's a chance this was the wolf who killed the woman?" That was something because Spencer remembered that Carter's jealous ex-girlfriend had never revealed who she'd hired to commit murder for her.

"Grace seems to think so." Carter still slumped in the chair like a man with the weight of the world on his shoulders.

"What? There's something else?"

"Yes, Spencer, there is. The Hannahs happened to mention that they'd also heard Blue Garrett has been missing for over a week. I called back to London and confirmed that."

That got Spencer's attention. The drag queen had been in a relationship of sorts with their cousin Joe, until it was revealed that he'd plotted with Kim Foster. Joe had been so disgusted after that he'd refused to see or talk to him ever again.

"Wait. Blue is missing. Grace thinks the dead wolf might be the one who was hired to kill her and Francesca Woods. Where the hell is Kim?"

Kim Foster had once dated his cousin, Carter Annis, and she was the person responsible for the death of Francesca Woods and the attempts to kill Grace.

Even after they knew the reason why, it had shaken them all up a bit to know that one of their own had been responsible for the heinous acts. Kim had hired another wolf, whose identity was still unknown, to do the dirty work for her. She'd thought to thwart pack prophecy by killing the woman it said would come to them and reveal through a pack mating ritual the identity of the new alpha.

Kim had suspected, as many had, that Carter would be the new alpha. She was willing to do anything to prevent that woman from becoming Carter's mate. If she had been successful, her hope was that Carter would return to her.

Yet Kim hadn't thwarted anything. The prophecy had come to pass. They found Grace and managed to keep her safe. The mating ritual revealed Carter to be the pack's next alpha and Grace's mate, a good thing since he was already besotted with her by then.

Grace herself was a snow leopard and that brought powerful blood to their pack as the prophecy said it would. It was also foretold that their pack would be restored to prominence among their kind in Europe, but they'd have to wait and see how that played out.

What Spencer really wanted to know is what their kids would be. Snow wolves? Wereleopards?

"I haven't been able to reach anyone up there," Carter explained.

Spencer's mind was spinning. Carter hadn't killed Kim though most of the pack thought he should. Instead, he'd sent her away to one of the pack's smaller holdings in Wales. He'd decided that since she wanted to be the mate of a pack's alpha so badly, she could be one there. Carter had her married off to Winston, tasking him with the responsibility of making sure she did no more harm to anyone. A couple of other wolves that Carter trusted took their families and went as well to keep an eye on things. The prospect of beginning a new pack and establishing positions of authority for themselves had been quite appealing.

And by all accounts, Kim had done very well there. She hadn't produced cubs yet, but she had supposedly been working hard and beginning to enjoy her new life. "Were they invited to the party?" Spencer wanted to know.

That earned him a look. "Be serious, Spencer. Do you honestly think I'd invite that woman after she tried to have Grace killed?"

"Point taken." Spencer slowly began to piece it together. "So out of the three parties involved in the plot to kill Francesca Woods and Grace, the only one we can account for is the dead wolf."

"Exactly."

"A little coincidental, yes?"

Carter had to be thinking the same thing. If this was a case of the three of them being targeted, who would be next? Would Carter and Grace be at risk? It was a chance the pack couldn't afford to take. "If Kim and Blue *are* really missing and *if* the dead wolf is in fact the hired killer, it's one hell of a coincidence," Carter admitted. "I've got people looking for the missing ones. We have no way to prove the wolf that was killed last night is the same one who killed Francesca Woods."

Spencer immediately thought of the woman sleeping in his bed. Perhaps they did have a way to prove it after all.

"Spencer?" Carter's voice pulled him from his thoughts.

"Yes?"

"Who's that outside?"

A flash of red went by the window, heading straight for the cars.

*Shit! So much for being able to awaken Helen properly.*

"If you'll excuse me," he told his cousin.

Then he sprinted, in a most undignified manner, out the door in his robe.

## Chapter Eight

"Leaving so soon, Helen?"

She screamed at the voice that came out of nowhere. Spencer stood up to lean against the driver side door, grinning at her, wearing only a thin robe of dark navy blue. His tawny hair gleamed in the morning sun and the noticeable protrusion at the front of his robe let her know he was happy to see her.

"I have to leave, Spencer." God, she didn't want to leave. "Please get away from my car."

He didn't move a muscle, forcing her stop right before him. "*Why* do you have to leave? Is there another lover you have to get back to?"

Helen snorted. As if.

"Then why?"

"I'm not going to tell you."

"Because it isn't allowed, right? You aren't supposed to make contact with those you're sent to spy on, and you aren't allowed to talk about them or the people you work for. Am I right?"

So Grace had talked. How else did Spencer know about the agency? What else did he know? Well, if he thought now she'd relent and tell him all about it because of his in your face bluntness, he was dead wrong. "I have to go, Spencer. Please don't be difficult. You agreed to this."

"That was before."

"Before last night?" Helen didn't know whether to slap his smug face or throw herself back into his arms. "I was like no other woman you'd ever experienced and one night won't do. Right?"

Spencer didn't react at all to the sarcasm in her tone. He just watched her with those incredible blue eyes, completely unflappable. "Well, there is that. But overnight another situation has developed and we need your help."

Caught totally off guard, Helen stared at him. Her heart pounded so hard in her chest that she was certain he could hear it. "Excuse me? *We*? What we? Who did you tell about me? This?" she demanded.

"I haven't said anything to anyone about you yet, Helen." His eyes locked with hers, his features set by determination. "Whether you stay or go is your choice."

"Thank you."

"I'm rather hoping you'll decide to stay."

"Because you want my help?" She hated herself for asking that.

"No, because one night with you isn't enough."

"Smartass."

Spencer's grin widened. "I'll prove you wrong later."

Helen wanted to stay with him. Oh, but she knew better. Sure, Spencer was standing there with a hard-on, telling her he wanted her to stay. But for how long? A week or two? She couldn't give up her career for that. If she didn't leave right now, this moment, she risked fucking up the career at the agency that she'd worked so hard for. At thirty-five, starting over wasn't something she wanted to do.

Damn, he wasn't making this easy.

And now she was curious as shit about what he'd meant by needing her help.

"You won't trust me, but I'm going to trust you, Helen. I'm going to tell you that a werewolf was found murdered last night in Devon. Someone shot him in the head. He wasn't part of our pack but fortunately some members of our pack were staying at his hotel. They recovered the body and contacted our alpha so the humans wouldn't find him. He died in wolf form, you see, and allowing humans to have that sort of evidence of our kind is something we can't have happen."

Helen stared at him as he spoke. His charming smile vanished.

"And?" They didn't need her to deal with that.

"And we have reason to believe that he was the wolf who murdered Francesca Woods."

Now she was interested.

"Grace was at the murder scene where Francesca's body was found. She remembered an irregularity in the bite wounds on the body. She's seen the body of the dead wolf and he has a broken tooth. We need to find out if the wolf that killed Francesca and the one shot dead last night are one in the same."

"Who killed him?"

"We don't know. But we do know that Blue Garrett has been missing for over a week and now we can't get in touch with Kim Foster either."

Shit. This was a big development. "So, it's possible we may have someone targeting the three people responsible for Francesca Woods' death."

"And they plotted to kill Grace."

"Yes, but she lived. And if there was someone on her side of things who wanted some payback for that, she'd probably be aware of it. As it is, she's has no one outside of this pack. That points to Francesca. Who in her life wanted payback?"

Spencer's expression was still and serious. "I hadn't thought of that. What I'm concerned about is a potential threat to Carter and Grace. What if this party decided to take Carter out for not dealing with Kim, before or after Francesca's murder?"

"Or they might simply want to eliminate anyone who could track them down."

"Precisely." Spencer blew out a deep exhale. "Will you help us?"

Help them? Was he kidding? "If I don't get out of here this moment, and I've already said way too much, I won't have a career. A girl's got to make a living, Spencer."

"Only if they found out." That sly expression of his was back.

"Excuse me?"

"If we play this right, Helen, maybe you'll have a nice, shiny achievement to put on your resume."

Her heart leaped at that. Her mind was screaming at her to climb into the car through the passenger side.

"Perhaps something got your attention in your observations here early this morning. A phone call to Carter Annis. You followed him and Grace to the hotel where they took a look at the body of a dead werewolf. You overheard her comments about the possible link to Francesca Woods, and you wanted to verify this. Perhaps you even managed to obtain a sample of his DNA to run against any samples taken from the murder scene."

Damn him. It did sound plausible. If she'd been doing her job instead of fucking Spencer last night, it might have happened like that anyway.

"You also heard mention of Blue Garrett's disappearance so you wanted to investigate that as well since the two could possibly be related."

Helen nodded.

"This would interest them, yes?"

"Sure it would. This pertains to one of ours."

"Then what do you say?"

She wasn't going to let that gorgeous smile get to her. And she wasn't going to look at that tent his cock made out of his robe. She already had sore spots in places she couldn't name to remind her of last night and how much she still wanted him.

Her little thing with him was over whether she decided to help or not. It had to be that way. "If I agree to help you, it doesn't change anything. You and I can't—"

"Of course not."

She didn't believe him. His erection hadn't gone anywhere, and she knew better than to believe that Spencer Kingston was remotely capable of being as angelic as he tried to look just now.

"I mean it."

He smiled at her as he held out his hand for hers. "I understand."

# Chapter Nine

Helen drove back out to the Annis estate late that night. She dressed as she would have if she were still watching everyone fuck through the window, parked her car in the same place just outside the gate. She was going to smack Spencer in the mouth if he dared give her grief about any of it as she crept through the shadows with the black portfolio under her arm.

One really nice thing about the agency, they'd send information and files to agents just about anywhere via runners. It only made good sense because you didn't want to pull the agents away from their investigations at crucial points to return to the Motherhouse for the things they needed.

She'd handled everything just as she and Grace had discussed. She gave them the story, asked for suggestions on how to proceed and who to contact. If she seemed to know exactly what to do, she could give herself away. Her superiors had been most interested in the identity of the dead wolf, to see if he was Francesca's killer. They'd given her every concession they could.

A runner had delivered the reports this afternoon to her hotel. She hadn't stopped to look at the results. When she was certain that the runner was a safe distance away, she'd jumped in her car and had driven straight to the Annis estate.

Spencer was wearing that shit eating grin of his when he opened a side door to let her in. He always evoked an extreme response in her. She wanted to slap him for his mockery. She wanted to throw him down in the narrow hallway and fuck his brains out.

*Okay, get that thought out of your head right now. Not happening.*

"Are we going to play Catwoman and Wolfman later?"

"Shut up." Helen walked around him, remembering how to get to the parlor where she'd talked to Grace earlier.

"I love this outfit." Spencer kept pace with her, sliding his hand over her ass until she slapped it away.

"I just knew you'd give me shit."

"I enjoy it," he explained unapologetically.

"Yes, I realize that." Helen stopped on that note. "Spencer, this can't go any further. I told you that this morning and last night. I'm here to bring you the information you need and then our business is done."

Spencer moved closer, backing her against the wall. Helen was lost in the shadow he cast, feeling, at least to a small extent, overpowered by him.

"Don't you want to stay and help us solve the mystery?"

Helen tipped her head back toward the door. "I can do that out there."

"Do you really want to go back to the cold shadows when you can be warm in here, screaming in pleasure again and again?"

"Stop it!" Was the man trying to drive her insane?

"I can change your mind."

Helen didn't like the predatory expression on his face. Without permission, he lowered his mouth to hers and took her lips in a searing kiss that made her forget to breathe. The line of demarcation she'd tried to draw was gone as she wrapped her one arm around him, her hand snaking up into his hair as his tongue slid into her mouth.

"Ahem, it's good to see you again, Helen." Carter's voice had Helen pulling away and Spencer pinning his cousin with a murderous stare. "Won't you both join us in the parlor? There has been more news, I'm afraid."

Helen almost ran after Carter in an effort to get away from Spencer and the devastating impact he had on her common sense. One glance back over her shoulder showed her Spencer was following them slowly. Was he sulking?

Good. The man wasn't playing fair and he knew it.

Once Spencer reached the parlor, Carter shut the door behind him and they all took a seat on the sofas by the fireplace.

Helen had the portfolio ready on her lap, but the intensity she read in Carter's face convinced her to let him speak first.

"Blue Garrett is dead," Carter told them. "I just got off the phone with Joe. He'll be here later tonight."

"Shot?" Spencer asked quietly.

Carter nodded. "Old Maurice is getting the bullets for us. I'd be willing to bet they match."

"What do you have for us, Helen?" Grace asked.

"I haven't read this yet. The runner took forever getting there." Helen opened the portfolio, her eyes scanning the pages she found inside. Grace leaned forward in the chair to her left, trying to read with her.

"There it is," Grace whispered.

"The DNA is an exact match," Helen announced. "The dead wolf was known as Clyde Bradford. It's believed he came from an obscure pack in Scotland, but there is little known about him. The one thing we do know is that his DNA matches the werewolf DNA found on the body. He killed Francesca Woods."

"And whoever killed him has likely also killed Blue Garrett," Grace added.

"Any word on Kim?" Carter asked. "We've heard nothing on this end."

Helen frantically searched the pages again. "Ah, they actually have an agent up there, but we don't have a current report. That's strange."

Grace nodded. "It is. Agents are supposed to submit a report daily. When was the last report from the region?"

"Not good. Five days ago."

Helen caught the worried look Grace flashed Carter. No word on Kim was likely bad news. And if she'd been eliminated, what did that mean for Grace and Carter?

"We've got added security around the estate and more coming for the masquerade tomorrow night. We'll be fine," Carter told Grace, his tone reassuring. "We'll find out who is behind this."

*Masquerade?* Shit. Something else from her dream.

"Well, I'd best be going," Helen told them on that note. "I'll call if something else comes in from the Motherhouse."

"Why don't you come to our party tomorrow night?" Grace smiled at her. "It is a masquerade. You'd be safe attending that, I would think."

Oh, wasn't that asking for trouble? She'd dreamed about Spencer and that masquerade for some reason. It had ended like a nightmare so that may have been a warning not to go, right?

Spencer, who'd been sitting silently through the entire discussion, watched her with narrowed eyes. She knew he wasn't pleased about their kiss being interrupted in the hallway. Well, it was his own fault. Beyond last night she hadn't promised him anything.

She sure as hell wanted to though.

She would be able to wear a mask, right? And she'd probably have news from the agency to share anyway.

"Perhaps I will," was all she said.

Carter and Grace thanked her and bid her a good night as she stuffed papers back into the portfolio and rose to her feet.

"I'll see you out," Spencer offered, already at the door.

"That's okay."

A muscle twitched at his tightened jaw. "I insist."

Helen made her way out of the parlor and did her best to ignore Spencer. When he came marching down the hallway behind her, she knew he wasn't about to let that happen.

"Where are you going?" he demanded.

Helen didn't break her stride. "Back to my job."

"You're not going to at least kiss me goodbye?"

Damn him to hell. Helen whirled around to glare up at him. She'd had enough. "You know what would happen if I did, Spencer."

His blue eyes glittered in triumph. "You want it too."

"Maybe I do." She held out a hand to ward him off as he took a step closer. "But what we want isn't always best for us, is it?"

Spencer moved even closer, a predator stalking his prey. She loved how he smelled, the heat from his body.

"What are you afraid of, Helen?"

"Afraid of?" She *was* afraid.

He leaned down to brush a kiss on her forehead, nothing sexual. Yet her body ignited from that simple touch, burning to have him devour her.

"You are afraid," he whispered, his lips brushing her mouth now. "What if you give it all up and find yourself wounded and alone within weeks, days? Isn't that what you're thinking?"

Well, yeah.

"Won't I be?" she had to ask.

Spencer crushed her against him, his lips slanting down over hers hard. He was wild, ripping at her clothes and growling with the same desperate need that ran through her. His strength was amazing as he hauled her up and ran down the hall with her to his rooms.

Once they'd reached his bedroom, he turned her face away from him at the window and quickly began to peel off her cat suit from behind her. Her heart raced with excitement as she let him do it, the powerful lust she thought last night would cure her came back with a vengeance. Spencer's teeth nipped at her neck and she shuddered. His rough hands pulled her back against his warm smooth flesh, letting her know he'd taken off his clothes too.

The heat between them escalated, his flesh burning her back like flame. Bending her forward, he entered her without preamble. His balls slapped against her when he thrust inside her to the hilt. He seemed larger tonight if that were possible, but he felt so fucking good filling her pussy with his cock. The angle of his penetration hit pleasurable places she didn't know she had, and she hung onto the window sill for dear life as he withdrew and slammed back into her.

"Oh, I wanted this," she whispered as pleasure and pain blurred. His cock was so deep within her that she felt like she might split in two. His hands were everywhere on her body, his mouth and teeth an added torment that she craved as their bodies slapped together.

"Can you walk away from this?" he demanded in a strange, guttural voice. "Can you walk away from me?"

She didn't want to. It terrified Helen to realize how much she craved him and she barely knew him. Release was coming up fast and her pussy clenched around him like a fist. Spencer answered that by pounding into her furiously, making her scream as her body trembled and pulsed. The orgasm exploded in her body with an intensity that eclipsed even last night. She felt faint, struggled to breathe.

Spencer wasn't through with her yet. Dropping to his knees, he buried his mouth in her pussy. He licked and sucked her until she started screaming. When he started tongue-fucking her, she came again. The blast waves of her release shook her until she thought her sanity would shatter.

Helen's thighs trembled and her knees gave way after that. Spencer followed her to the floor, pulling her down to straddle him. Once again his thick cock filled her, butting against her womb as he began to drive into her.

"Fuck me, Helen," he growled.

His hands guided her and lent her strength as she rode him with abandon. His blue eyes were wild as her body milked his cock, flashing at her with an intensity that took her breath away. He moaned and growled beneath her, bucking under her ass to deepen the thrusts as his fingers dug into the flesh of her hips.

When she was about to climax again, his body went taut beneath her. She came a split second before he threw his head back and jerked violently beneath her, flooding her pussy with his sperm. He thrashed and howled, holding onto her with a grip that was nearly painful.

Helen collapsed on top of him, too exhausted to do anything else.

Spencer's arms wrapped around her, his voice a sleepy murmur. "Don't leave me, Helen. Stay."

## Chapter Ten

Helen shivered in the chilly air, the long skirt of her black evening gown whispering around her ankles as she walked up to the front of the Annis estate for the masquerade ball. She could barely remember trick or treating as a child, much less going to a Halloween party as an adult. She had to admit to being a little excited as she walked through the door and handed her stole to the uniformed man who waited just inside.

Each slow step she took, slowly following the crowd toward the ballroom, made her aware of a dozen little sore spots and she warmed as her thoughts drifted to Spencer. He'd loved her long into the night, until she thought she'd expire from ecstasy. He'd finally allowed her to sleep in the early morning hours, but he'd awakened her to more sensual kisses not long before noon, making love to her again. Only that time it had been easy and slow.

When she showered and dressed, Spencer had followed her around like a puppy dog, wanting to play, teasing her. When she went to leave, he reminded her of the masquerade but made no effort to stop her. Only when he'd kissed her did she taste his longing. That and the words he'd whispered to her the night before had haunted her mind for the rest of the day.

*Don't leave me, Helen. Stay.*

After a couple of hours she went from trying to write off Spencer as another life experience to thinking that it probably wouldn't hurt anything to go the ball. She'd be wearing a mask after all, and there would be so many people and so much activity. Would anyone really notice if she disappeared with Spencer for a while?

She'd left her hair down because she knew he liked it that way. The mask made her feel different. The anonymity it offered making her feel sexy and more confident. She made her way through the throng of werewolves, her eyes scanning the room. When she didn't see Spencer right away, she decided to linger near the entrance of the glittering ballroom, just inside it. She did spot Carter and Grace dancing at the center of the dance floor. Carter looked handsome in his sharp tuxedo and Grace was stunning in a sleek dress of dark red.

"I knew you'd come."

Helen's eyes slid closed at the sound of his husky voice. Spencer's presence sent a shiver running through her body.

She turned to face him and heart lurched in her chest. Spencer was a vision from her dream, smiling at her just as she remembered. He looked incredible in his tux, a black mask covering his eyes.

"You look beautiful, Helen." He held out his hand for hers. "Dance with me."

Placing her gloved hand in his, Helen felt her excitement and happiness at seeing Spencer fading to the background. She couldn't shake the terrible feeling that something bad was about to happen as he led her to the edge of the dance floor. Something bad had happened in her dream, hadn't it?

Normally attempting to dance would be scary enough for her, but since her mind wasn't on it, she seemed to do well enough. She let Spencer lead as they began to dance to the beautiful strains of music provided by the small orchestra in the corner of the room. Masked couples danced all around them like a sea of satin and sequins.

"Are you all right?" His voice was a soft intrusion on her thoughts.

Helen couldn't stop her gaze from darting around the room. In her dream she remembered laughing with Spencer, feeling carefree until darkness had swept through the room.

The darkness *was* there she realized, spinning around the dance floor in Spencer's arms. Instead of sweeping through the room it passed through her body in a cold shudder and she recognized it with eerie clarity.

"Helen?"

She chuckled nervously. "It's nothing. I guess."

His eyes fastened on hers through the black mask he wore and concern clouded them. "What's wrong?" He pulled her closer to him as they danced. "Why do you look as if you'd seen a ghost?"

"You'd laugh," she told him. Wouldn't he? How did she expect him to believe she'd dreamed of this evening before she'd ever known about it? The dream had occurred before they'd ever made love.

"No, I won't."

The confidence of those words convinced her to give it a try. "Spencer, this is going to sound insane, but I've dreamed of this night. Of this dance and being with you. I dreamed about it the night before I met you for dinner. I had no idea there was going to be a masquerade ball, I promise."

Gentle strokes of his hand on her back helped to calm her. "That happens sometimes, sweetheart. Everything is fine."

Helen stopped dancing, her sense of foreboding undiminished. "I don't think so. That dream didn't end well. I don't know what happened exactly because I woke up. Something is going to happen here, Spencer. I can feel it."

"Your witch senses are tingling, are they?" he teased.

"Don't be an ass!" Why did he have to give her shit now of all times? "If something were to go down tonight, here in this room, what's the worst case scenario in your mind?"

Spencer led her off the dance floor, and she heard his exhale over the din of the room. "That something would happen to Carter or Grace."

"Let's get them out of here then. Please." Helen hated the pleading in her voice but her heart began to race now. "Trust me."

Helen had clutched his hand in hers at some point and he squeezed her fingers. "Let's do it then."

Helen watched as Spencer scanned the dance floor for his cousin. Once he spotted him, he headed in that direction, taking Helen with him. She stayed close behind him, her grip tight on his hand. They had to weave through the crowd of dancers, one couple catching Helen's eye. A tall, eerie man wearing a skull mask danced with a woman who appeared to be so drunk she could hardly stand up. She eyeballed them as she followed Spencer with sick fascination—like staring at the scene of a horrible car crash, unable to look away.

"Carter!" Spencer called.

The head of the man in the skull mask jerked up at that. He steered his partner in their direction as Helen's heart threatened to break free of her chest.

"Spencer! That's him!" Helen yanked hard on his arm and pointed toward the approaching figures. The woman's feet weren't moving. Her head fell back and Helen felt sick as she got a good look at her bluish pallor.

The woman was dead.

Spencer stopped abruptly as the man in the skull mask dropped the dead woman to the floor Grace and Carter's feet with a sick thud. Her small, lace edged mask tilted crookedly on her slender face, her dark hair fanning out on the floor. "My God, it's Kim," Spencer whispered.

The man in the skull mask pulled out a large hand gun and pointed it at Carter. Startled gasps and screams erupted from the crowd and the music faded away. No one made a move.

To Carter's credit, he showed no fear. Slowly he pulled Grace behind him and glared at the unknown party. "Who are you?" Carter demanded.

"No one you would know." The man spoke with a crisp British accent. With his free hand he easily pulled the mask from his face, grinning at Carter like a man who'd lost his mind.

Grace stared at the man in recognition. It took Helen a moment, but then she recognized his face from the case file. Lawrence Thompson. He was with the agency! He'd been a close friend of Francesca Woods.

"If you kill me, you have to know there are well over a hundred werewolves in this room who will rip out your throat," Carter warned.

"Do you really think that I'm afraid of death now?" Lawrence taunted. "You all took away the only thing I loved in this world. Once you're dead, I'll be happy to die. My revenge will be complete."

Slowly Helen lowered her hand to her skirt, carefully pulling up the lightweight fabric. The other agent focused on Carter Annis. He hadn't so much as glanced in her direction. Good.

"What did I take away from you?" Carter asked, his tone calmer now.

"Why Francesca, of course." The man's hand was steady on the gun, never wavering. "She and I were lovers, you see. We had been for many years. You have no idea how long I had to wait for that."

Carter flinched when the man cocked his gun. Helen tugged at her skirt a little faster. Just a little bit more...

"I'd loved her since we were children. I almost lost her when she joined the damned agency. I had to join myself just to keep track of her. By then she was married, but I still didn't give up hope and I was right. That fool of a man she married slowly started to lose his mind and I was all too happy to be there to lend comfort. She was mine. I allowed her to pursue possible cures for her husband, knowing she wouldn't find anything in time to save him."

Helen felt Grace's gaze on her as found her gun, tucked in the holster she'd strapped to her thigh.

"What I hadn't counted on was losing her," Lawrence went on, kicking the woman on the floor. "This bitch had her killed just for you, Mr. Annis. And that worthless lout I shot in Devon was nothing more than a mindless killer, but he didn't have to rip her apart as he did. There was no need to be so merciless with my Francesca."

Grace nodded to Helen as she slowly slid her glock out of its holster.

"And that other person who couldn't decide whether to be a man or woman? He'd plotted along with them to try to keep his lover. My Francesca meant nothing to him. Killing him was quite easy."

Helen's muscles tensed as Thompson took a small step closer to Carter. "Killing you, in front of your entire pack, will be quite easy, too."

Helen rushed him, pointing her gun at his head. Thompson noticed her at the last minute. Startled, he fired his weapon. Grace pulled Carter to the floor a split second before the bullet would have plowed into his skull. Screams filled the room around them.

"Drop it!" Helen ordered, ignoring the flurry of activity behind her. "Drop it now."

The man laughed then in a way that told Helen he'd completely lost his grip on reality. "I've seen you," the man taunted, his grip tightening on the gun. "I don't know who you are but I know who you love."

Her heart leapt into her throat as he pointed the gun at Spencer.

"If you keep me from completing my quest," the man warned, "I'll take him away from you. I have nothing to lose."

Helen swallowed hard as her eyes locked with Spencer's. The thought of losing him was crushing. As important as she thought her career at the agency was, it hadn't done anyone in this room a lot of good. Grace had been a loner, concealed within their ranks, until she'd found Carter. This man had been ultimately robbed of the woman he loved because of the world of the Thoth Agency. If she ended lost Spencer, she knew she could never return to the agency.

And then everything became crystal clear in her mind.

"Make your choice," Lawrence yelled at her.

Helen pulled the trigger.

Spencer dove for the floor along with those left around him as the killer's gun discharged, the sound of the gunshots filled the room. Lawrence Thompson crumbled to the floor, blood pouring from his head.

Gripping her pistol for all she was worth, Helen stepped around the man she'd felled as Spencer rose to his feet. She was shaking violently all over when she walked into his waiting arms. "Are you okay?" Helen pulled back to look up into his face.

"I'm just fine, love," Spencer told her, stroking her back. "I'm not hurt."

"He could have—"

"But he didn't." Spencer's smile was gentle. "You stopped him, sweetheart. And the next time you tell me you dreamed of something that you think is happening, I'll bloody well pay attention."

Her dream. Had it been the real reason she'd brought the gun? Had it been part of the reason she'd come to the ball? Was it meant for her to stop the killer?

Was it meant for her to save Spencer?

"The elder members of our pack assign great importance to dreams. You should talk to my grandmother, Margaret, about that one day."

Could that possibly mean she was meant to be with him? Part of this pack?

"It's all over now," he whispered.

Helen gazed down at the gun in her hand. Spencer followed her gaze and she held it out to him. She didn't want to see it right now. She'd just shot a man, and even though she was justified in doing so, it was a horrible feeling. "Take this."

He did. Putting the safety on, he tucked it into the pocket of his tuxedo. "Let's get you out of here, Helen. We'll go to my room so you can rest, okay?"

She looked around to where Carter and Grace kneeled on the floor, holding each other. Neither appeared to be hurt. A quick scan of the floor revealed no other casualties among the guests who'd remained.

"Everything's fine. Let's go," Spencer urged her.

He wrapped an arm around her waist, holding her tight. Murmuring voices surrounded them as they made their way out.

When they reached the room, Spencer led her straight to the bedroom and urged her to sit on the bed. Kneeling in front of her, he removed her shoes. "Lie down," he told her.

Going around the room, he closed the drapes and turned out all but one small lamp. He shrugged out of his jacket, and then the bed dipped with his weight as he climbed onto the bed next to her.

Spencer said nothing. He just pulled her into his arms and held her. "You saved me," he said quietly.

"I know."

"Why?"

"Because I couldn't stand the thought of losing you."

"So you need me as much as I need you?"

His words had her heart squeezing in her chest. "I think so," she admitted.

"Stay with me, Helen."

It was her undoing. Helen began to cry quietly against his chest, the enormity of what had just happened and what could have happened overwhelmed her. Spencer let her cry, brushing kisses into her hair and rubbing her back until exhaustion finally pushed her into sleep.

# Chapter Eleven

"What are you doing?"

Helen turned around at the sound of Spencer's voice, grinning at him. "I'm closing my account at the paranormal dating site."

Spencer walked up behind her, looking over her shoulder at the monitor of her computer. "Do we have to?"

"We should," Helen pointed out. "I don't know about you, but I'm off the market."

Spencer nodded. "I'll do it later. I like your desk here."

Helen had been more pleased than she could say when he'd offered her the room in his London home for her personal study. All of her belongings were now here and unpacked. A good thing too. Now that she'd accepted his proposal, there was a wedding to plan and Grace was already putting together quite an event. "So do I," she told him.

Spencer read the words on the screen over her shoulder. "So you're going to say that you've found a lifemate?" he asked.

"Actually, I was thinking I'd check 'Too expensive.' I'm unemployed now."

Playfully Spencer nudged her. "You won't have to work, unless you want to. Besides, there are plenty of things here that need your attention."

"Such as?" Helen teased.

"Come here."

Spinning her in the chair to face him, Spencer dropped to his knees and pushed her thighs apart. Yanking up the hem of her peignoir, he ripped off the filmy little matching panties. His nostrils flared as he breathed in her intimate scent and a shudder passed through her. Helen was already quaking inside. Her body seemed to be in an unrelenting state of readiness for him. And that was convenient because Spencer wanted sex often, any time of the day, anywhere in the house.

His light growl was the only sound in the room as he parted her with his fingers and licked her. His tongue was a restless devil that roamed from her opening to her clit where he lingered, flicking against her.

Pausing only to suck on her labia or clit, Spencer licked her over and over. He devastated her clit with hot kisses and lashes, his teeth, tongue and lips driving her insane. Helen writhed in the chair, her hands clutching the arms so tightly, her knuckles were white. His strong hands at her hips held her in place for his greedy mouth. The wet lapping sounds and her soft whimpers filled the room, driving them both on.

When her pussy walls clenched, he seemed to sense it. His long tongue speared deep into her wet opening and began to thrust into her like a cock. His tongue fucked her, in and out, while his fingers found her throbbing clit. Helen cried out at as she drew closer and closer to release.

"Spencer!"

The orgasm was a powerful explosion that ripped through her body. Her blood boiled, darkening her skin with heat from her cheeks to her cunt. Her thighs trembled around his face and the tremors shook her endlessly as she held onto the chair.

Spencer's eyes burned into hers, yanking her forward in the chair.

"See how you taste?" His mouth claimed hers with a kiss of pure possession.

While the room spun around her, he hauled her up from the chair and stole her seat. He began fumbling with the fastenings of his slacks, freeing the thick, ready length of his cock. Helen was still reeling from the orgasm when he pulled her down to straddle his lap.

Spencer positioned her over his straining cock and slid easily inside her, using the juices that had gathered between her thighs. Helen moaned as his cock filled and stretched her cunt until he was sheathed balls deep inside of her.

Helen would never get enough of him.

She pressed a kiss to his mouth as she began to ride him slow and easy. Even in this position, Spencer took control, thrusting up into her hard enough to make her want more without hurting her.

The chair squeaked in protest from the power of their thrusts. Spencer growled and moaned as he neared his climax and Helen sank her fingers into his hair and held on. Her pussy walls quivered and tightened around him, pulling a sharp groan from him. His fingers dug into the flesh of her hips and his teeth sank into her shoulder as his thrusts grew in speed and force. The light sting of pain was all it took and the powerful tremors of orgasm began again as he thrust into her so deeply she felt as if she would split in two.

Spencer came with her, rocking against her until both of their bodies were spent. They panted in each other's arms, Helen resting her head against Spencer's strong shoulder, his shirt warm and damp beneath her cheek.

"What were we talking about?" he asked, his breathing ragged.

Helen laughed. "I haven't a clue."

Behind Spencer, the screensaver wiped the Paranormal Mates Society site off Helen's computer and she decided that was fine. She'd close her account later.

# Isabella Jordan

Isabella Jordan is a lucky lady who spends her days with her family, doing volunteer work and writing. She loves creating new stories of all kinds and chatting with readers and friends.

Isabella would love to hear from readers! Visit her on the web at http://isabellajordan.com.

# Changeling Press E-Books
## Quality Erotic Adventures Designed For Today's Media

More Sci-Fi, Fantasy, Paranormal, and BDSM adventures available in E-Book format for immediate download at www.ChangelingPress.com—Werewolves, Vampires, Dragons, Shapeshifters and more—Erotic Tales from the edge of your imagination.

### What are E-Books?

E-Books, or Electronic Books, are books designed to be read in digital format—on your computer or PDA device.

### What do I need to read an E-Book?

If you've got a computer and Internet access, you've got it already!

Your web browser, such as Internet Explorer or Netscape, will read any HTML E-Book. You can also read E-Books in Adobe Acrobat format and Microsoft Reader, either on your computer or on most PDAs. Visit our Web site to learn about other options.

# What reviewers are saying about Changeling Press E-Books

## Jingle Buns — Judy Mays

"The sex was stupendous! I would have loved to be there to watch."

—*Marcy Arbitman, Just Erotic Romance Reviews*

## Mistletoe High — Alexis Fleming

"Mistletoe High is a lovely lighthearted Christmas romp with enough heat to keep your hearts and toes warm."

—*Mahaira Fatima, Just Erotic Romance Reviews*

## The Office of Kink and Karma: Love Me — Celia Kyle

"This, the fourth in an already great series, has to be my favorite. Packed with some deliciously juicy scenes, Love Me really couldn't get any better."

—*Hayley, Fallen Angels Reviews*

## Dravidian — Sierra Dafoe

"Smooth, flowing plot, endearing characters, and hot erotic scenes ensure Dravidian is going onto the keeper pile."

—*Hayley, Fallen Angels Reviews*

## Union in Blood — Madeleine Oh

"Union in Blood is an intriguing tale that mixes splashes of wit with deep space adventure."

—*Roxy Blue, Just Erotic Romance Reviews*

## Ainen Chronicles: Jordan's Quest — Kyla Logan

"It's a joy to discover an author who writes paranormal romance with a different twist. Jordan's Quest is rich in detail and arouses all your senses with the mating of Jordan and Micaela."

*— Lisa F., The Romance Studio*

## Troll's Blog: Troll Under The Bridge — Shelby Morgen

"Wow! This is one hot read! Not only does the sexual tension between the troll and the cop begin immediately, it's also thick enough to cut with a knife. This encounter between the two characters is absorbing. The steaming sex and unexpected ending will keep you smiling long after you finish The Troll Under The Bridge."

*— Trang, Fallen Angel Reviews*

## Driven to Justice — Alice Gaines

"The plot is tense, the dialogue tight and the characters are heart winning. Ms. Gaines has again written a winning story that is creative and different."

*— Valerie, Love Romances and More*

## Camille Anthony -- Women of Steel 4: Strawberry Daiquiri

"I am once again amazed at Camille's talent for world-building. She's a master storyteller, crafting characters for readers to fall in love with…. Strawberry Daiquiri is amazing and a must read!"

*-- Sharyn McGinty, In the Library Reviews*

www.ChangelingPress.com

LaVergne, TN USA
27 August 2010
194864LV00001B/76/P